P9-DFT-796

DISCARD

Place your initials here to remind you that you have read this book!

A M			
A B			

Naked Came
the Phoenix

 This Large Print Book carries the
Seal of Approval of N.A.V.H.

Naked Came the Phoenix

Nevada Barr, J. D. Robb,
Nancy Pickard, Lisa Scottoline,
Perri O'Shaughnessy, J. A. Jance,
Faye Kellerman, Mary Jane Clark,
Marcia Talley, Anne Perry,
Diana Gabaldon, Val McDermid,
Laurie King

edited by Marcia Talley

A SERIAL NOVEL

Thorndike Press • Waterville, Maine

Published in 2002 by arrangement with St. Martin's Press, LLC.

Thorndike Press Large Print Basic Series.

The tree indicium is a trademark of Thorndike Press.

The text of this Large Print edition is unabridged.
Other aspects of the book may vary from the original edition.

Set in 16 pt. Plantin by Minnie B. Raven.

Printed in the United States on permanent paper.

Library of Congress Cataloging-in-Publication Data

Naked came the phoenix : a serial novel / by Nevada Barr . . .
 [et al.] ; edited by Marcia Talley.
    p.   cm.
   ISBN 0-7862-3639-6 (lg. print : hc : alk. paper)
   1. Blue Ridge Mountains — Fiction.   2. Health resorts
— Fiction.   3. Large type books.   I. Barr, Nevada.
II. Talley, Marcia Dutton, 1943–
PS3600.A1 N35 2001b
 813′.6—dc21   2001053497

To the millions of
breast cancer survivors everywhere,
in hope of an imminent cure

Acknowledgments

The making of this novel has been, in every way, a collaborative effort.

First, to the thirteen amazing women who said 'yes' when I called — Nevada, Nora, Nancy, Lisa, Pam, Mary, Judy, Faye, Mary Jane, Anne, Diana, Val, and Laurie — thank you for your talent, enthusiasm, cooperation . . . and patience.

To my agent, Jimmy Vines, for giving me the idea and sticking with me every step of the way while I ran with it — thank you for the countless hours you spent helping me put the project together and keeping it on track.

Thanks to Jennifer Weis at St. Martin's Press for giving us a good home.

And to the dozens of authors' agents and assistants who juggled a seemingly endless stream of contracts, schedules, correspondence, and e-mails . . . thanks, we couldn't have done it without you.

Introduction

When my agent first suggested that I try my hand at putting together a novel like *Naked Came the Manatee*, a collaborative effort first serialized in the *Miami Herald* by a baker's dozen of top Florida journalists, including Carl Hiassen, Dave Barry, and Edna Buchanan, I smiled. I remembered — because yes, I am that old — a 1969 literary hoax perpetrated on the reading public by Mike McGrady and twenty-four of his Long Island *Newsday* coworkers; an unabashed sexual romp entitled *Naked Came the Stranger* that succeeded beyond McGrady's wildest dreams. In fact, "Naked Came . . ." is now synonymous with a collaborative novel written serially.

"Penelope Ashe," *Naked Came the Stranger*'s fictional suburban housewife/author, wasn't the first to pen such a collaboration, of course. The roots go back much further, to 1931 Britain and *The Floating Admiral*, written by "Certain Members of the Detection Club," including Dorothy L. Sayers, Agatha Christie, G. K. Chesterton, and other giants of the mystery genre. Wouldn't it be fun, I thought, to assemble a group of modern mystery and suspense writers — all women — write such a novel, and donate a portion of our royalties to breast cancer research? I sketched a cast of characters, plopped them down in an exclusive health spa because, let's face it, there are dozens of interesting ways to bump off a character in a health spa, and *Naked Came the Phoenix* was born. Twelve women accepted my invitation, Nevada Barr picked up her pen, and six thousand words later, the game was afoot.

The rules were simple. Each chapter was to be written in the third person and, in the spirit of *The Floating Admiral*, with a definite solution in view, even though we were well aware that subsequent authors might take — indeed were expected to take — the plot in divergent directions. "It was dangerously liberating to know I didn't personally have to deal with the consequences of whatever I put in my chapter," wrote Nancy Pickard.

Although authors were cautioned to avoid cliff-hanger endings that would require Houdini-like efforts on the part of the next author (and our heroine), "the real fun" comes, according to Laurie R. King, "in seeing thirteen sweet-tempered lady crime writers stab each other thoughtfully in the back." Nancy, too, "loved the diabolical feeling of cooking up an outrageous plot twist and cackling, 'Heh, heh, heh, let's see what you do with *this*, Lisa!' " Because, as the game is played, there is no going back. No fair asking a previous author to change a clue. Against the rules to beg her to bring a promising character back to life. *Pssst! Hide this bloody knife in the potted palm in chapter two, will you?* is simply not allowed. Each writer is left to plant a new clue, target a fresh victim, point the finger at another suspect, introduce a new character, catch another in a lie, overhear a heated conversation — on and on — until it falls to the hapless writer of the final chapter to pick up all the problematic threads and tie them off in a nice, neat solution. I am deeply grateful that Laurie R. King volunteered for this task and that she did it so brilliantly.

And we had fun. Anne Perry enjoyed the discipline of writing about characters already created and thinking, "What can I do with them to give the story a twist and stay within the bounds set?" For her and others, it was the chance to try out a completely different time and place setting — the present day United States, for example, as opposed to Victorian London or sometime in the future. Still others relished the opportunity to experiment with new characters and new voices. What I enjoyed most was borrowing a character from my Hannah Ives mystery series and giving him a job at Phoenix Spa. And, of course, we all felt it necessary to do exhaustive, firsthand research in luxury health spas all across the country.

As *Naked Came the Phoenix* goes to press, it pleases me to learn of a new link with *The Floating Admiral*. We have come full circle, with one of our sisterhood, Val McDermid, being elected to membership in the famed Detection Club.

Val's a professional. And as Laurie reminds me, it takes a professional to play the game well. I think you will find thirteen of them here.

MARCIA TALLEY
Annapolis, Maryland
May 2001

1

She went through life like an open razor. Caroline couldn't remember where she'd read that phrase, but there was little doubt in her mind that it had been inspired by a woman like her mother. Maybe Hilda herself had been the muse. She cast a long shadow, Caroline knew firsthand; she and her father had lived in it, Hilda always center stage between them and the light.

Two weeks before, Hamlin Finch, Caroline's father, had finally been set free. Throat cancer, brought on, Caroline was convinced, by decades of angry words unspoken, had killed him. Now she hoped he was standing in the light. Hoped, not believed.

She toyed with the idea that her father watched them. Because Sunday school had left its benign scar across her psyche, she pictured him in his battered La-Z-Boy, Frosty, his beloved Siamese cat, across his knees, the newspaper in an untidy heap on the puffy white cloud supporting his chair.

The sky above was impossibly blue, the clouds TV-commercial white, the sun gold and sentient.

Would he be pleased that after thirty-seven years of berating him for ruining her life, his wife had toppled into a bleak depression once he died? Or would he, like his daughter, wonder if it was another of Hilda's cunningly executed manipulations to get what she wanted?

This time what Hilda had wanted was a ten-day stay at one of the most exclusive — and expensive — spas east of the Rocky Mountains. And she'd gotten it. Douglas had paid for it.

Douglas. Thinking of her husband, Caroline smiled. *Husband.* The word was still magical. In the eleven months they'd been married, she'd often thanked the gods for bringing this man into her life. Douglas, a freshman congressman from the state of Tennessee, was handsome, respected, admired. And he was kind. It was the kindness Caroline loved most. He'd found the twelve thousand dollars to send them to Phoenix Spa because he believed Hilda was in pain and he was a good man. Caroline had agreed to accompany her, not because she was a good daughter, but because she was afraid that Hilda's increasingly bizarre behavior since Hamlin's death would reflect badly on Douglas's career.

Phoenix Spa was so exclusive that it was booked two years in advance. Once Hilda knew Douglas would foot the bill, she'd wrangled two spots in less than a day. Claudia de Vries, the spa's owner, had been Hilda's roommate her first — and only — year at Brown University. Hilda said Mrs. de Vries made room for them because of old friendship. Judging by the bitter undercurrent that soured her greeting when they'd arrived, Caroline couldn't help thinking it might have had more to do with a spot of petty blackmail.

Caroline looked across the table at her mother. She didn't bother with a covert glance. Hilda liked to be watched and courted attention. Hilda was in her element, or what she'd always believed her element should be. Phoenix was a favorite hideout for the rich and famous and those who wanted to be rich and famous. They paid for the promise of the motto carved in gothic letters across the massive stone arch at the entrance: *Incipit Vita Nova* — the new life begins.

To Hilda's left, elbows planted heavily on the crisp white tablecloth, was Howard

13

Fondulac. Claudia swooshed by their table, dust and fawn silks fluttering, exquisitely applied makeup doing a fair job of camouflaging the sharpness of her eyes and an age she surely lied about, and introduced Fondulac in what was apparently the most important factor at the spa: not who you were but what you were. Caroline was "Congressman Blessing's wife." Fondulac was a "leading Hollywood producer." Claudia listed highlights from Fondulac's résumé: a Mel Gibson film, movies by two of the Baldwin boys, one with Sarah Jessica Parker. If Caroline remembered right, the most recent had been made six years ago.

Claudia de Vries was more of a politician than any congressman Caroline had met in her time as a political wife. Small of stature and big of ego, she had dragged herself up from poverty to become an arbiter of health and fashion for the privileged few. Hilda, smug in her own upper-middle-class heritage as a podiatrist's daughter, said Claudia went to Brown on scholarship. Not even having enough money for a nice dress for homecoming, she had to borrow one Hilda had worn in high school.

In a flurry of silks, Claudia moved on.

Caroline looked back at the movie producer. "Nerves" was the explanation he gave for being at the spa. Alcohol was Caroline's guess. Watching him stare morosely into his water glass, forlornly clinking the ice cubes against the side, she could almost smell his whiskey wish. Despite the aging properties of the booze, at fifty he was still a handsome man in the craggy school of Robert Mitchum and Kirk Douglas.

Hilda loved the movies. Lived life like she was writing her own script as she went along. At the moment she played her newest role to perfection. The attractive widow in flattering weeds: subdued, grieving, but not sloppy about it. Bitter tears stung Caroline's eyes.

"Are you okay?"

So deep was she in reverie, it took Caroline a moment to realize she was being addressed. Turning to the speaker, she smiled. The woman was younger than she, twenty-two at most, and achingly pretty. Caroline had seen her, dressed in expensive clothes that hung like empty sails from her angular frame, peeking out from magazine covers. Her name was Ondine, just Ondine, and she'd held pride of place in the fashion industry's pantheon of waif

15

goddesses for nearly six years. Like a professional gymnast, she had the undeveloped body of a girl denied puberty. Her hair was as fine as corn silk and as pale. Tonight she wore it down, adding to her trademark look of a lost and ethereal child. A faint brown discoloration covered her right eyelid and ran in an irregular stain to the corner of her mouth. That was never seen in the photographs.

Caroline was no slouch in the looks department. Light brown hair, softly curled and kissed by the sun, skimmed her shoulders. Her trim, almost boyish body was sleek and strong and usually did what she asked of it. Partisan politics in the Nashville Philharmonic Orchestra where she'd played cello for seven years had honed away the roundness of her face and carved lines at the corners of her hazel eyes. Age looked good on her; it brought out the fine bones of her face. Caroline knew she was pretty.

Ondine was not pretty. She was stunning. Because of the girl's beauty, Caroline was sufficiently shallow that she wanted to hate her but, instead, found herself feeling protective.

"I'm fine," she said and felt better because Ondine had asked. "It's all so . . . so much."

To her relief the model laughed, and for a few seconds the two of them looked around like awestruck teenagers on their first trip to Bloomingdale's. Phoenix Spa didn't stint on luxury. The tablecloths and napkins were linen, not polyester spun to look like it. The tables were set with fine china, plates, cups, and bowls ringed in a lapis pattern set off in gold. The dining room's decor was white and wood and glass; clean, modern; a perfect backdrop for the huge urns of cut flowers that fed the eye's need for color and the soul's for anarchy.

The dining room captured that rare blend of spaciousness and intimacy — just large enough to comfortably seat the spa's thirty pampered guests but two stories tall. Peaked cathedral windows framed a view of the lake and the grounds.

"*Too* much?" Ondine asked, arching a manicured eyebrow.

"I could get used to it," Caroline admitted.

"I am used to it," Ondine confided. "I'm here to see if I can't hang on to it at least a few more years."

"How so?" It was a personal question and one Caroline usually would not have asked on such short acquaintance, but

Ondine had an openness about her that made them friends with a single shared admission of lusting after the finer things.

"I've got to lose this." Ondine brought both fists down on her midsection.

Weight. It took a second for the meaning to register in Caroline's brain. Ondine was here to lose weight. Had it not been for the low clatter of forks and tongues, Caroline was convinced she would have heard the clack of Ondine's wrist bones hitting her pelvic bones when she struck herself. She was that thin. Suddenly Caroline was afraid for her.

She looked at the plate in front of the girl. The small square of salmon, lifted from mere food to an art form by the fan of baby asparagus spears and a drizzling of dill sauce that Jackson Pollock would have been proud of, was largely untouched. One tiny corner had been disturbed as if a mouse nibbled briefly before being frightened away. Caroline had sucked her own dinner down and had to refrain from devouring the nickel-sized orchids used as garnish.

Caroline was a musician. She knew nothing about medicine or diet. But she knew skinny when it poked out of a silk sheath in the chair next to her. Ondine was pathologically skinny, her perfect bone structure all too apparent beneath translucent skin. Not flesh, the woman had none of that, just skin.

Casting about for something to say, she settled on careful inquiry. "Have you planned out your diet with Mrs. de Vries?"

"Oh, yes." Ondine laughed; a breathless sound. "She and Raoul have promised to lock me in my room and keep me on tofu and water if that's what it takes. My manager would probably call out the Virginia state troopers if they ever did that!" Ondine's face took on the pouty cast of a spoiled child but remained lovely.

"Is your manager here?" Caroline asked, already liking this caller-out of the troops.

"Always. Everywhere. Endlessly. Ubiquitously." Ondine smiled shyly. "I just learned 'ubiquitously,' and it fits Christopher Lund to the eyeteeth. That's him over there sitting between Raoul and that guy who looks like a roadie for Alice Cooper."

Ondine pointed ostentatiously, clearly hoping her manager would see her doing it. Playing along, Caroline stared, taking her time studying the occupants of the next table. Raoul was Claudia de Vries's husband. From the scraps of gossip Caroline had picked up since their arrival, that's

19

how everyone thought of him, but he didn't look like a second fiddle. He wore his tux like a man born to it, and his face was shaped by a long line of aristocratic genes. Self-assurance hung on him like a shimmering cloak. Opposite Raoul was the man Ondine had characterized as a roadie. Caroline knew better. Her mother had pointed him out in excited whispers not two minutes after the valet had taken their car. King David, a rocker from the seventies, who still toured, still brought in the crowds, though his fans were now approaching the age of his grandkids, presuming the man had grandkids. Passing years had honed King's look: dangerous. Body lean from exercise or heroin, long hair streaked with iridescent greens and tattoos in the shape of lightning bolts at the corners of both eyes made him ageless and intimidating.

The man between King and Raoul, the one Ondine pointed out as her manager, was in profile, his attention fixed on his plate, making a workman's job of the delicate dinner. Noting the conservative suit, tie carefully knotted, short, neatly brushed brown hair, and bland unapologetic face, Caroline said, "He looks out of place."

"He won't have an ounce of fun. Count

on it. He's here to protect his interests," Ondine said scornfully. "If I'm not careful he'll be force-feeding me chocolates when Raoul's not looking. Raoul's the doctor here. I thought Christopher was going to deck him when he found out Raoul had okayed three hours of aerobics every day to get the fat off me. You'd think Christopher of all people wouldn't want me blown up like a blimp. I'm his meal ticket."

Caroline barely heard the last. She was staring at Raoul de Vries. Tomorrow she had an appointment with him. "A complete physical by the spa's own physician." It was in the brochure. She made a mental note to take a look at his walls for medical degrees. What kind of doctor would prescribe hard exercise for a woman who was clearly teetering on the brink of anorexia?

"Newcomers' moonlight walk." The words pattered down like light rain, surprising an unladylike grunt from Caroline. Claudia de Vries had wafted to their table on soundless wings of peach chiffon. Everyone at Phoenix was encouraged to dress for dinner. Slightly ill at ease in a clingy burgundy spandex number gussied up with black bugle beads and a velvet shawl, Caroline had the bad grace to wonder if it

21

had been thus decreed not to "celebrate your own personal glamour" as the brochure said but so Mrs. de Vries could float about in Hollywood confections à la Ginger Rogers.

Claudia drifted on, Caroline and her mother following in her wake. The woman was definitely eccentric, perhaps even a touch absurd, but the force of her personality could not be denied. Claudia was one of nature's true charismatics.

In Pied Piper fashion, she played her fluted voice and called Phoenix's newcomers to follow. From the table where Ondine's manager sat with Dr. de Vries and King David, the group gathered in a short, stout woman with cropped iron-gray hair and an evening dress of the same no-nonsense shade. The dress was brocade, the stiff kind Caroline had seen on her mother's old prom dress when she dragged it out of the attic to illustrate the story about how she could have married the boy who was now CFO of WorldCom.

With a start, Caroline realized that the wearer of brocade was Phyllis V. Talmadge. The recognition was spurred by Ms. Talmadge's latest bestseller, *Flex Your Psychic Muscles*, lying near her plate, her picture, unsmiling and intense, glaring up from the back cover.

As Claudia de Vries led them on, Caroline was relieved to see the book retrieved by King David. Had Phyllis V. been toting her own tome around, Caroline might have lost her composure.

The image of this uncompromising chunk of womanhood stumping through the spirit world in her all-purpose formal wear and Sears Roebuck foundation garments, the lavish unreality of the dining room coupled with the diaphanous presence of their hostess — a businesswoman in butterfly's clothing — were working on Caroline like cheap champagne at a wedding. Laughter, broken in pieces by an adolescent inappropriateness, threatened to explode in uncontrollable giggles.

A sudden and too familiar sense of falling hit Caroline. For her the room turned cold, the colorful people surreal, as if normalcy was a gift others shared without her. Hilarity turned abruptly to the icy pinch of an anxiety attack.

Four more spa clients were swept up by Claudia's passage, but Caroline was only peripherally aware of them. She breathed slowly, concentrating on pulling the air in and pushing it out as her therapist had taught her, a way of anchoring herself in the present when an attack threatened to carry her away.

Caroline's panic attacks had started three months ago, when her father was first diagnosed with cancer. Stress, her therapist had told her. *Not me,* she'd thought. The therapist listed the changes in Caroline's life: new marriage, husband's election, traveling to Washington, leaving her job with the symphony, her father's death. *Not me,* Caroline had insisted. *Straight-A student, magna cum laude from Juilliard, youngest first chair in the philharmonic. Always in control.*

Unfortunately, logic had little effect on the process. Feeling fear pour through her veins, shatter her thoughts, Caroline had to accept that she was only human. Stress was real.

Perhaps she was due for some world-class pampering. For the first time since they'd driven through the imposing front gate and up the winding drive, she was glad to be at Phoenix Spa.

Her terror receded slowly. At length Caroline could breathe again. Eyes opened fully to the beauty of the night and the place, she finally allowed herself to laugh; not the hysterical giggling that threatened earlier but a full-throated woman's laugh that she didn't feel obligated to explain to anybody.

Hurrying to catch up, she ran down the shallow steps flowing from the dining room to the brick walk circling the lake. The others had stopped at the shore to admire the view. As Caroline rejoined the group, Hilda smiled and held out her hand. Her mother was so small, her figure, still perfect, straight and proud in her new midnight velvet dress, her never-to-be-gray hair in a classic French twist. Maybe it was a trick of the moonlight, but Caroline thought she saw something new in her mother's face — a softness she remembered from when she was a very little girl. Caroline took her hand and squeezed it briefly before letting go.

"The lake is twenty-five acres," Claudia said in good tour-guide fashion. "Fed by natural springs."

Purposely, Caroline tuned out the statistics. Like a poem, the night should not be dissected into mere meter and rhyme but enjoyed in its wholeness.

Claudia prattled on. Caroline let the musical voice babble around her, taking in a word or two when interest stirred. The lake was nestled in a hollow formed by the rumpled skirts of the Blue Ridge Mountains. Around it, scattered at odd angles to fit in with nature's artful chaos, were A-frame cottages, each different in design but all echoing the cathedral windows of the main hall and dining room. Ground-level lights, shuttered to shine only on the walkways, ringed the water and branched off to the cottages, creating a spiderweb of light.

The air was warm for late October, but an indefinable tang of autumn dispelled summer's somnolence. In the morning the palette of black and silver would be burned away by a conflagration of fall colors blazing in the ancient hardwoods that pressed close around the spa's grounds.

The spa's services were housed in four centers, one set on each side of the lake, Caroline learned as they walked. The square they formed, Claudia told them, created a proper feng shui pattern guaranteed to enhance mental and physical well-being.

The first was the bathhouse. "An old-fashioned name," Claudia said as she pulled a ring of keys fit for a jailer from a beaded evening bag. "Though we welcome the new, we've been careful not to throw the baby out with the bathhouse. The old methods of soothing the soul and stimulating the spirit carry with them a special alchemy."

Claudia must have given this talk a thousand times, yet her love of the place breathed life into the worn spiel. While Claudia talked she opened three locks on the bathhouse doors. Two were dead bolts; Caroline heard them slide free and wondered at such heavy-duty security measures. What in this idyll, tucked away from urban areas and the fly-by crime of the turnpikes, needed to be kept out? Or in?

The double doors swung open and the lights came on, either triggered by the movement of the doors or an electric eye. Caroline joined the others in an appreciative, "Ahhh."

The architect had managed a harmonious marriage of Swedish modern and the stained-glass-and-tile opulence of a vintage nineteen-thirties bathhouse. A fountain, sprung to sudden life with the lights, sparkled under a high ceiling cut through with skylights, each of the panels depicting a flowering herb in jewel-toned glass.

Claudia arranged herself prettily in front of the falling water. "I won't show you all the facilities tonight, but I wanted to give you a glimpse of the world you entered into when you chose Phoenix Spa." She went on to list the wonders that awaited behind the closed doors: mud baths in stone tubs from the turn of the century, steam rooms with aromatic and healthful plant extracts added to the boiling water, massage rooms, facials. Most of the treatments were standard, made unique to Phoenix by the addition of herbal therapy. Herbs, plants, and flowers, all, Claudia insisted, gathered from the surrounding woods by an expert in botany brought over from Bombay specifically for his arcane knowledge of how to use plants for spiritual enhancement.

Caroline couldn't help but wonder what a guy from Bombay could know about the plants of the Blue Ridge, but she didn't interrupt. She liked good theater as much as anyone and had to admit the concept intrigued her.

"Plant materials are used in many of our treatments," Claudia went on. "By using only those indigenous to the area, the harmony of persons, places, and things brings harmony between the spirit and the flesh of each of you precious people who have come to us for succor."

The rhetoric was getting a bit thick. Caroline's attention wandered as they returned to the lakeshore and Claudia triple-locked the bathhouse doors behind them. With a wave of a beringed hand that set her evening wrap, a shawl of a thousand scraps of feather-light fabric, to quivering like an aspen in a windstorm, Claudia led the troop onward.

Caroline found that she had fallen in step with the stalwart psychic. Phyllis Talmadge's head barely came to Caroline's shoulder. She couldn't have been more than five feet tall even in her sensible one-inch pumps.

"Hah!" the little woman puffed.

"I beg your pardon?" Caroline said politely.

"Hah!" she repeated for Caroline's edification. "Herbal, schmerbal. What bullshit. They'd better not go smearing any of that muck on me. Bombay. Hah."

Caroline snorted unbecomingly, a startled laugh that went up her nose when she tried to smother it. "What brought you here?" she asked, since it didn't seem to be the promise of youth-rejuvenating vegetative wraps or the energizing properties of aromatherapy.

"*They* told me to come," Phyllis Talmadge replied enigmatically. "The center is threatened. It may not hold." With that garbled quote from Yeats, she trundled on, a small female tank with a mission.

Caroline slowed, letting the others move

ahead so she could better enjoy the play of the light on water, the stealthy promises whispered by the wind as it passed through dry leaves.

"You hear it, too?"

The voice in her ear was as smooth as the autumn breeze and as hard-edged as winter's first bite. Shying in the time-honored way of startled colts, she bumped into the man standing as close as a lover behind her. He had appeared without a sound, without her sensing him, and it scared her. Either her survival instincts were at low ebb, or he was as conversant with the night as Count Dracula.

"Easy." He caught her by the shoulders as she stumbled over the hem of her evening gown. He was tall, six-four or -five, and lean without weakness or frailty. His dark hair fell in a wild mass past his shoulders, the green highlights creating the illusion of seaweed. King David. The rocker. What had she read in *Rolling Stone*? Ah. That he'd gotten rabies biting off the heads of live bats at a concert in Detroit in 1979.

"Easy," he said again and smiled. The effect was electric. The lightning bolt tattoos at the corners of his eyes crinkled and straightened, and his very white teeth flashed. Pure animal magnetism boiled off the man. For an instant Caroline was afraid she was going to swoon like the heroine in a cheap romance. No wonder he was still packing stadiums with shrieking fans after thirty years.

Carefully, as though he'd long been aware of his effect on the weaker sex, he let go of her arms and watched to be sure she could stand on her own two feet.

"Did I hear what?" she snapped in response to his earlier question. Humiliation was turning her hostile.

"The music," he said softly. "You're a musician. You hear it."

The wind in the leaves, the minute skittering as those already fallen whispered across the brick walk: the music she'd been listening to when he'd come upon her. "How did you know?" she demanded, suddenly afraid that this strange man knew all her secrets.

He caught her left hand in both of his. Running his thumb over her fingertips he said, "Calluses. Violin?"

"Cello." His touch was paralyzing. She willed herself to snatch her hand back with some show of indignation, but nothing happened.

He released her. She felt relieved, bereft, and ridiculous. A gust of wind whipped the hair across King's sharp features, then pulled it away. A dark curtain closing on one scene and opening on another. The lightning sewn into his skin flashed, his eyes narrowed, and he said, "Musicians are mad, you know."

She was aware that he spoke not only of himself but of her.

"Not cellists," she retorted. "We aren't amplified."

He laughed and she was drawn into it. Annoyed that a man old enough to be her father was giving her vapors, she began to walk toward her cottage. *He's good at this,* she thought. *It's a game he's played for longer than I've been alive.*

Without being invited, King fell into step alongside her.

"Why are you at Phoenix?" She asked the most banal question she could think of to reintroduce normalcy into what was becoming a seriously peculiar evening.

"The same reason you are," he replied in his ice and honey voice.

"And why is that?" Irrationally, she was afraid of what the answer might be.

"I'm looking for something that once belonged to me."

Caroline walked faster. Refusing to take the hint, he stayed beside her, his long stride easily matching hers.

"You don't have to walk me to my cabin." Caroline was aware she sounded desperate but was unable to do anything about it.

He smiled again. She wished he'd stop that. "My cabin's there." He pointed to the A-frame next to the one she shared with her mother. "I'm going to bed."

"Oh."

"Enjoy the music." He touched her cheek as lightly as a leaf blowing by and turned away.

When she realized she was standing where he'd left her watching him leave, she shook her head and whispered, "I've got to call Douglas." She was up the walk and opening the door before she remembered that Phoenix Spa cottages had no phones. Guests were even encouraged to check their cell phones when they registered. The same went for laptops.

Feeling adrift and disconcerted, she let herself into the cottage. The A-frame had two bedrooms, one downstairs and one in a loft reached by a spiral staircase made of beautifully polished and treacherously slick hardwood. The loft overlooked the living area with its small fireplace and grand view of the lake.

A single lamp was lit. Hilda sat under it in an old morris chair refinished to a rich gleam. She still wore the velvet gown, every hair lacquered in place. With both hands on the chair arms, knees together, feet flat on the floor, she looked like a miniature monarch. Caroline half expected a curt, "Off with her head!" as she entered the room.

Needing to sort out her feelings, Caroline intended to slink by and flee up the spiral stairs to bed. A faint glistening on her mother's cheek stopped her. Hilda was crying.

Caroline tried to remember the last time she'd seen her mother cry and couldn't. Maybe never. The tears shocked her, made her awkward and dumb, but she could not ignore them. Kicking off her shoes, she padded across the thick white carpeting and sat on the footstool by her mother's chair. Neither spoke. Caroline wanted to take her mother's hand, offer her some crumb of love and comfort, but she couldn't. She didn't know how.

"I wasn't a good wife to Hamlin," Hilda said, the tears continuing in their course.

"You did —"

"No," Hilda said quietly, "I wasn't. In the beginning I might have been, but something changed. I changed. I thought I needed to be more than a wife and mother and ended up being less.

"I loved your father." She looked at Caroline for the first time. She needed desperately to be believed; it was in her eyes. So Caroline believed her.

"Those weeks and months when he was dying, I was so angry. He never gave me what I needed and now he was leaving me. Just like that. He seemed so tired, and I couldn't be kind."

The tears fell faster. Hilda made no move to brush them away, and Caroline resisted the temptation to run for the Kleenex box. Her mother needed to cry, long and hard.

"I'm going to miss him," she said simply. "I'm going to miss being the wife I could have been, and now it's too late." Hilda swallowed a shuddering sigh and said, "I haven't been a good mother to you, sweetheart."

The old endearment, seldom used in recent years, struck into Caroline's heart like a firebrand, melting the ice she'd been keeping there. She took her mother's hand. Holding it felt strange but right.

Hilda manipulated. Perhaps it had been the only way she'd known to get what she needed to survive. Caroline had met her grandmother — Hilda's mother — a total of three times as she was growing up but remembered her as a harsh woman wrapped tight in a religion that used God as a rallying cry and the Bible as a bludgeon. Maybe Hilda wasn't acting. She'd married Hamlin when she was nineteen. For nearly four decades they'd slept in the same bed, worried over the same bills and, each in his or her own way, centered their lives around their only child.

Looking at her mother's face, turned slightly as if she looked back down the years, it occurred to Caroline that, to the best of her heart's ability, Hilda might have loved Hamlin, might even now love her. A wave of compassion broke with such force tears came to Caroline's eyes.

Perhaps, here, now, for mother and daughter, a phoenix would rise from the ashes and a new life would begin.

2

Caroline woke dreaming of pizza. She'd have sworn she could smell it — that first heady rush of spices and sauce and melted cheese.

It was a huge disappointment to wake in the dark, without the pie. The perfume of the hothouse roses that bloomed out of a crystal vase on her dresser was lovely, subtle, and sweet.

But she couldn't eat the damn roses.

Caroline rolled over in the huge bed and willed herself back to sleep. Hunger was a demon gnawing greedily at her insides, but she'd just have to wait until breakfast to satisfy him. Surely it was nearly time for breakfast by now. She opened one eye, looked at the bedside clock, and moaned. How could it only be two in the morning?

She flopped over on her back and stared at the ceiling. She'd think of something else. Of anything else. Food had never driven her life. Of course, food had always been easily available. It was the absence of it that had changed the complexion of things.

Would a cracker be too much to ask?

No, no, she was here on a program. It would be good for her to be more regimented about her diet and her health, those things she took entirely too much for granted. It would be good for her mother. More, it would be good for their relationship.

Maybe they'd actually *have* a relationship by the time they went home again.

Her mother was grieving, really grieving, and that was unexpected. It shouldn't have been, Caroline admitted. She hadn't given her mother — perhaps not even her father — enough credit. More than thirty-five years of marriage stood for something, and those outside of it — even a child born from it — didn't always understand what went on inside that intimate bubble.

She'd try to be more sensitive to her mother's feelings, more patient with her annoying habits. They'd bond over herbal wraps and mud baths.

She'd be a better daughter, a better wife, a better human being. If she just had a damn sandwich.

On a muttered oath, she switched on the light, rolled out of bed. When a desperate search of her purse, her bags, her pockets turned up nothing but half a tin of breath mints and one ancient piece of hard candy, she dropped into a chair, scowling at the walls.

It was a beautiful room, meticulously decorated with soothing pastels and gleaming wood with the added charm of original watercolors of the mountains and valley. She'd have traded it for a six-by-six concrete bunker, if the bunker came with a decent meal.

There was nothing to do but tough it out. She couldn't very well sneak out of the cottage and execute a quick sortie on the spa's kitchen.

Could she?

Of course not. That would be rude — and against the rules. She always followed the rules.

Yes, always, she thought. Always did what she was told, followed directions, behaved as expected. The only time she'd ever let herself follow her instincts and be swept along by feeling, she'd ended up with Douglas.

She'd ended up happy.

And when she started comparing her marriage to a middle-of-the-night snack, she was in trouble.

New life, she reminded herself and got to her feet. All right, then, she was going to take that seriously, take that literally. It was about time Caroline Blessing embraced her new life. If that meant sneaking a chicken leg at two in the morning, so be it.

She shrugged into the thick, soft folds of the spa's complimentary pale green robe, belted it like a woman girding herself for battle. Her heart was pumping fast as she tiptoed out of the room, crept down the spiral stairs to the main level. She could feel the edges of the panic attack scraping along her courage with sly fingers.

Go back to bed. Turn off the light. Be a good girl.

Be safe.

She nearly did. Pausing at the base of the stairs, she listened to the sound of her own labored breathing, felt the rise of that panic fighting to gush into her throat. It wasn't just the hunger that pushed her forward now. It was the need to prove that she could take the step, that she could risk doing something foolish. And fun.

Her first reward was stepping outside. The air was crisp and fresh. She could smell the lake and the woods, and could hear the quiet breathing of the night. Over-

40

head the sky was clear as polished glass and alive with stars.

She was alone. Wonderfully alone and alive. The thrill of that had her standing a moment, eyes closed, while the light breeze fluttered over her face and hair.

She might have been content with that, if her stomach hadn't let out a rumble. Wincing, she pressed a hand to it and looked hastily, guiltily around. However loud the sound had seemed to her, it didn't appear to have disturbed the other guests.

She noted that a light still burned in the next cottage. King David either had insomnia, she thought, or a fear of the dark. The idea that he might be awake, could look out his window and spot her, sent her moving briskly down the path.

She backtracked, reversing the route she'd taken during the moonlight walk. A part of her wanted to stroll, to detour by the lake, to revel for just a little while in this exciting sense of freedom.

She looked toward the lake and was startled to see two figures at the far curve of it. One wore a spa robe, as she did, and looked so painfully thin Caroline assumed it was Ondine.

She heard a sound drift back to her over

the water. Either laughter or weeping, and definitely a girl's. She couldn't be sure who it was the girl walked with, wasn't even sure if it was a man or a woman, though it seemed to her the shadow of shape was male. Then it occurred to her that if she stood there staring long enough to make out the identities, they were very likely to turn around and spot her.

The goal was to get into the kitchen, grab enough to sustain life until breakfast, and get back to the privacy of her room. Without getting caught.

She got moving.

Though most of the cottages she passed were dark, she noticed other lights here and there. Had she left the one burning beside her bed? She thought she had. Maybe when she got to the kitchen, she'd find all the other guests inside, wild-eyed and foraging.

The image amused her so much she began to chuckle as she passed the bath-house. Tomorrow, she thought, she was going to make good use of those facilities. A long swim, a leisurely whirlpool. And that mud bath that seemed so decadent and fascinating.

She supposed Claudia kept it triple-locked so guests wouldn't be tempted to dive in after hours.

Which, Caroline thought, would be wonderfully exciting. Maybe if she got away with tonight's breaking and entering, she'd try her luck with the bathhouse.

She was becoming a real wild woman.

She stopped dead when she reached the doors of the main hall. What, the wild woman thought, if they were set to alarms? What if she tried to open the door, and sirens screamed, lights flashed, and the staff came bursting out of the night with guns? And snarling dogs.

She'd come this far, she thought, rubbing her suddenly damp palms on her robe. She wasn't going back without doing her best to get food.

Holding her breath, shoulders braced for attack, she pulled the door open.

Silence.

Of course, she thought as she crept inside, there could be a silent alarm. Even now police officers in two states were being deployed. She'd be arrested with a bowl of carrot pasta in her trembling hands. The media would salivate.

Congressman's Wife Arrested in Kitchen Raid!

The evening news would carry pictures of her being dragged off, handcuffed, with a dab of low-fat sauce on her chin.

But at least her stomach would be happy. She smiled to herself.

She tiptoed through the dining hall, heading for the doors where the wait staff had slipped in and out during dinner. Gathering her courage, she groped for the light switch, then blinked as the overheads flashed on.

Everything was blindingly white and silver. Gleaming acres of white counters, sparkling seas of chrome. She made the dash to the enormous subzero refrigerator, yanked open the door. Then nearly wept with joy.

It might have been health food, but it was food. And there was plenty of it. She snatched a bunch of gorgeous green grapes, snagged a small block of nondairy product masquerading as cheese, a carton of low-fat yogurt. Dumping them on the counter, she popped grapes into her mouth while she searched the cupboards.

Fat-free crackers, whole-wheat bread sticks. She stuffed some in her robe pockets for the stash she intended to build in her room.

Fifteen minutes later, she let out an enormous sigh. The hole in her belly was filled. Drunk with power, she selected a few more nonperishables, weighing down her pockets. When she was satisfied, she cleaned the counter, washed the utensils she'd used, and meticulously replaced them precisely as she'd found them. She hunted up crumbs and buried all evidence of her raid in the trash.

At the door, she scanned the kitchen one last time. The perfect crime, she decided. Maybe she had a talent for petty larceny. She switched off the light, then hastily switched it back on and used the sleeve of her robe to wipe down the plate. No point leaving fingerprints.

By the time she was outside again, she was euphoric. Not once during the actual deed had she panicked. She'd been cool-headed, focused, skilled, and successful.

She had the full stomach and bulging pockets to prove it.

She was so proud of her triumph that she didn't hear the voices until it was nearly too late. Instant and full-blown panic froze her to the spot. Self-preservation, a stronger instinct than she'd realized, uprooted her and had her bolting off the path and all but diving into the perfectly trimmed shrubbery.

"Do you think that matters to me?"

Recognizing Claudia's voice, Caroline

tried to sink into the ground behind the weeping yews. The idea of being caught crouched behind a shrub, pockets crammed with pilfered food, had her covering her mouth with her hands to quell a burst of laughter.

"Do you honestly think that's going to make a difference as to what I do and how I do it?" The laughter that followed the statement was scalpel sharp, the kind that flayed to the bone. No longer amused, Caroline stopped breathing and willed Claudia and her companion to move away.

Had it been Claudia with Ondine down at the lake? What the hell were they doing out at nearly three in the morning? Which, of course, was exactly what Claudia would ask her, if she was discovered squatting in the evergreens.

"I've given you all I can, for as long as I can." The second voice was no more than a whisper, harsh but colored with a great deal of passion.

Caroline strained to identify the speaker but couldn't be sure if it was a man or woman. Her curiosity piqued, she tried to shift, just a little. But even the slight movement caused the bushes — and the stolen goods in her pockets — to rustle.

"You'll find more, and for as long as I

say." Claudia didn't bother to keep her voice down, so it rang out. Clear and vicious. "Really, darling, you can't afford not to. And we both know it. So let's not play this game anymore."

"If you keep pushing me —"

"What?" There was challenge in the single word Claudia spat out. Challenge, Caroline thought uneasily, and a great deal of ugly amusement. "You'd best remember who's in charge here. Our relationship remains as it is. You should relax. Temper and stress are death on the system and begin to show, all too soon, on the face. I suggest some meditation and a nice aromatherapy massage. I'll put them on your schedule for tomorrow."

"Bitch." It was no more than a hiss. "I could kill you."

"So you've said before. Really." Claudia let out a heavy sigh as the footsteps passed just on the other side of the bushes. "Redundancy is so tedious. I have things to do. *Ciao,* darling. Sleep well."

"At least give me more time."

"I already have." Claudia's voice faded as she moved down the bricked path. "Time's up."

Caroline listened to the footsteps recede. Nasty business, she thought. Nasty, *per-*

sonal business she wished she hadn't overheard. She didn't know what Claudia was
talking about, but it had sounded uncom-
fortably like blackmail of some kind. She
gave a little shudder and wondered if there
would have been more than a little embarrassment to face if either Claudia or her
companion had discovered her eavesdrop-
ping.

Cautious, she stayed exactly where she
was, counted slowly to twenty, then eased
to her feet. She could see no one and let
out a long breath of relief. They'd obviously rounded the curve to the bathhouse.

Which was, of course, exactly the path
she needed to take to get back to her cottage. She'd have to detour, then, go around
the back of that facility and make a dash
for her own front door.

With one eye on the path, Caroline
bolted to the left, swung into one of the
manicured garden areas. Mums were a
blaze of color in the shadowy light, and red
salvia speared up with its blood-red
blooms. She caught a scent in the air.

Flowers and . . . other. Tobacco, she
thought. Someone had passed this way not
long before and had been smoking.

Wasn't anyone tucked into bed where he
or she belonged?

Praying she'd picked the right direction, and that whoever else was awake and about in the night had chosen another one, she hurried along the meandering path.

She heard a door slam, sharp as a gun shot, and had to lean over and put her head between her knees to get the blood back in her own head.

Now panic came as a giggle that wanted to bubble and burst out of her throat. She tried to swallow it, told herself firmly it was inappropriate, even dangerous. But it trickled out of her as she fled, her rich brown hair flying, her robe flapping cheerfully around her legs.

The bathhouse stood, a majestic shadow under starry skies. She heard nothing from it, saw no figures as she streaked to her front door. She slipped inside, then peeked out through the crack.

King's light was still on, a single beacon in the dark. Hers, she thought, was going out. As soon as she hid her stash.

As she climbed the stairs toward her room, she was grinning.

All in all, it had been one of the most exciting hours of her life.

Her mother's voice sliced through her sleep like a laser. Caroline groped for the duvet, was about to drag it over her head, when Hilda tugged it away.

"No, you don't, lazybones. This is our first full day at the spa. We don't want to waste it sleeping."

"I'm not wasting it. I'm wallowing in it. Go away, Mom."

"Up! Up and out. We're going for a walk. I signed us up for a sunrise stretch class. Didn't I tell you?"

"No. If you'd told me, I'd have killed you."

Hilda let out a bright laugh — reason enough for murder — and patted Caroline's head. "Douglas is paying good money for us to be here, Caroline. We're going to make sure he gets his money's worth."

That was exactly the right weapon out of her mother's considerable arsenal. Heavy eyed, Caroline sat up. Her little nighttime adventure had cost her nearly two hours' sleep. If she was foggy and out of sorts this morning, she had no one to blame but herself.

She focused on her mother's face, then angled her head in consideration. Hilda might have been in full makeup, her hair ruthlessly styled, but the softening Caroline had noticed the night before was still there. "You look rested."

"I am. I'd say that crying jag last night did me a lot of good. Sweetheart, I'm so glad you're here with me. I — no," she said and shook her head briskly. "I'm not going to start that again. No tears today. We're in this fabulous place, and we're going to have a wonderful time."

Because there was something almost desperate in the declaration, Caroline got quickly out of bed. "You're absolutely right. We're going to get oiled and polished and pampered and stretched. We're going home new women."

"And thinner ones. Caroline, if I don't eat soon, I'm going to *die*."

"Well . . ." Fighting to keep her face composed, Caroline opened her lingerie drawer and slid her hand under a neat stack of bras and panties. "Want a bread stick?"

Hilda gaped, blinked, then grabbed the treasure her daughter offered. "How did you get this?"

"Don't ask." Caroline waved her away. "Go, enjoy. I'll toss on my exercise gear, pack up my bathing suit, and be ready to stretch in five minutes." She was already pulling her hair back into a ponytail. "I want a long swim, too — and a look at the much-lauded mud baths."

True to her word, Caroline came down the stairs five minutes later. Only to find her mother back in her room engaged in a bitter self-debate over which bathing suit to take.

"Presentation is vital," Hilda explained after the royal blue tank scattered with red poppies had been selected. "Everyone here is *somebody*. Even my daughter," she added, hooking an arm through Caroline's. Hilda wore hot pink designer sweats. Caroline wore faded and baggy gray. "I want to create the right impression. I mean, honestly, sweetheart, did you *see* that psychic creature's outfit last night? Horrid. I don't want to end up like that."

"Not a chance. You're beautiful, Mom. You've always been beautiful."

"I've always needed to be. And what's wrong with that?" She laughed, threw back her head. The mountains were jewels of colors in the pink dawn light. The day was just beginning. "You were always beautiful. A beautiful baby, beautiful child, beautiful woman. But you never needed it. Maybe it was because you had your music."

"I never felt beautiful." She hadn't meant to say it. Wasn't sure why she had. And would have shrugged it off if her mother hadn't stopped, turned.

"Caroline." Hilda took her daughter's face in her hands. She realized as she did so that it was a gesture she'd denied both of them. "You are beautiful. And if you don't feel it every time Douglas looks at you, you're not paying attention."

"I love him so much."

"I know. I'm happy for you. I should have told you that before. I should have told you a lot of things before. I'll probably forget to once we're back to our own lives again."

"You told me now."

"I —" Hilda glanced over as the door to the next cottage opened. She saw King briefly as he poked his head out of the door. He wore sunglasses, jeans, and a black leather vest over a bare chest.

He did not look rested.

He slammed the door shut again even as she started to wave.

"How odd."

"Plenty of odd around here," Caroline murmured. She began to walk again. "These people might be rich, but they still make a motley crew."

"Think of all the wonderful gossip we'll have to take home."

"Gossip isn't . . . well, look at that."

Using the toe of her shoe, Caroline prodded the empty pint bottle of Jack Daniel's lying beside the pristine path. "I don't think this is on the spa's menu."

"If Claudia finds out which one of the staff's been drinking, she'll fire him or her on the spot."

"I'd say guest rather than staff. And," Caroline added when the bottle rolled and uncovered a cigarette butt smeared with lipstick, "maybe more than one guest."

"She'll still have a fit. Believe me, I know her. When Claudia says no alcohol, no tobacco, no drugs, no cell phones, she *means* it. Claudia has a vicious temper. Vicious and cold."

"I believe it," Caroline mused, remembering the barbs in Claudia's voice early that morning. "You never told me how you convinced her to find spots for us here."

Hilda flushed a little, avoiding Caroline's eyes by staring out at the lake. "Let's keep that my little secret. Look, who's that?" Grateful for the distraction, she gestured toward the figure standing on the shore of the lake.

"I couldn't say." Caroline blocked the strengthening sun from her eyes with the flat of her hand and studied the slim redhead dressed in sweater and slacks. Like

King, she wore dark glasses and had added a pale green scarf over her tumbled hair.

"Oh my God! Caroline, that's Lauren Sullivan." Hilda let out a muffled squeal and dug her fingers into Caroline's arm. "*The* Lauren Sullivan."

"Oh, it can't be. Hollywood queens don't come all the way to a little hollow in Virginia for a spa. California has plenty of them."

"I'm telling you, that's Lauren Sullivan. Why wouldn't she come here? It's one of the top spas in the country and probably more private than any in California. Sometimes a person wants to be three thousand miles away from where she lives. Look at that profile. That's her."

There was no mistaking it, not when the woman turned her head. The mass of flame-colored hair under the gauzy scarf, the trademark chin coming to that foxy little point below a full, wide mouth. "You're right again, Mother. But it's just so odd seeing her here instead of on the movie screen."

"She looks so romantic," Hilda said with a sigh.

"Lonely," Caroline disagreed. "She looks lonely to me, and sad. Mom, there are bruises on her face. You can see them, just under the sunglasses."

"Face-lift." Hilda whispered it and couldn't prevent the zing of excitement from jumping out. "She's had a face-lift. That must be why she's here. Recovering. Hiding out. And why we didn't see her at dinner last night. She wouldn't want to let it get out she's had plastic surgery."

"But she's young and beautiful. Why would she want —"

"Let's go talk to her. We'll just stroll down to the lake."

"No." Caroline gripped her mother's arm. "We will not."

"But, sweetheart . . ."

"She's entitled to her privacy." And, Caroline thought as she dragged her mother down the path, she would get it. That lone and lonely figure on the beach had struck a chord with her.

"It's not as if I was going to ask her for an autograph," Hilda complained. "Right this minute."

"Making a good impression means being much too cool to accost a movie star at dawn. You'll see her later and smile breezily and ask her how she's enjoying her stay."

"That's good. Very good." Impressed, Hilda studied her daughter. "How did you think of that?"

"You learn a lot being a politician's wife. The bathhouse is unlocked," she announced. The door to it, triple-bolted the night before, now stood partially open. "Let's go in."

"Now?"

"I'm dying to see it. And I'd much rather have a swim than stand and stretch with a bunch of other yawning guests. It'll be fun. Just you and me splashing around in the pool."

It was so unusual for Caroline to suggest doing something on impulse, or for fun, that Hilda let herself be pulled inside.

The fountain was on, spewing up its crystal water. The room echoed with the music of it. The early sunlight sprinkled through the jewel tones of the skylights and sparkled on the polished tiles.

Fresh flowers stood on the low tables near the deep-cushioned sofas and lounge chairs of the waiting area. Pillows were plumped and glossy magazines artistically fanned.

Luxury, waiting.

A wide glass display across the room held the many products, all in the spa's trademark silver packaging, that were available for sale. Scattered among the boxes were spears of dried herbs and flower petals and bits of polished stone.

A cathedral to that luxury, Caroline thought as she crossed the tiles and opened one of the doors. Inside was a changing area, complete with lounge, generous closet, and thick white towels. A small counter held a mirror and a supply of spa products.

"I found the pool," Hilda announced.

Caroline wandered back out and joined her mother in front of wide glass doors. Through them was a beautiful stretch of blue water under high white ceilings. The walls were covered with colorful mosaics depicting mythical scenes. Gods and goddesses frolicked in naked abandon.

And a man, very much flesh and blood, walked around the skirt of the pool laying fresh silver cushions on the lounge chairs. He wore nothing but a minuscule electric blue triangle, low on his hips.

"Oh my," Hilda managed. "Oh my goodness."

He was tall, muscled, and tan with a mane of black hair that spilled nearly to his shoulders. Caroline's mouth fell open when he turned his back to them and she saw that the triangle was a very thin thong.

"I guess we skip the swim."

Hilda purred. "And I was just thinking

what a terrific idea you'd had."

"We can't go in there now. He's practically . . . he's really built well, isn't he?"

As if he'd heard her, the man turned. He had a face that belonged carved on a coin and eyes both bold and black. He skimmed them over her, smiled lazily.

"We're going," Caroline announced and, mortified, turned the wrong way. She shoved through another door. And into the mud baths.

It was everything it had been hyped to be. And standing there, studying the stone troughs and black mud, gave her the time to regain her composure. The smell was . . . thick, she decided. Thick and rich and secret.

There were four of them, each mounted on its own individual platform and tucked into a corner where seeded glass doors could be closed for privacy. The curved stone was long enough for a grown man to sink into.

High padded tables stood beside them. Sparkling chrome-and-glass shelves held still more products she imagined were used during the treatment.

Music was playing softly, something with lots of strings and pipes. The lights were turned low and carried a faint amber hue.

It was a quiet, relaxing glow she imagined was part of the sensuous experience offered here. In the center of the room another fountain bubbled, a charming counterpoint to the music. Warm, slippery mud, perfumed air, music, soft light, and the relaxing notes of water striking water.

Yes, she'd very much like to try it.

She stepped to a trough, dipped a finger in. "You'd feel like Cleopatra, wouldn't you?" she mused. "But once you get in, how do you get out? Much less get the mud off."

She walked around the tub, saw the stone steps built into the far side of the trough. "Well, that solves the in and out part, I suppose. They must have showers or scrub rooms or something."

"We'll make sure we get in on this right away," Hilda began. "I want a full paraffin, too. And the deep-pore facial. No, the collagen facial. Hell, I want *everything*."

"Someone forgot to clean this one up," Caroline said absently as she wandered toward another trough. Ribbons of mud ran down its sides and into untidy pools on the floor.

"Claudia'll have someone's head for that. We'd better get going if we want to make that class. Unless you change your mind and we go for that swim with that Adonis. You know, Caroline, it's all right to look at gorgeous male specimens, even after marriage."

All Caroline heard was a buzz in her head. Her mother's words had turned into a messy tumble of sound. She stared down at the trough. And at the mud-streaked hand that dangled from its lip.

The hand wore a ring. A square diamond caked with drying mud.

She screamed. In her head, she screamed — one long, loud shriek. But her mother's voice continued, cheerful nonsense, babbling nothing. Caroline stumbled forward, plunged her arms into the trough. And met cold flesh.

"Help me. Oh, God, Mom, help me!" The flesh slithered through her hands. Panting, she fought for purchase even as Hilda ran over.

"Honey, what in the world are you . . ."

Out of the sucking mud came a head, a face. Grotesque as a gargoyle with its coating of black.

Now it was Hilda who screamed. Her screams cannoned off the walls, careened from floor to ceiling while Caroline struggled to hold on.

"Get help!" she ordered, fighting to clear

her own vision as it threatened to gray. "Hurry. Get help now!"

"It's . . . It's . . ."

"I know." Caroline's arms were trembling, with both effort and fear. "Hurry, Mom. Please."

While Hilda fled, screaming still, Caroline braced herself and stared down in horror at Claudia de Vries's mud-bathed and very dead face.

3

Help came half naked.

"Oh!" exclaimed Caroline, when her mother returned with the man in the turquoise thong. Directly faced, as it were, with the skimpy patch of electric blue, she nearly slipped her oozing grip on Claudia's body. Blushing as if he had arrived to ask her to dance instead of to assist her in a grisly task, she bleated, "Help! I can't hold her up any longer."

He bent down quickly and slid his forearms under Caroline's. For a terrible, intimate moment, they were locked together in a slippery embrace with the corpse.

"Do you know CPR?" Caroline squeaked.

Adonis shifted slightly, cradling Claudia's upper body with his arm and supporting it from below with his knee. He bent his magnificent head over the victim's muddy face, and for a long minute Caroline held her breath while he listened, as if waiting for Claudia to say something.

Then he laid two fingers against the spa owner's neck. He shook his head gravely. "Let go," he whispered, and she thought she heard an accent.

Caroline slid her arms out from under his, and backed far enough away to be able to lean against a wall. Even a lifetime of holding a cello propped between her legs had not prepared her for bearing the weight of a dead body. Her arms quivered with exhaustion. Her knees began to tremble, so much that she thought she was going to slip ingloriously to the floor and have to put her head between them to keep herself from fainting. *Calm down!* she directed herself. If she could play Beethoven in front of a thousand symphony lovers, if she could sit on a political platform smiling up at her candidate husband while three hundred people cheered, if she could steal food from a deserted kitchen, surely she could keep her composure for this.

Douglas!

The thought of her husband made her heart race, partly out of longing for his sweet presence in this moment of emergency but also out of fear of the headlines in tomorrow's tabloid newspapers: *Congressman's Wife Drags Corpse Through Mud!*

Caroline chided herself for her self-absorption. Her stunned gaze fastened on the spectacle of the body being pulled out of the clinging embrace of the mud bath.

On his knees now, with his feet braced against the wall, the Adonis was tugging, dragging the body out of the muck. He freed her with a grunt and one great clean-and-jerk, as if Claudia were a barbell and he were a weight-lifting contestant. Now only her high-heeled shoes still dangled in the muck. He took one step backward, so that her body was completely clear, but the shoes were left behind. Caroline hurried forward to grab them before they could sink again. For an awful moment, the strength in her legs gave way, and she was terrified that she was going to tumble facefirst into the "grave."

"Got 'em?" her mother crowed, as Caroline saved the shoes.

She peered over at Hilda, marveling at her mother's ability to wrest the trivial from the profound in virtually any circumstance. Where was the hint of new sensitivity she thought she had detected in her mother this morning? She should have known better than to get her hopes up. One good cry did not a better woman make. It was said that a person's true character emerged in crises, and this was a crisis if ever there was one. And here was the old familiar Hilda, bobbing to the surface like a rotten egg in a pan of boiling water.

I knew it was too good to last, Caroline thought.

She put the shoes down by the edge of the bath.

"Those could be saved," her mother said, with a fastidious frown. "Although they might have to be re-covered in a new fabric."

When Caroline turned and looked up, she saw that the young man was still clasping the body to his chest, and looking as if he didn't quite know what to do with it. He and Claudia were locked in a stiff embrace that looked to Caroline as if they were caught in a moment of dancing a macabre tango. For one wild moment, she thought he might whirl the body in his arms, press his tanned cheek to its muddy one, and step smartly out into a Latin rhythm.

"Put her down on the floor," Hilda commanded him.

Gently, he followed her directions.

"Caroline, turn up the lights in here," her mother ordered, and when the dimmed lights came up to their full brilliance, painfully illuminating the scene as if it were an operating room or a morgue, she exclaimed, "Good grief, she's still in that same dress."

Caroline heard an acidic note to her mother's comment, as if this were a judgment on Claudia's fashion sense instead of on the timing of her demise. For surely this meant the spa owner had never gone to bed last night. With a shiver, Caroline remembered the voices she had overheard on her own adventure — the raised voices — and wished she knew who had been taunted by Claudia only a few hours ago on the moonlit path among the trees.

"Why would she take a mud bath in her dress?" Hilda asked in the peevish, superior tone of someone who might have said, "Why would she wear a cocktail dress to a morning wedding?"

Caroline stared at her mother and then looked up at the Adonis. He was shaking mud off his arms, flinging it off onto the tile floor. A glob of it landed on Claudia's still breast. Another bit struck Caroline's own cheek, just missing her eye, and she flinched when it stung her skin.

Didn't they see what she saw?

Couldn't they see the obvious, terrible truth?

With a chill that increased her shivers, Caroline realized she might have overheard the final argument between Claudia de Vries and the one who killed her. For there was no doubt in Caroline's mind that this was no "natural" death. Claudia's peach chiffon dress was plastered to her body. But it was her lovely shawl of a thousand scraps of fabric that told the murderous tale: It was wound around and around her neck, pulled tight as a cello string tuned almost to breaking, and tied with a strangling knot.

"Go get Raoul," Hilda imperiously told the muddy Adonis.

He cast her an unreadable look but then turned to do as he was bid. As he brushed past Caroline, he muttered, "Your mother acts as if she owns the place." She cast him an apologetic glance that her mother couldn't see. Caroline had to agree that even for Hilda, her mother was being uncommonly bossy. His accent, she was startled to hear, was English, and not just any old Cockney, either, but decidedly upperclass. What in the world was that accent doing with those black eyes, that wild hair, and that swimsuit?

"What was that?" Hilda demanded when they both jumped at the shock of a loud splash in the adjoining room. "What's he doing?"

Caroline walked on shaky legs to the connecting door and opened it.

Adonis had plunged into the swimming pool to wash off.

She watched him swim the length of it, fast as a shark, graceful as a dolphin, as smooth in the water as if that were his natural habitat instead of land. *I've never felt that sure of myself,* she found herself admitting with a shock of piercing regret, *not even as a musician, certainly not as a daughter, a wife . . . a woman.*

"Caroline?" her mother called out behind her.

Without turning, she answered, "He's washing off the mud."

By the time he climbed out — with a single muscular lunge, his entire weight supported on one hand — his body was gleaming and clean again though a dark trail lingered behind him in the turquoise water. He shook himself, casual and efficient as a dog, but this time it was only water that flew off him. She watched him stride toward the front door, open it, and go off into the morning light without closing the door behind him. He didn't amble, but neither did he race. There was no visible urgency to his mission, nor did he appear to be the least bit self-conscious about walking around half naked. Rather, he moved across the ground with measured, graceful strides, as if he were merely moving to the side of a pool to scoop out a bit of litter that happened to be floating there.

Well, Caroline thought, forgivingly, *it isn't as if hurrying is going to bring Claudia back to life.* Her heart suddenly contracted painfully with sympathy for what Claudia's husband was about to hear and to endure. If it were Douglas who was dead, God forbid, she would want the Adonis to take his time, take forever, if possible, to walk from here to there, so that for all of those remaining moments she would still believe her husband was alive.

"Caroline!"

"Just a minute, Mother," she pleaded, still without turning.

Go slowly, she whispered silently to the handsome young man whose name she did not know. *Don't hurry to tell Raoul this awful news. Give him a little more time before he learns his world has shifted on its axis.*

Only at that moment did it occur to her that Adonis had not said a word about his employer or her death. Nor had he asked a single question, not even, "What hap-

70

pened?" He hadn't asked, "Is she dead?" although perhaps that was all too easy to see at a glance. He had simply followed directions; he had silently and efficiently moved to do what needed doing. Perhaps that was not a bad example to follow, Caroline decided, after a moment's thought about it.

She took another moment to compose herself.

Then she turned back to the mud bath room, her mother, and the body of Claudia de Vries.

"Mother! What are you doing?"

Her mother looked up from her crouched position beside the body of her old college roommate. "Nothing. I just wanted a closer look. I think somebody killed her, don't you?"

So her mother did realize the truth.

"You amaze me, Mom. You're so cool about this."

"Hysterics won't help, will they?"

"No, but . . ." Caroline couldn't say what she was thinking, that hysterics hadn't helped when her father died, either, but that hadn't kept Hilda from having them. "What are you doing, Mother?"

"Just checking something."

Caroline felt a sense of unreality. The

71

piped-in music was now playing a Celtic tune. The fountain still burbled in the center of the room. This couldn't be real. This wasn't a spa with a dead body in it. That wasn't really her mother down there, bent over a corpse, turning its head this way and that as if it were a turkey she was inspecting for the holidays.

"Mother! Don't touch anything. The police . . ."

"Well, why not?" her mother retorted. "You and that Hercules have already pawed all over her. I just wanted to see if what I suspected was true. . . ."

"What you suspected?" Caroline's heart began to pound again. Was her own mother on the verge of solving a crime before the police detectives even got here?

Hilda sat back, looking triumphant. "Yes. She *has* had a face-lift. I thought so."

Caroline found a chair and sat in it.

"Why doesn't anybody come?" her mother fretted, after they had waited what seemed an eternity alone with one another and the body of Claudia de Vries. Where only moments before she had seemed lost in her own thoughts, now Hilda turned and arched an eyebrow at her daughter. "You look like something the cat dragged in, Caroline. What if someone takes photographs? What if they print it in a newspaper? How would that look for Douglas to have his wife seen like this? Clean yourself up before somebody sees you."

Caroline looked down at her clothing and her arms, which were coated with thick, damp mud. She had hardly been aware of herself since she sat down, so stunned was she by the events of the past twenty minutes. But now, as much as she hated to obey Hilda, suddenly she couldn't bear to leave the mud on herself for an instant longer. Spotting a basin and faucet, Caroline hurried to rinse off as much as she could. She thought about taking off her clothes and putting on one of the terry cloth robes that hung on hooks but decided she didn't want to meet the police that way, wearing something so intimate as a bathrobe. In lieu of that, she scrubbed her face and neck and arms until they stung and the water ran clean into the basin and down the drain.

Her mother, she noted, didn't have a dirty drop on her.

Caroline had just sat down again in the leather chair when suddenly it seemed as if everybody was there all at once in a great loud chaos of discovery and dismay.

Claudia's husband, Raoul de Vries, came rushing in first, followed by several of the guests.

"Claudia!" he shrieked upon seeing his wife's body.

He didn't go to her, however, but drew back in a way that looked almost superstitious to Caroline. The man looked, she thought, as if he were afraid this death might be catching.

His next utterance sounded horrified. "How could this have happened?" He stared suspiciously at Caroline and then at Hilda.

"We don't know, Raoul," Caroline told him sympathetically. She stood up out of respect for the widower and the occasion. "When we came into this room, we found your wife's body submerged in that tub, and we pulled her out." She was going to break the news that it appeared that his wife had been murdered, but Caroline paused at that point, feeling unsure of herself and suddenly wary of saying it in front of so many people.

Behind Claudia's husband, Phyllis Talmadge was shaking her head in a deeply resigned and unhappy way, as if something she had feared had, indeed, come to pass. When she caught Caroline's eye, she mouthed, "I told you so!"

King David had come in with them, too. Now he leaned back against a door jamb, staring at Caroline, so that she found herself stammering for that reason as well. He looked older this morning, she judged from the quick glance she gave him before looking away. His sybaritic face looked more deeply lined, the bags under his eyes were heavier, as if he hadn't slept. But in spite of that, there was such a magnetism about him that it was all she could do not to keep glancing at him. She continued to be acutely aware of his gaze upon her face.

Beyond the door, she heard a man raise his voice and say, "No, Ondine, don't go in there!"

But the young model plunged through the open doorway, coming even farther into the room than anyone else had, so that when she did see the body, she gasped, and then screamed, and ran away from it like a little girl. The man she had pointed out to Caroline as her manager walked into the room, put his arm around her shoulders, and led her out again, saying, "Are you ever going to listen to me?"

Caroline risked a glance at King David.

He smiled ever so slightly and slowly winked at her.

It seemed wildly inappropriate, even lewd under the circumstances.

Caroline looked away again and this time firmly kept her own gaze turned away from the grown man who called himself King but who still seemed to want to be a bad boy.

Hilda, she noted, was hanging back, saying nothing.

Thanks a lot, Mom, she thought, as she faced the widower alone.

Just then, Lauren Sullivan slipped into the room past King David and went to stand just behind Phyllis Talmadge. Her bruised eyes looked as wide and distressed as a wounded animal's, and her famous little chin looked quivery, as if she might cry at any moment. She was so quiet, so unobtrusive, she might have been a maid coming in to assist all the celebrities, Caroline thought. And yet she was probably the most famous one of them all. She was also, it seemed, the most loath to call attention to herself.

But she had King David's attention, whether she wanted it or not.

By accident, Caroline caught her eye and was amazed to see the wide, generous mouth curve up in a small, sweet smile. For just that moment, they seemed to

Caroline to be caught in a circle of compassion that this beautiful, shy woman exuded by her very presence. And then the breathtaking smile was gone. Lauren Sullivan moved behind the others, so that she was out of sight of everyone, including Caroline.

Caroline stepped closer to Raoul, wanting to speak only to him. "I think you need to call the police," she suggested quietly.

His response was anything but quiet in return. "The police? Absolutely not. Why would I do that? Claudia would kill me. *The publicity* . . ." He turned slightly and clapped his hands once. "I want everyone to leave now. This is a private affair. I appreciate your concern, but this is a family matter. If you will all please step outside the room, I'll handle this. . . ."

At that moment, Hilda finally did step forward to speak. "No, Raoul," she said. "I'll handle this."

He turned his handsome, aristocratic face toward her, looking surprised, condescending, even slightly amused. His distress seemed to have given way to brisk management, Caroline observed.

"You'll handle it?" he asked Hilda with insulting politeness. "Is that what you said?

77

Well, thank you, Hilda, I'm sure that's very kind of you, but there's really no need for your assistance. I may be distraught" — he didn't look it, Caroline thought — "but Claudia was my wife, and I am now the owner of this spa, and —"

"No, Raoul, you're not," Hilda announced in the same strong, bossy tone. Behind him, his famous guests gaped at the little scene that was unfolding. Hilda cast a quick glance at her astonished daughter before saying, "You are not the owner of this spa, or at least you are not the majority owner. I am. I am sorry for your loss, Raoul, because I know what it's like to lose a spouse, but I must tell you that you have lost more than you realize. I am the new owner of this business, and I will take charge of everything from this moment on."

"Mother!" Caroline urgently pulled Hilda aside after a furious Raoul de Vries had been ushered out by the Adonis in the swimsuit who now, it appeared, worked for her very own mother. "Is this true, Mom?"

"No, I made it all up," was her mother's sarcastic reply.

"You've got to tell me more than you told them!"

"All right, come over here where he can't

hear us." Hilda cast a queenly look at her employee and called out to him, "What *is* your name, anyway?"

"Emilio."

"Emilio what?"

"Emilio Constanza, madam."

With that accent, Caroline thought, she wouldn't have been surprised to hear him say his name was Winston or Basil or Frederick, something as British as double-decker buses.

Her mother, who had honed her giving-orders skills on Caroline and her father for years, was already proving adept at taking charge and issuing edicts. That was the one part of this incredible turn of events that didn't surprise her daughter in the least. She'd always suspected that her mother must have been Napoleon in a former life.

Hilda ordered King David to call the police immediately, an assignment that he appeared to accept with relish and sardonic amusement. "Great publicity," he murmured, as he sauntered off to accomplish the job.

"Black forces still threaten us all," declared Phyllis V. Talmadge.

"Oh, mind your own business," Hilda snapped.

The psychic departed in a huff of outrage.

Hilda then shooed Christopher Lund and Ondine out of the building as well.

The only guest who hadn't appeared on the scene at all was Howard Fondulac, the producer Caroline suspected of being an alcoholic. So at least there was one guest whom her mother hadn't yet managed to order around or offend.

Now only Emilio remained with them. He stood with his back against the door, instructed by Hilda to keep out everyone except the police.

Caroline was determined to demand answers from this astonishing woman who was her mother. She had already heard Hilda tell Raoul that she herself was the majority stockholder in this privately owned company that was the spa. But what Hilda hadn't answered yet to anybody's satisfaction was, "How? Why? Mother!"

Hilda smiled in a satisfied, superior way. "Claudia and Raoul always thought their benefactor — their majority owner — was a wealthy attorney in Atlanta."

By the door, Emilio looked openly interested in this.

"But it wasn't? Was it you and Dad?"

"Not your father, dear, just me. It was

80

my secret little investment that I made long ago with money your father gave me when I asked him for it."

Of course, Caroline thought, Hamlin Finch gave his wife anything she wanted to try to keep her happy, to try to keep the peace.

"But why did you keep it a secret, Mother? Why didn't anybody know? Claudia was your old roommate, for heaven's sake. Why didn't you tell her?"

"She was my roommate but not my friend."

Hilda glanced at their "guard" and pulled Caroline deeper into the room, away from his listening ears. And then in a few terse sentences, Hilda delivered to Caroline the biggest shock of her life. "Didn't you ever wonder why I stayed at Brown for only one year?"

"Well, no, I —"

"You thought I left to marry your father, didn't you? That was true, as far as it went, but that came later. The real reason I left was to have a baby."

Her daughter gasped, and the man at the door looked at them curiously, though she thought he was surely unable to overhear their conversation.

"My parents knew, and my roommate

knew, but nobody else — not even the father — knew about it. I had the baby, and I put it up for adoption —"

"Oh, Mom," Caroline murmured, sympathy overcoming shock. But then she blurted in amazement, "I have a sister? A brother?"

"One of the above," her mother said, with a hard, brittle humor that Caroline suspected hid her real feelings. At least, Caroline hoped it did; she would have hated to think her mother could really be *that* cold and unloving. "I didn't want to know if it was a girl or a boy. I made them take the baby away without telling me. And then I let your father court and marry me, because I was afraid to go back to college."

"But why?"

Hilda cast a lingering glance at the woman whose mud-covered body still lay on the tile floor. "Because she said she would tell everyone what I had done. She hated me, she was jealous of me, and she didn't want me ever to return to school. I was afraid of her after that, always expecting her to divulge my secret someday. And then one day years later she called me and said she would tell your father about the baby if I didn't give her enough money to start this spa."

"Oh, Mom!" Caroline tried to clasp her mother in a comforting embrace, but Hilda didn't want it and pushed her away. Still, Caroline whispered, "I'm so sorry."

"Never mind that. The important thing is that I vowed my own revenge on that terrible woman. I began to buy her out, using an attorney, and she never knew it. It took me twenty years, but this year I finally did it. I finally became the majority owner of this place. And now I intend to run it my way." Her mother's smile was cold. "It's the best revenge, Caroline."

The owner of Phoenix Spa was dead.

The new owner was her very own mother.

But her mother was wrong, Caroline thought, even in the shock of the moment. That wasn't the most important thing. Not at all. And it never would be. The most important thing was that all those years ago another baby had been born and then disappeared, perhaps into another family. *She has another child! And I have a sister or a brother.*

Caroline's heart felt suffused with a warmth that nearly brought her to tears. But she saw at once that her mother wouldn't appreciate any show of emotion or, worse, sentimentality. And then a very unsentimental thought occurred to her like a cold wind that froze the warmth in her heart.

If the police were looking for a good motive for murder, her own mother certainly had one.

4

Detective Vince Toscana surveyed the scene. A bunch of people who were already too beautiful, standing around a beauty spa that had more marble than the Vatican, and all the people were covered with mud. In fact, they had paid good money to be covered with mud. Vince didn't get it. Back home in Philly, if some knucklehead threw mud on you, you wouldn't *pay* him for it, you would break his face, no question. You would have to break his face just to save yours, and you both would be better for it. Vince had learned that lesson from the boys on the corner, which is where he learned every lesson that mattered in life.

Vince sighed inwardly and wished, not for the first time, that he had never moved out of the city. He didn't belong in Virginia. There wasn't enough graffiti. Strangers greeted him on the street. People said "please" and "thank you" like it was going out of style. And now the mud people. It was crazy. But Vince loved his wife, Mary Elizabeth, who was from here, and so he had transferred, even though he was pushing sixty, two years from retirement, and the farthest south he had ever lived was a brick rowhouse on South Street.

And though Vince liked his fancy new house with the plush lawn, he often felt like the only Italian in the Confederacy. By day, he would find himself yearning for a steaming cheese steak and a growing crime rate. At night, his dreams were filled with the happy honking of congested traffic and the screaming of police sirens. He woke up relaxed when he had his recurring dream, the one where the cabbie cut him off and then cursed him out for it. Vince Toscana was homesick.

But now he had a job to do, and Vince loved his job almost as much as his wife. He flopped his tie over his shoulder, hitched up his khaki slacks, and eased onto his good knee beside the muddy body of Claudia de Vries. Vince suppressed his sympathy to serve his profession and appraised the lovely woman, now lifeless, with a critical eye. The medical examiner would determine the time of death for sure, but the pallor of the body and the tension in the facial muscles told Vince that rigor mortis had set in but not disappeared, so the murder was probably committed late last night. Plus the lady wore a fancy cocktail dress, like the kind his wife would wear at night. Then Vince noticed something strange. Down by the woman's manicured hand, the filmy dress concealed an object behind it, formless as a shadow.

Vince slid a ballpoint from his breast pocket and edged the cocktail dress away from the hand, exposing the article clenched in its death grip. What the hell was it? Vince leaned closer. The hand held a piece of clothing that looked for all the world like a skimpy bathing suit. He probed it with his pen, ignoring the surprised murmuring of the mud people behind him.

The swimsuit was made of white jersey, with some sort of bright gold pattern, and Vince couldn't tell without disturbing the suit if it belonged to a man or woman; it could have been either a man's suit or the bottom half of a woman's bikini. Vince wouldn't touch the suit until it had been photographed in place, so he had to settle for eyeballing it from the other side of the body. A swatch of material bulged through the corpse's thumb and index finger. A big yellow dot. A polka dot.

"An itsy-bitsy, teenie-weenie, yellow polka-dot bikini," Vince said aloud, almost involuntarily, as the song sprang instantly to his mind. He heard more murmuring behind him, which he disregarded as his thoughts returned to the body.

What did it mean? Was it a clue? Did the color matter? Did the dead woman rip it from the killer? Or was it presented to her, in some sort of confrontation, as proof of an affair? Perhaps she was just doing her laundry at the time she was killed? A *bathing suit?* Vince could feel the mud people hovering over his shoulder at the discovery. "Please, step back," he said. He waved them off as politely as possible, not wanting the scene contaminated more than it had been, until he heard a well-bred snort.

"I assume we can leave now," a woman's voice said, and Vince squinted over the top of his bifocals at a broad who had introduced herself as Hilda Finch. She was a definite number for her age, but too high-rent for Vince's taste. Next to her stood her daughter, Caroline, who managed to look pretty even with mud covering her clothing and a frown tugging at the corners of her mouth. She looked confused at the sight of the suit, as if she hadn't seen it before, or was too young to know the song, and Vince made a mental note.

"Mrs. Finch," he answered, "you don't have to stand here, but please wait for me in the front room, with the others. I will want to ask you some questions. For example, do you recognize that bathing suit in her hand?"

"Questions?" Hilda Finch peered down her small nose at Vince. "Detective, we don't know anything about this matter. Caroline and I simply discovered the body. That's the extent of our involvement."

"I understand, but we will need a formal statement as part of our investigation." Vince rose to his feet with difficulty. His knee hurt more, down South. All this clean air, and nobody had shot at him in a year. And it hadn't escaped his notice that Mrs. Finch didn't answer his question about the bathing suit. So much for Southern hospitality. "The department likes to do a thorough job, Mrs. Finch."

"That is not my concern, Detective."

"See what I mean?" Vince ignored her and gestured to the door, where an army of techs in blue jumpsuits and white booties entered, carrying stainless-steel cases of crime detection equipment. Their appearance had nothing to do with anything;

Vince was stalling Hilda Finch with his Crime Scene 101 lecture. She was an obvious suspect, and he didn't want her going anywhere. "These people, they'll gather the physical evidence from the crime scene. It will give us clues as to the killer. Your statement can help us, too, Mrs. Finch. The department would appreciate it."

"Detective, you can't be serious, detaining me. Don't you know who I am?" Hilda Finch fixed a cold gaze on Vince. "I am the owner of this spa, and my daughter Caroline is the wife of a very important person, a United States congressman."

Vince nodded, no-nonsense. "In my book, if you two found the body, that makes you both important people. I have to talk to you about the circumstances of this homicide."

Next to her mother, Caroline looked confounded. "Aren't you curious?" she asked. "I mean, about how Claudia was murdered?"

Vince looked from one woman to the other, waiting for the answer but acting casual. It wasn't easy to act casual around such classy people, and Vince wasn't a casual man to start with. In fact, Vince hated casual. Casual meant nothing mattered, and to a detective, everything mattered.

Hilda Finch batted her eyes, recovering quickly. "Of course I'm curious, but I'm not morbid. I refuse to stand here, gaping like some fool at a car wreck. I trust Mr. Toscana will tell us what we need to know." She glanced at her jeweled Rolex. "Besides, I have an appointment in fifteen minutes. We can chat after that." She turned away from a startled Caroline, and Vince didn't need twenty-five years' experience to figure that this was the first the daughter heard about any appointment.

"Appointment, Mrs. Finch?" Vince asked. "No problem. I can accommodate you. Normally I would examine the scene first, then talk to witnesses, but we'll talk now. Then you can get right to your appointment."

She pursed thin but glossy lips. "Detective, I will not be delayed. I have a business to run, and the next few hours are critical to its success. I'm sure the word is already out on what happened. There is much to do to make a smooth transition."

Vince decided to let her go. She could run, but she couldn't hide. Joe Louis had said that, or was it Cooch, from the corner? "Suit yourself, Mrs. Finch. If I need you, I will subpoena you."

"Send it to my attorney, Detective." Mrs. Finch took her daughter's hand more rudely than necessary. "My daughter and I are leaving right this minute."

"Why your daughter?" Vince glanced at Caroline, who looked like she wanted to cooperate. "She doesn't have an appointment, or a spa to run." Vince addressed the daughter directly. "Do you?"

Caroline reddened slightly, then cleared her throat. "No, but I think my mother's right, Detective. As the wife of a congressman, I probably shouldn't be speaking with you, at least without talking to my husband first. I have to think about the press, for his sake."

This Vince didn't like. The daughter had information, he could tell. "A woman has been murdered here, ma'am. You may have information that can help me bring her killer to justice. In fact, the murderer may still be among us, right here, in the spa." At this, the mud people recoiled in offense, but Vince ignored them. It was homicide that offended him, not honesty. "You're not gonna talk to me, Caroline? With human life at stake?"

"I can't," she answered, her forehead wrinkled with conflict.

"You may be putting all of these people in danger."

"I know, but —"

"If you have information for me, that puts you at greatest risk, do you understand that?"

Caroline looked torn, but her mother showed no ambivalence. "I'll leave the name of our attorney for you at the desk," Mrs. Finch said. Then she turned and walked off, dragging her daughter away as if she were a small child leaving a petting zoo.

Watching them go, Vince decided that Hilda Finch was the type of person who didn't care about others in the least, not even about her daughter. People like that, they were the most dangerous of all.

Vince had arranged to use a spare conference room in the spa for questioning the witnesses, which suited him fine. He didn't believe it would be real productive but it was procedure, and he'd have to make a record anyway. He could interrogate these characters on their home turf, which he hoped would put them at ease, and the room was nicer than the Ritz. Who knew what would happen? A black granite table, round as a black hole, dominated the room, which was otherwise completely white. Black leather chairs ringed the table, and as soon as Vince sat in one, the pain in his knee disappeared. The chairs were called something — *ergonomically correct,* Vince remembered, and figured he might ask for one of these babies for Christmas. They made his ergonomics feel better.

He eased back in the chair as a uniformed cop ushered in the first of the mud people. He would see them in no particular order, but they had been kept separate by the uniforms, per directive. The first witness was a young model named Ondine, one name only, if Vince had heard her correctly outside. She was gorgeous but so skinny she needed emergency ravioli. Vince watched with concern as she crossed legs thin as spaghettini and all but disappeared into the cushy chair. "I'm Detective Toscana. Can I get you anything?" he asked on reflex. "A drink, or maybe a meatball sandwich?"

The model set her puffy lips. "I cannot answer that question on the grounds it might incriminate me," she answered, with a straight face, and Vince didn't understand.

"What?"

"My lawyer told me not to talk to you. Also my manager, Chris Lund? He said to pound sand." She got up instantly and walked out the door with a speed surprising in the malnourished.

Vince rubbed his forehead. It was going to be a long morning.

Vince waited while his next interview, a man who looked a lot like George Hamilton, sat down opposite him. It was Raoul de Vries, the husband of the dead woman, and he didn't look unhappy enough at being suddenly single. Vince was instantly suspicious. The spouse was always the prime suspect. He leaned over the table toward Dr. de Vries. "My name is Detective Toscana, and I'm very sorry about your loss, sir."

"Not as sorry as I am. And that concludes this conversation." Dr. de Vries leaped to his Gucci loafers.

"Huh?"

"I will not discuss this matter further, on advice of counsel."

"But, Doctor —"

"You heard me," DeVries said and left even faster than the model, owing to his normal caloric intake.

Vince sat a minute in the glossy, quiet

room, suddenly cheered. He was getting so much crap, it almost felt like home.

Vince straightened in his wonderful chair at the appearance of King David, who strode through the door as if he were taking center stage. Vince had never heard King David's music, but he knew that the kids were wild for him. The rock star sat in the chair with such a theatrical flourish Vince was tempted to ask for his autograph, even though he didn't like anybody who would name himself King, on principle. It seemed vaguely sacrilegious. Plus what do you call him for short?

"King?" Vince began, taking a flyer. "I'm Detective Toscana."

The rock star laughed softly. "You don't really think I'm going to answer your silly questions, do you?"

Vince drummed his fingers and stared at his empty pad until the door opened and Howard Fondulac, the Hollywood producer, entered the room. The producer didn't even bother to sit down and stood inside the door only long enough to announce:

"I take no meetings without my lawyers."

Then he left, his cell phone ringing.

"Pleased to meet you," Vince told the young muscleman, and tried not to notice that the man was wearing only a black bathing suit, thin as a strip of electrician's tape. Vince wondered if the swimsuit was the same type as he had found on the corpse, but didn't want to spend a lot of time staring at the young man's crotch. Otherwise the guy had biceps out his ears and nipples that seemed to be winking at him. It was scary, even for a homicide detective. "I'm Vince Toscana," he said nevertheless.

"Emilio Costanza here," said the man, and Vince broke into a happy grin.

"You're Italian? A *paesan?* In *Virginia?*"

"I still ain't talking, goombah. I know my rights."

Vince nodded, understanding.

Vince was about to give it up when Phyllis Talmadge, the psychic author, chugged into the interview room like a diesel-powered tugboat. A red-lipsticked smile dominated her plump face, and her eyes burned an intense and alert brown. Her short hair bounced as she grabbed a chair and plopped down, oblivious to its ergonomic benefits. "I know *just* what you're thinking!" she boomed, and Vince smiled, startled.

"You should. It's your job."

"Damn straight it is." The psychic author burst into merry laughter. "You're thinking that these people are too rich for their own good. You're thinking that they have too much ego and not enough brains. Or heart. Am I right or am I right?"

Vince laughed. "Yes."

"You're thinking that, for once, you wish you had an easy interview. Someone who actually wanted to talk to you. Who could work with you. Who could put it all together into a nice, smooth story."

Vince laughed again, in wonderment. "That's exactly right."

"You want to meet somebody with useful information, who can throw out all the irrelevant facts, highlight the ones that matter, and just get to the point already."

"True!" Vince said eagerly. Her enthusiasm was catching.

"Well, I am that person! I can answer all your questions and wrap it up for you in a neat package. Most of the time, I can answer a question in eight words. That's a trick my media coach taught me. Go ahead. Try me!"

Vince frowned. "Media coach?"

"Come on, ask me a question, any question."

Vince glanced at his notes. "Well, I do have a series of questions and we —"

"Ask me what my new book's about, for starters."

Vince shrugged. He'd play. It *was* nice to have a witness cooperate, for a change. "Okay, what's your new book about?"

"Using your psychic powers to change your life." The author clapped for herself, with delight. "You're amazed, right?"

"Well, yes."

"You're so easy to read!"

"I am? I mean, I am." Vince leaned over, intrigued. He had never met a psychic, but a buddy of his in the department back home had. That psychic had helped them clear a major case, a double homicide. Maybe the psychic author could help on this case. "Are you really psychic?" he asked.

"Of course. I have the sixth sense. That's why I sell so many books. I'm on the list with the latest, it's goin' on eighteen weeks. Got three million in print and my backlist is going bazoogies. I'm givin' those Chicken Soup clowns a run for their money. I'm in a very competitive business, you know."

"But you're not a businessperson. You're an author, right?"

"Same difference. For example, take my latest, *Flex Your Psychic Muscles*. It flew outta the stores on the lay-down date."

"Lay-down date?" Vince didn't know the term, but it sounded important, if not clairvoyant. Or literary.

"After I did *The Morning Show*, we went into a fifth printing. I told my publisher, who needs Oprah? Print those suckers! Hold contests! Give incentives! Co-op ads! Rebates! Post me on the Web site, bounce me off the satellite, shrink-wrap me with the Sugarbusters, do whatever it takes. Just move product!"

"You mean your books?"

"I'm following up with a video, for people who hate reading, like me. Who has the time? And who needs it, really?"

"You don't read?" Vince asked, but the author appeared not to have heard him.

"My publicist thinks we can take John Gray, hands down, if we can just get the media in LA. Nobody gets media in LA, she says. She tells me you gotta be blonde. It's a visual medium, she says, but I say, *to hell with that!* I'm a promotable author, even though I'm not blonde. Where is it written you gotta be blonde? Look at Faulkner!"

100

"Uh, well —"

"Not blond. Also Hemingway — not blond."

Vince was growing impatient. He had met felons with better manners. "But Ms. Talmadge —"

"And Papa shoulda missed a few meals, if you know what I mean. The man had a beard like my aunt, but he moved product. You gotta admit, the man could move product! He *still* can and he's dead! And not even blond!"

Vince halted the author with a palm. He wasn't getting anywhere, and he had a job to do. "Yes, well, I wanted to talk to you about the murder of Claudia de Vries. Where were you last evening, between the hours of six o'clock and midnight?"

The author's enthusiasm vanished in an eye blink. "Why do you ask?"

"It's my job."

"Is *that* what you want to talk about?"

"Yes, of course."

The author looked confused. "You don't want to talk about my books?"

"Frankly, no. I'm a detective." Vince caught himself. He hadn't introduced himself because of the way she had barged in. "I'm sorry, my name is Detective Toscana."

101

"*You're* the detective?" The author gasped. A pudgy hand flew to her mouth. "This isn't my preinterview for *The Today Show*? They said they'd meet me here, at the spa. I thought the detective was next door. Wait'll I get a hold of that publicist!" She jumped to her tiny feet and plowed through the door, leaving steam in her wake.

Left alone in the interview room, Vince mentally regrouped. So nobody would talk to him without a lawyer. He should have expected as much. Rich people didn't expose themselves to risk, and they were used to layers of protection. He would have to approach the crime another way. Outside the room, the coroner would be examining the body of Claudia de Vries, and the techs would be vacuuming for fibers, hair, and other trace evidence. In a mud bath, there could even be muddy footprints. The crime scene would talk to him, even if the witnesses wouldn't. He had no time to lose.

Vince rose quickly to go and, in his haste, bumped into a white board resting on an aluminum easel. The easel toppled over and the white board fell off with a clatter, knocking into a closet door. Embarrassed, Vince hurried to right the easel, and as he bent over, noticed the closet door had been knocked ajar. Hmmm. He didn't have a warrant and had a lousy argument for a consent search. But if he found pay dirt, he'd go to the judge and get the warrant, then come back later and "find" the stuff. Vince had no problem with the Constitution, when it served justice. He opened the closet door.

The Sharpie letters on one of the boxes read "Dead Files." Vince lifted the cardboard lid of the box and peeked inside. A lineup of manila folders, all tabbed with different names and colors. Vince, whose color coding was limited to pink for girls and blue for boys, was dazzled by the array of chartreuse, cerise, and puce. He gave up cracking the color codes and pulled out the first folder.

"Leticia Finnerman" read the name on a lime tab, and Vince opened the folder. It had the name and address of a woman who lived in Newton, Massachusetts, and who weighed exactly 112 pounds. There was a chart that contained a detailed account of everything Mrs. Finnerman had eaten for a ten-day period. Vince closed it in disgust. Not a pasta dish among them. It broke his heart. And it didn't help with the case, either.

He riffled through the other folders, and they were all similar: records of spa menus for the length of the guest's stay. Then Vince remembered the skinny model, with the legs. Ondine One-Name. Had she been here before? What the hell could she eat? Water with ice? Vince flipped to the *O*'s and found a file. *Ondine*. He yanked it out and it flopped open.

But it wasn't a record of Ondine's menus. It was something else entirely. A ten-day stay, all right, but on each day, where the other guests had their food intake recorded, Ondine's chart showed a record of cash payments. The first day of her visit, which was October 31 of last year, she received $125,000, and she got $100,000 every day after that.

Vince blinked. Could it be? Did this kid get over a million dollars in ten days? But why? And from who? Whom? How much was she getting this visit, which was around the same time of year? Did it have anything to do with the de Vries murder?

Astonished, Vince looked up from the file just as the door to the conference room opened.

After her encounter with Detective Toscana, Caroline walked in a stiff silence with her mother, neither speaking until they had left the crowd at the mud baths behind and reached the flagstone path to their cottage. Caroline's emotions churned within her, as did so many questions. Why was her mother acting so strangely? Why didn't she tell the detective what she knew? And why didn't she want Caroline to talk to the authorities? She couldn't contain her thoughts a moment longer. "Mother, you told the detective you have an appointment. What appointment do you have?"

"I have things to do." Hilda Finch picked up the pace and her eyes remained straight ahead, confusing her daughter further. "I've had a telephone installed in our cabin, for one thing. I have a business to run. The transition has to be smooth."

"Mother, for heaven's sake. It's a spa, not a country. And a murder has been committed."

Hilda Finch pivoted on her heel, her face contorted with anger. "Don't you *dare* tell me what to do. Or denigrate my efforts. The spa is my business, just as you have your business. I don't make jokes about your cello playing, do I?"

Caroline was stung. "I wasn't making jokes. I was just trying to understand you.

This is a murder we're talking about, the murder of your friend. Don't you feel bad for her? And aren't you concerned for all of us? Why don't we go back and help the detective? What about justice?"

"Justice!" Her mother snorted. "Do you have any idea how much money this spa grosses a year?"

"Well, no."

"Swedish massages at a hundred and fifty dollars a half hour. Victorian manicures at forty-five dollars. All we do is put a foreign name on it and we charge extra."

"We?"

"Yes, we." Her mother's anger seemed to dissipate, and she leaned over confidentially. "The profit margin here is obscene, especially considering what we pay the help. I'm going to run this place even better now. I'll be more hands-on. Downsize, merge, and franchise."

"But you don't know anything about —"

"I don't? Does Mrs. Field know cookies? Does Mary Kay know mascara? Why shouldn't I have my own spa business? Who knows more about beauty than I do?"

Caroline gathered that the question was rhetorical. Her mother was the vainest woman alive, but was that a job qualification? Caroline couldn't shake the sight of poor Claudia, clutching that absurd bikini, even in death.

"With a clever accountant and some elbow grease, I'm planning to make Phoenix Spa into a chain. Breathe new life into the old bird." Her mother's eyes focused for a moment on some faraway bottom line, and Caroline couldn't take it anymore. A woman was dead and her mother was dreaming of franchising facials.

"You know what, Mother?" Caroline snapped. "I don't know you at all. And what I'm coming to know, I don't like very much. I think we should go right back to that detective."

"I will not!"

"Then *I* will."

"You will *not!*" Her mother's eyes flared in renewed anger. "I forbid it! Douglas forbids it!"

"You can't forbid me. I eat solid food now, have you noticed?"

Her mother didn't bat an eye. "I can still forbid you, and I do. Do it and you'll hurt me, destroy your family!"

"But how?"

"I don't want a new business at the center of a murder case, and if you don't care about your own mother, think of

Douglas. He loves you. He's a politician. You think he needs his wife being the star witness in an ugly murder case?"

Caroline tried to imagine it. It would be awful for Douglas. But being accused of obstructing justice could be worse. Caroline felt torn, but her mother ranted on.

"Picture this scene. Every press conference dominated by questions about you. Your name in the headlines, linked with a strangulation. And a bikini. God knows how they'll play it up, the possibilities are endless. He'll never get reelected!" Her mother drew a quick breath. "Now stop this foolishness and go to your room!"

The command struck a familiar chord. Without another word, Caroline broke away from her mother and hurried up the staircase to her room in their cottage. She was so angry and confused, she had to be alone. To think. To sort it out. To make a decision.

She threw herself facedown on the puffy duvet, like she used to when she was a teenager. When was she going to grow up? Why did she still let her mother control her? She didn't know. But she had to talk to Douglas. Maybe he would tell her. She had to get him up to speed on what had happened, so he could protect himself.

And what about this news, about her having a sister or a brother? Was that related to the murder? She had so many questions, so much to think about. It was all too much to process by herself. She needed help.

Caroline padded downstairs, poked around until she found the cordless phone that had been newly installed on her mother's desk, and punched in Douglas's personal number. Only she had the number; it was his wedding gift to her. She hated to disturb him at their country cabin, but she had to. He was working on a speech and always went into isolation at their cabin to write. Surely this was important enough to interrupt his solitude. She knew he would understand.

Still Caroline couldn't keep her thoughts from racing ahead. She had overheard Claudia's conversation last night. Did her knowledge put her in jeopardy? As the phone started ringing on the other end of the line, she eyed the glass sliders to the patio with new concern. The room was open to the lake. Anybody could break in. She tucked the cordless under her ear and hurried over to double-check the lock.

Good. The lock was in place. The phone was ringing. Douglas would know what to do. She loved him like crazy, and he was wonderful to her. He always seemed to have all the answers, and being married to him for the past eleven months was the best time of her life. Soon it would be their first anniversary. How would they celebrate? She would have to think of something. The phone was finally picked up. "Douglas!" Caroline said, almost breathless.

But the voice on the other end of the line was equally breathless. And it wasn't Douglas's voice. It was a woman's. "Hello?" the woman said, in almost a whisper.

"Douglas?" Caroline asked, taken aback. It couldn't be Douglas's phone. He was alone at the cabin, and nobody else had this number. "I'm sorry, I must have a wrong number."

"No, you wanted Doug? This is his phone."

Caroline's mouth went dry. Her face felt suddenly aflame. She didn't understand. *Doug?*

"He's sleeping, right here, but I'll wake him if it's important. Is this his office?"

Caroline couldn't answer or speak. She didn't get it. Was Douglas at the cabin with another woman? It couldn't be. He was going up alone, he'd said. He always did. Their marriage was sound, wasn't it?

"Hello? Anybody home?" breathed the woman's voice, then laughed lightly. She sounded young. Fresh. *Thin.*

Caroline's fingers tightened around the cordless. So Douglas hadn't sent her here for her benefit, or for her mother's. He had done it so he could be alone with this woman. It had all been planned. Premeditated. And was it the first time? Douglas always went to the cabin to work. Was this woman with him all this time? Caroline felt her heart wrench within her chest, but it wasn't pain, it was anger. Rage. *Fury.* She felt like exploding. For the first time in her life, Caroline felt like an adult. Like a *woman.*

"Would you give Doug a message for me?" Caroline asked, her voice surprisingly strong.

"Fer sure. I'll get a pencil."

"You won't need one. Just listen."

"Okay. Whatever."

"Tell that jerk I want a divorce for my anniversary," Caroline said abruptly, then pressed the button for End.

5

"Bravo!" The phone clattered to the floor. Caroline whirled around and saw King David in the doorway clapping, his head seeming to scrape the top of the door frame. "Couldn't have said it better myself," he added and came toward her.

She took a step backward toward the bathroom.

He stopped and held his hands up as if she had a gun on him. But he was smiling. "Did I scare you?" he said. "I just wanted to have a minute to talk to you. It's not easy, with your mother . . . anyway, can I sit down?"

Caroline shook her head. He was too big for the room. It wasn't just his extraordinary height, the long ropy arms, the snakelike hair coiling around his shoulders. Power bristled around him like microwaves. It came from decades of people pouring love into him in huge stadiums, writing him letters, waiting for him outside stage doors; from the critics arguing about him in *Rolling Stone* and *Spin*; from the judges letting him off one more time; and from the gossip columnists and girlfriends and agents.

He put his hands in his pockets and sighed, lounging comfortably in place.

"For all I know, you killed Claudia," Caroline said.

"Maybe I did," he said and laughed. "In one of my famous drug-induced frenzies. Don't think I was having one last night, but then, the frenzied one is always the last to know. Look, let's go outside. We can stay in full view of the police the whole time, if you're really worried about me. I really have to talk to you."

She hesitated, searching herself internally for the flood of emotion that ought to be paralyzing her. Shouldn't she be wailing and weeping and taking to her bed about now?

Why did she feel so . . . so liberated instead, as if she'd been living in a cage, well fed, well housed, for the past year? Her mouth opened a little and she looked down at herself. Her hands were on her hips, her chest sticking out so the top button of her shirt had unceremoniously popped out of the buttonhole, her bare feet standing apart on the rug. She felt galvanized, not

113

stricken. The giant only a few feet away raised his eyebrows and she saw the tattoos in the corners.

"That must have hurt quite a bit," she said, tapping her temples with her fingers.

"Anything for art," he said. "So?"

"So let's go outside."

As she passed through the doorway after him, the phone began to ring. She closed the door on the ringing, no slam, no acknowledgment of it at all. King did the eyebrow thing again, then turned and walked over to the path by the lake. Following him down the path toward the water, she felt grateful for his ironic smile and cheerful cynicism, because she had responded to it with some unknown part of herself that was saving her now. That conventional part of herself hadn't taken over, the part that would have been hoping she was wrong. If King hadn't come along she would have answered that phone and listened to whatever story Douglas told her.

Listening with one ear she heard the phone finally fall silent. What could Douglas have said? She would have to be a moron not to comprehend the tones of the girl's voice, the lazy assurance in it, the estrogen-soaked attraction of that breathless soprano.

Now, trotting behind the tight jeans and wide leather belt that strode ahead, she let the waves of angry realization wash over her one by one. Douglas hadn't been home for dinner more than twice a week for the past three months. He'd been on the road or at meetings or in legislative sessions. Someone important needed his advice, or a crucial campaign donor needed a pep talk.

And she, she had been proud that he was so important. She'd closed her eyes and ears and especially her mouth, because Douglas was everything she wanted, her mother said so, everybody said so. Somehow, she must have felt that way, too.

She bit her lip. She'd left her hard-won position in the symphony, left her home in Tennessee, without a second's regret, gladly even.

"Shit!" she muttered. She had known Douglas since high school, but the gawky kid in the glasses had metamorphosed into a sophisticated, charming man who wore Italian suits and knew how to talk to a woman. He had always said he supported her music, even envied her talent, and he went to her performances, but somehow his work had become the primary work. She had allowed it, had actively collaborated in it. She was a fool!

Caroline and King had reached the lake. Mallards rode the calm water, gossiping in low quacks. Haze veiled the trees in the distance. No one seemed to be around, though the parking lot on the other side of the property was full of cars, including the police cars that had been there since dawn. Detective Toscana must still be hard at work in his conference room.

"You know, now that I don't get loaded anymore I find that running works well to take the edge off the bad stuff," King said. "We could go around the lake."

"No." Actually she was so furious at her stupid naïveté right now that she felt like going into the lake, not around it, but she wasn't going to tell that to this complete stranger with his Medusa hair and wicked grin. "What did you want to talk to me about?"

"About Claudia. Sit down." He sat on the grass and indicated the place beside him with a long hand, but she stood in front of him, her hands plunged in her pockets, still locked in anger at Douglas and herself. She felt like somebody else, somebody who didn't care about her manners and who wasn't about to be impressed by this stale old rocker with his muscles and big lips.

"Let's get it over with," she said.

"All right." Sprawled out on the grass he wasn't quite as formidable. "I'm going to tell you something I didn't tell the police. And then I want you to tell me something."

"We'll see."

"Hmm. All right. I told you that I was here for a reason, a reason that had nothing to do with massages and mud baths."

"Yes. You said you were here to get something that belonged to you." Slowly, her mind began pulling away from Douglas as she returned to the indelible, shattering fact of Claudia's death.

"Claudia has it — had it. The thing I was looking for. She died before I could get it. I had been looking for it for a long time, and when she called me I was . . . I took the first plane."

"You knew her before?"

"Quite well. Pre-Raoul. She knew how to reach me and how to get me here on short notice is what I'm saying. When I arrived, Claudia put me off. I had to stick around, and I started talking to people. Actually, people talked to me. I'm used to it. They do that."

"I'll bet they do." She couldn't keep the scorn out of her voice. "What exactly is this mysterious thing you came here to find?"

"Not important to anyone but me," he said, sitting up and folding his legs. His jaw set and the cheekbones popped into prominence. Under all the hype he was an awfully good-looking man, the sort of man who in the past might have even been said to possess beauty. She now saw a certain purity and cleanness of feature, as though the dissolute lifestyle hadn't even touched him. Sitting like that on the grass, talking calmly, his long hair stirring briefly in the morning breeze, he didn't look dissolute; he looked like a Tibetan lama.

"Women like you always hate me," he said. "I guess I seem unpredictable. The funny thing is, you scare me as bad as I scare you. You seem so sure of yourself. Makes me feel fraudulent somehow."

"Women like me," Caroline repeated. "What is a woman like me?"

He looked surprised. "Well, mainstream women. Who go to good women's colleges like Wellesley. Who marry well and do good works, not for pay of course, and have one point six beautiful —"

"Stop!" she interrupted. "You don't know anything about me!" She felt ashamed to hear her life described like that, ashamed that anyone could reduce her to just that. And yet an hour before she had been proud of her marriage, looking forward to beautiful children. *What's wrong with what I am?* she thought. *Who have I ever harmed? Did Douglas ever love me at all?*

"Sorry," King said. "Whatever I say seems to make you dislike me more. And from what I heard on the phone, you've just had a hell of a shock."

She breathed out. "It's okay. I suppose I've got you hopelessly stereotyped, too."

"I did do it. Bit the head off a bat. It was performance art. I was young and trying to make it any way I could. I'm forty-four now, and I study classical piano, and I contribute to the Humane Society, and I'm a vegetarian. But people still remember me and the band, the bras flying onto the stage, the screaming, the heroin. . . ." He stopped and folded his arms around his knees.

"I'm a cellist," Caroline said.

"So you said."

"I loved it. Love it."

"Fantastic," King said. "Do you have it with you? Your cello? It'd be a kick to hear you play."

"No."

"Why not?"

She almost didn't answer, but he seemed genuinely interested. He was a musician, too. "I gave it up. When I got married. Isn't that a riot? I sold my cello." Thinking about her cello finally brought out all the emotion that had been roiling inside her. Angry, frustrated tears stung her eyes. She felt King's big hand on her arm, and she shivered.

"You were saying that you knew Claudia," she said, pulling her arm away.

There was a pause, as if they were re-collecting themselves. Caroline realized that she really wanted to spill her guts about her life, to weep on his shoulder and tell him intimate details about her marriage.

People talk to him, she thought. King was staring down at his shoes, which she was happy to notice were not the lizard-skin pointy-toed boots she might have expected but beat-up Adidas sneakers, size fourteen at least.

"Claudia. Yes. When I first met her, she was a nutritional counselor at a very exclusive facility that catered to a lot of very well-known people," King said. "This was about twelve years ago. She did favors, you know? And then she'd come back to you, sometimes years later, and want a favor in return."

"I see," Caroline said. She was thinking about the word he had used earlier. *Heroin.* Was that what the "facility" treated? Or was it one of Claudia's "favors"?

"She got me to come here to the spa, and when I arrived yesterday I recognized two of the other guests. They had both been at this other . . . place. I asked them if Claudia had asked them to come, rather than them just happening to sign up. And they both said Claudia had put the pressure on."

"Who are you talking about?"

"Well, Howie. Howard Fondulac, the producer."

She remembered. The man who seemed to be a drinker.

"And Phyllis Talmadge."

"The writer. The New Age lady."

"Right."

"So what?" Caroline said. "What has that got to do with me? Why tell me this?"

"So I thought this was peculiar. I decided to check with some of the people I didn't know. I just happened to be talking to Ondine's manager, what's his name —"

"Christopher Lund, I think he said —"

"And I asked him what really brought Ondine here. He told me that Claudia had invited them both to come and waived all

121

fees. He thought the idea was that she would find a way to get some publicity from having Ondine around, but he actually hasn't got a clue about why they got this invitation. Then he said when they got here, he could see that Ondine already knew Claudia."

"Okay," Caroline said slowly.

"That covers four of the people who came just before Claudia was killed. So, what about you and your mother, Caroline? Why are you here?"

"My mother wanted to come. She decided."

"And you came along like a good girl," King said. "Did your mother know Claudia too, before she came here?"

"Yes. They were roommates for a while in college. A very long time ago." Careful, she told herself. Don't say any more, don't mention the baby. That was far too private. She had so much thinking to do!

King was watching her struggle to say no more. "And what about you? Did you know her?" he said.

"Not at all. I didn't know who ran this place. I just —" I just blindly followed, she thought.

King said nothing. He rubbed his chin.

"So all of the new guests either knew Claudia before or came with someone who did," Caroline said. "As though Claudia had some purpose in mind in gathering together this particular group."

"She didn't do it as a friendly get-together," King said. "Not her style."

"Tell the police," Caroline said.

"After I find out who killed her."

"You? But why should you?"

"Because her killer took the thing I came here for. I need to get that back. Then the cops can have whoever it is."

"That could be dangerous."

King threw back his head and laughed. A product of who knew how many brawls and riots, he obviously wasn't afraid of much. Then he said, "I'd like that to mean you care about what happens to me."

She got to her feet, and he jumped up and again was standing too close. She had gotten up too quickly — or was it his proximity making her dizzy? — and a fantasy blew into her mind, born of resentment toward Douglas as well as King's slow smile. Any second now he would stretch out his arms to her, pick her up lightly, run off with her into the woods and —

"Caroline?" he said, still smiling, embarrassing her, knowing somehow what she was thinking.

"Yes?"

"What were you doing last night at two a.m.? I saw you go by my cabin."

"I — I —"

He leaned down and put his mouth to her ear, and she could smell the scent of him, woody and slightly pungent.

"I won't tell," he whispered. "Just give me the key you took from her."

"No! It wasn't me!" She stared at him, wide-eyed. His eyes with the lightning bolts gleamed like the lake, and suddenly she thought she caught something cold and terrible in there. He could easily kill Claudia, the way he had lived for so long, lawless and wild. And he was a magician, the way he held you with his eyes and touched you and fascinated you, a master of misdirection.

"You found Claudia, didn't you? You had time to take it. Don't be afraid, I won't tell anyone else. Our secret. But I need the key."

"Maybe you killed her and didn't have time to take this key you're talking about," she said, breathing hard. "But I sure didn't."

He cocked his head, held her eyes, then nodded. "I believe you. Then your mother must have it."

Caroline felt the memory like a knife,

saw it all again, her mother touching Claudia's body.

No!" She shoved him hard, taking advantage of his surprise to get him out of her way, and took off running. The long rays of sun jabbed through the haze here and there, striping the path in dark and gold, confusing her. She ran on in what she hoped was the direction of her cabin, every sense occupied with getting there and avoiding a misstep.

Through her ragged panting she could swear she heard another breath, a panting behind her, rhythmic and determined. King David?

Or someone else?

Vince leaned back in his chair, which he found cloyingly comfortable, put his hands behind his head and his feet up on the granite, and listened to the noise in the corridor outside. The first one to arrive had barged right in, and Vince had kicked him out just as fast.

All the lawyers had arrived by now, in rapid succession, importantly, noisily, tethered to their attachés, raising hell with the patrolman outside for making them wait.

Vince did not budge. He twisted his lower lip and thought. After a while, a skittish police officer finally knocked and edged in, locking the door behind him.

"They all out there yet?" Vince said. "Let's see, we got lawyers for the Hollywood boozer, the husband, the macho employee, the rocker, the Madame Blavatsky lady, and the supermodel."

"There's five Hermès ties and one pair of Manolo Blahnik spike heels out there, sir. The suits are all gray and black. Two of them have been waiting almost an hour. The woman lawyer just got here."

"Fine."

"They're starting to froth, sir. Staring at their watches and barking into their cell phones. The woman has her laptop out, but the men may try to beat the door down if you don't see them soon."

"I hear you, Mike. Did you offer them anything to drink?"

"No, sir, like you said —"

"Good, good."

"Sir?"

Vince was looking out the window again. He had a nice view of the lake, not a hint of the smog up here. Birdies twittered outside and the whole scene was like a postcard. Yeah, staged for the photographer. Ten minutes before, King David and the congressman's wife had been sitting by the lake having a heavy discussion. Then she jumped up and ran around a turn in the path, and he had lost sight of them. "Huh? Yeah?" he said.

"How long before I start bringing them in?"

"Listen, Mike," Vince said, not taking his eyes off the view. "Three hours ago I asked those important people outside to answer a few questions about a murder in their freakin' midst. And you know what they did?"

"No, sir."

"They were disrespectful and uncooperative. They tried to jack me around."

"Not good, sir."

"Right you are. So I gave them time to round up some local mouthpieces, and I applied myself to other freakin' aspects of the case. Because we got a duty, right, Mike? Rich people, that's the problem. Exercisin' rights poor people don't even know they have."

Knock knock knock. "I need to see the detective," an authoritative baritone announced.

Vince motioned with his finger for Mike to come closer. "Fifteen more minutes, Mikey," he said. "Let 'em stew in it, okay?" He turned back to the papers on the table.

"Yes, sir." Mike threw open the door. A balding man in a thousand-dollar suit was standing there, his Adam's apple bobbing up and down in fury. "Step back," Mike ordered. "Step back there. Detective Toscana is not ready for you yet."

Fifteen minutes later a slightly less balding man entered, ushered by Mike, clutching a heavy briefcase as if he'd already drafted a bunch of briefs and wrapped the whole thing up. The wait had fired him up and he started talking before he even sat down. Behind him came Howard Fondulac, unshaven, uncombed, and undone. Vince switched on the tape recorder.

"Outrageous," the lawyer was saying. It was a routine lawyer greeting. Sort of like "hello."

"Please," Vince said, feeling better than he had in hours. "Take a seat, gentlemen." They sat down in front of the table and right away the producer, if that was what he really was, Vince was going to check him out, spoke up. "I don't know anything. I've got to go back to LA right away. Important business. Meetings. Commitments."

"I'll do the talking," said the lawyer.

"Well, tell him."

128

"My name is Eric Derrick." He handed Vince a card engraved so deep it was practically coming apart. He had a slow Southern accent that gave Vince time to grind his teeth between words. "Mr. Fondulac was sound asleep from ten p.m. until eleven a.m. this morning. He is shocked and distressed at this situation, and he fears for his own safety since a killer appears to be running free on the property. He has booked a flight leaving in two hours, and —"

"He's not going anywhere," Vince said.

"But Mr. Fondulac has important business —"

"His current business is right here. Nobody's leaving at the moment."

"But you can't — there's a murderer loose!"

Vince just sat there and looked at him and let the inanity of that statement sink in. Eventually even the lawyer got it, if the merest hint of a blush on the top of the ears was any indication.

"Yeah, you got that right, and we're trying to do something about it," Vince said finally. "Like talk to the witnesses. You mind?"

"But I don't know anything!" Fondulac said.

"What do you do in Hollywood?" Vince said. "I've never been there myself."

"I'm a film producer." Vince let him explain that and came to find out that old Howard was sort of retired right now, hadn't done a movie in the last several years, in fact. He confessed he'd had a few health problems. Vince sympathized and told him about his arthritis, and Fondulac started relaxing and even getting a little garrulous, which made Derrick jump in, and old Howard shushed him this time.

"I guess a week or two at a place like this would be good for me, too," Vince said, patting his belly. "But I couldn't take the chow, I'd miss my pasta."

"Oh, there's pasta. Just no oil, you know. No cheese."

"I'd rather die young," Vince said. "No, give me my food and my liquor, you know? Speaking of which, you got a good one going this morning. Hangover, right? You ever try vitamin C for that?"

"Mr. Fondulac certainly does not have a hangover. He did not come here to be —"

"Give it a rest, counselor. Well, Howard? Big night last night?"

"That's exactly why I don't know anything," Howard said. "I'm afraid I had too much to drink. I missed breakfast. And all the rest of it."

"Do that often, do you, Howard?"

"More than I should. I know I wasn't supposed to bring liquor in at all. I admit it, I've got a problem. I've been admitting it and surrendering and making amends and relying on my higher power for twenty-five years now, and I've still got a problem."

"What's your poison? Let me guess, Chivas?"

"Jack Daniel's."

"Good sippin' bourbon, if I do say so. So where's the bottle from last night? And by the way, how big a bottle are we talkin' about?"

"A pint? I think a pint."

"That's interesting, because we just picked up this pint bottle on the path by the bathhouse where the lady was strangled." Vince held it up in its wrapping. "The security man says he made a round at midnight and there was no bottle. He saw it runnin' in to see the commotion when the body was discovered. So it got laid down last night."

"Now wait just a minute," Eric Derrick said.

"That couldn't be my bottle," his client

131

said in a choked-up voice.

"Great," Vince said. "Then you won't mind us taking your fingerprints just so my superiors don't yell at me. Mike outside has the kit."

"I don't think that would be appropriate at this time," the lawyer drawled.

"Oh, yeah? I'll decide that," Vince said and gave him the patented Toscana glare. "You know, if we get involved in a lot of formalities, legalisms, that sort of thing, Mr. Fondulac could be here for a long, long time."

Fondulac and Derrick hastily convened on the far side of the office. Whispers flew. Vince looked out the window again. Strong sun now, not a soul out there enjoying the path by the lake. Eventually, the lawyer allowed as how Mr. Fondulac would give fingerprints, seeing as how he wanted to cooperate and get home.

And they all knew he didn't have a choice. Vince put on a cheerful look and said, "That's great. So let's get back to the location of that bottle."

"I certainly didn't leave it there. But if my fingerprints are on it, maybe someone took it out of my trash."

"Ah." They figured his prints would be on it and so the next line of obstruction had come up. They were making progress. "So you put it in the trash?"

"Yes."

"And where is the trash located?"

"In my room, of course. The plastic can in the bathroom, actually. It had a swinging lid."

"You specifically remember putting it in the can?"

"Yes."

Vince showed his teeth. "Then we're all set. All we have to do is confirm that. Dust the lid for prints."

"Maybe it didn't get into the trash can. I might have left it on the floor. I was drunk!"

"So you're saying somebody came in your door late at night while you were crashed and took your empty bottle and left it on the path by the bathhouse?"

"My God," old Howard said in a surprised voice, turning to his lawyer. "Someone's trying to frame me! That's just what must have happened!"

"Now who would do a thing like that?" Vince went on, not missing a beat.

"I — I can't imagine!"

"You had an enemy here, Howard. That must be how it went down."

"Yes! Yes! Raoul! That sneaky bastard. I'll fix him. He hates me. Because I — because of a money thing. Years ago. We had a dispute. He said I owed him two hundred thousand dollars. We lost that money fair and square. It was a joint venture, a tax thing, and Claudia told me Raoul had forgotten all about it. But now I see he's just been biding his time. Eric, you have to do something!"

"How long ago was this? The money thing?" Vince asked.

"Ten, twelve years ago."

"You and Claudia and Raoul were tight, huh?"

And out it came. "Tight? We were business partners, that's all. Claudia worked at this health place I went to and we got to talking, and she told Raoul about this film I was producing. I had Kevin Costner practically attached, this was before the water flick and the futuristic Pony Express one. Raoul and Claudia had some money from somewhere and they were looking for an investment."

Vince nodded sagely. "Hollywood," he said.

"The project tanked, they tank sometimes, but they took it personally. And about the same time the deal soured, Raoul got this idea that Claudia was sleeping with me. He was madly in love with her. He was insecure and jealous. So anyway I was damn surprised when she called and invited me to come, but I really needed to get away, and when she told me Lauren Sullivan was here and looking for a project, it was perfect, and Claudia said — God, she said —" He stopped and a horrified expression came over his face.

"Well, what'd she say?"

"She said I deserved the full treatment."

"And had she started giving it to you by last night?" Vince asked.

"He thinks I'm lying," Howard said to his lawyer. "You check it out, Detective. It was her husband. He killed her. I don't know why he killed her, but he got me here to frame me."

"But she was the one who said you deserved the full treatment," Vince said.

"He got her to invite me," Howard said, less assurance in his voice. "He's a subtle one, he is."

Vince said, nodding again, "I hate subtle people. All those hidden agendas."

"So are you going to do something about him? Arrest him?"

"We'll check for his prints on the bottle."

"He'll have wiped them off," Eric Derrick said.

"You sure you didn't take a midnight

stroll last night?" Vince asked. "I get lit, I do funny things sometimes. Decide I need some air."

"I'm quite sure I never left my room," Howard said.

"Is there anything else?" said the lawyer, leaning forward.

"Well, I have to ask, you understand. Whether you did sleep with her way back when in the Kevin Costner days. Since it might have inflamed the husband."

"I never laid a hand on her."

"Oh, come on, how could you resist? You were all going to get rich together, you were at this relaxing place together, hot tubbing and all that, she was a fine-lookin' lady. And it would explain a lot better why the husband would go after you."

Howard said, "Well, just the one time."

"One time only. Sure."

"Once or twice. She really wanted me. I was damn attractive in those days." He smoothed back his neat, thinning hair, as if remembering thicker, more unruly days.

"I bet."

"Come on, Howard," Eric Derrick said. "Are we finished?"

"For now," Vince said.

"Who's next?" Mike said, sticking his

136

head in. Behind him was a talking head, irate.

"The husband."

Raoul de Vries came bounding in like he was aching to beat some butt on the tennis court. His tan and good health made Vince feel vaguely pissed off. He must be the stiff-upper-lip type, or else he didn't give a flyin' fart that his wife was dead, whatever he might have felt about her before, because there was no sign of red eyes or sadness. The second lawyer was just like the first: tall, balding, portly, and young. Vince waved them to seats and took the card. "H. David Derrick," it read.

"Your brother out there, H.?" Vince asked the lawyer.

"Yes. It's a small town. We aren't in the same firm."

"You guys could be twins."

"We are."

"What's the *H* stand for?"

"Herrick. Can we move on?" He was even more humorless than his brother.

"I bet you're the older one. By ten, fifteen minutes," Vince said. The devil made him do it.

"I am the younger. Is this relevant?"

"I guess not," Vince said. "But I don't know what else we're gonna talk about. Because your client told me this morning that he wouldn't talk to me on advice of counsel."

"I said without advice of counsel," de Vries interposed. "Let me explain. A long time ago a lawyer told me to say that if I ever found myself in a police situation. It's not that I don't want to cooperate. My wife is dead. My heart is broken. I'm at your service."

"I'm happy to hear that. Really. Because it looked bad," Vince said. "So what was this police situation you were in?"

"I didn't say I was in a police situation. I said *if* I was in a police situation."

"You ever done time, Mr. de Vries?"

De Vries gave him an incredulous look and turned to Derrick Herrick or whatever the Mother Goose hell his name was.

"I fail to see the relevance," the lawyer said.

This parrot talk didn't go over very well with Vince. He ignored the lawyer and picked up the rap sheet in front of him and said, "You went to Soledad Prison fourteen years ago. For attempted murder. You tried to kill your then-girlfriend. Not Claudia." He turned to Derrick. "Relevant enough for you?"

"Go ahead."

He was ordering Vince around, the twerp, but Vince did want to go ahead, so he contented himself with a scowl and went on. "You served only two years, what with good behavior, good lawyering, and good connections. It's cryin' out for reform, our penal system."

"Is there a question pending?" asked Derrick.

"I didn't do it," de Vries said flatly.

"Yeah? You told the California parole board you did it. You gave plenty of details and said you were sorry. You said you were, let's see, in a rage due to her infidelities and didn't know what you were doing. You beat her up pretty bad."

"If I hadn't told them I did it, I'd still be rotting in jail," de Vries said. He had crossed his leg and was bouncing his foot up and down. He was counting the seconds until he could get out of there.

"Did you already know Claudia by then?"

"Yes. We were married two months after my parole. Which has expired, by the way."

"Where's she now? The girlfriend, I mean."

De Vries jumped up. "Why are we crashing around in this ancient history? My wife is dead! You should be finding her

139

killer, finding out how Hilda Finch ends up getting everything we worked for, everything we own. You should ask me where I was last night, when I went to bed, how we got along! Yes, I went to bed with her! No, we had no quarrel at all! Yes, she must have got up in the middle of the night and gone to check something or maybe meet someone, I don't know!" He covered his face with his hands and started to sob.

Bored, Vince sat back and waited for the curtain to fall. He didn't believe de Vries's performance. Vince was getting the idea that de Vries was a jealous, weak man with a definite place in his scheme of things for women as objects of desire and sources of financial security, who had learned a few things in prison.

Derrick put his arm around his client's shoulder and offered him the paisley handkerchief out of the chest pocket of his jacket. Next he'd be saying de Vries was too distraught to continue.

Time for a little consult with Laidlaw, Vince decided. Laidlaw was the accounting expert the department used in white-collar-crime investigations. Raoul and Claudia had a nice business here. He wondered where the money to start it had come from. Were they pulling down a profit? So much money they could lay almost a million bucks on that stick of a girl out there?

And Fondulac's story, was there anything to it? De Vries was all bent over now, bawling like a baby, getting his back patted. It was a good act, but nothing Vince hadn't pulled himself when his ma caught him stealing papers off the stoops in Philly and reselling them on the corner.

And he thought about ancient history. It had a way of rearing up and biting you on the ass. The whole case had a smell of ancient history.

6

Out of breath, Caroline slammed the cabin door behind her and then stood leaning against it, gasping.

"You never did learn to enter a room like a lady," Hilda said. "You came racing through the door like the devil himself was after you." Hilda was once more seated in the morris chair. Quickly she removed the pair of red-framed reading glasses that had been perched on her nose. She stowed them in one pocket of her pink sweats and then gathered up the sheaf of papers and photographs that had been spread in her lap. Those she shuffled back into a manila envelope. Once the envelope was closed, she used the metal fastener to hold it tight.

"Douglas called," she said.

Caroline barely trusted herself to speak. "And?" she said finally.

"He wants you to call him back. At the cabin."

"What did he want?" she asked. Even as she asked the question, it puzzled her why she was carrying on this charade and acting as though everything were normal when she should have thrown herself into her mother's arms and confided in her, telling her the awful truth — that she had already called Douglas that morning only to find another woman at the cabin. But the years of acrimony between Caroline and her mother had left too much of a void between them, too much distance to be crossed all at once.

Not trusting her knees to hold her upright, Caroline sank down into the desk chair and stared at the phone as though it were her mortal enemy.

"Well?" Hilda urged impatiently. "Are you going to call him, or are you just going to sit there all day looking at the phone?"

"I'm not going to call him," Caroline said.

"Why?"

"Because I don't feel like it." Even in her present mood, it sounded to her own ears like a childish, stupid thing to say.

"Caroline," Hilda said firmly. "You have to understand. Your husband's a politician. You need to talk to him so he can give you whatever directions you need for handling yourself in this kind of situation."

"You mean like send one of his staffers

out to bird-dog me and make sure I don't say or do something that could make matters worse?"

"Yes. Of course," Hilda returned mildly. There was another unspoken part to her mother's answer, the part about now that Caroline had made her bed, she would have to lie in it. And, of course, there was no need for Hilda to say it then because Hilda had said it so often, Caroline knew it by heart.

She felt her temper rising. The whole idea was absurd. Here was Caroline, an innocent bystander to a murder she personally had nothing to do with, but both her mother and her husband expected her to agree to being led around by the nose and told how to act, what to say, and how to say it. Meanwhile Douglas was free to do whatever he wanted. He had taken a woman with him to the cabin, a cabin that was, after all, half Caroline's. He was up there now, doing God knows what and giving no thought or care to any kind of scandal. The double standard inherent in that was simply too much.

All her life Caroline had been a good girl. She'd done what she'd been told and tried her best to live up to other people's expectations. Last night she had broken into the kitchen and taken food. This time, instead of knuckling under to her mother's pressure, Caroline found the strength to fight back.

"What are we doing here, Mother?" she asked.

"Doing here?" Hilda repeated. "What do you mean by that?"

"You know what I mean."

"We've both been through so much the last few months," Hilda replied smoothly. "I thought a getaway to the spa would do us both a world of good. A time-out, as it were," she added.

"Like when you used to punish me by sending me to my room?"

"A little, I suppose," Hilda agreed. "Only with better food. Back then, you made mud pies. You could just as well have been taking mud baths," she added. "You were that messy most of the time."

"This isn't funny, Mother," Caroline continued. "And it's no time for jokes, either. Why are we here, and who paid?"

"Why Douglas did, of course," Hilda answered. "You saw the check he wrote — twelve thousand dollars."

"If you own the place now, I'm sure we could have come for free."

Hilda shrugged. "Maybe we did — come

for free, that is. In fact, Claudia invited us to come, both of us. Douglas gave me his check to pay for it, and I did cash it, but I can tell you Claudia de Vries never saw a penny of that money. I made certain of that."

"What do you mean?" Caroline asked.

"Go upstairs and look in your closet," Hilda ordered.

"In the closet?"

"Yes," Hilda replied. "It came this morning. UPS delivered it to the office while we were all preoccupied with what had happened to Claudia. It was heavy, so I had the deliveryman carry it upstairs."

Without saying anything more, Caroline fled up the stairs and threw open the door to the closet. Inside, her clothing had all been shoved aside in order to make room for an enormous box. As soon as she saw the size of it, she knew what it had to be. Still, not trusting her own judgment, Caroline went into the bathroom and retrieved the fingernail shears she carried in her overnight bag. Then she rushed back to the closet. It took her several minutes to chop her way through layers of protective cardboard and plastic bubble wrap, but as soon as she saw the black case she recognized it for what it was — a cello. And not just any cello. It had to be her own cello. She recognized the worn but familiar case. She placed the case on her bed and then opened it to reveal the beautifully finished instrument inside. Tears of gratitude sprang to her eyes as she caressed the familiar lines and curves and ran her fingers across strings Caroline knew almost as well as she knew her own body. Somehow her mother had returned it to her.

Leaving the instrument lying on the bed, Caroline made her way back down the stairs. "Where did you get it?" she asked in a hollow voice.

"I remembered the name of the woman who had bought it from you," Hilda answered. "All I had to do was track her down. I offered to buy it back for four thousand dollars more than she paid you for it. Believe me, she was more than happy to make a deal. Who wouldn't be? And there went Douglas's twelve thousand dollars. Money well spent, if you ask me."

Caroline was stunned. "Thank you, Mother. I can't tell you how grateful I am, but why would you do such a thing?" she asked. "Whatever possessed you?"

"Giving up everything that's yours for a man like that — a man with that kind of power — is an entirely stupid thing to do,"

Hilda returned. "Surely you're not really that naive, are you?"

Even though Caroline had called herself "stupid" not an hour or so earlier, it hurt to hear her mother say the same thing. Under other circumstances she might have been overjoyed to see her beloved cello once more. Now she was overwhelmed. She bit back the tears that still threatened to wash her away.

"I have no idea what you mean," she said, still playing the game, still pretending that things were all right between her and Douglas when they were anything but.

"Maybe you should take a look at this, then." Lifting the envelope from her lap, Hilda held it out. Caroline looked at it but made no attempt to take it.

"What is it?" she asked. Her voice sounded wooden. There was an ache in Caroline Blessing's heart. She knew that whatever was in the envelope was going to be bad news, and she didn't want to touch it.

"Surveillance reports," Hilda answered. "From a private detective."

"Surveillance reports on whom?" Caroline asked.

"On Douglas, of course. Who else? Names, places, dates, times. I thought you should know all these things. And I thought you should have some idea which of your friends aren't friends at all. That's always useful information to have, to know where you stand. When it comes to this sort of thing, a woman can't afford to have too many surprises, especially in this day and age."

"You've been spying on Douglas?" Caroline managed to stammer.

"Spying's too strong a word," Hilda returned mildly. "I prefer to think of it as checking up on him. And it's a good thing I did, too. Your father certainly wouldn't have considered doing such a thing, although, in my opinion that's something fathers are supposed to do — protect their daughters. Now take it," she urged. "Even if you don't want to look at it, I still want you to have it now, before it's too late."

Caroline reached out and took the envelope. The paper should have been cool to the touch, but it wasn't. The surface of the envelope seemed to sear her skin. She held it for a moment, and then it slipped through her reluctant fingers and dropped to the floor.

"I don't want it," she said. "I don't want to know. I already told Douglas I want a divorce. I don't need to know any of the rest of it."

"You may think you don't want to know, but if you don't take this envelope and put it away, the rest of the world is going to find out all about it."

"What do you mean?"

"Oh, Caroline, please don't be so incredibly dim," Hilda returned. "Why do you think I refused to talk to the detective today?"

"You said you had a spa to run."

"The detective may have been dumb enough to fall for that, but he'll get over it soon enough. I expected better than that from my own daughter. What I had to run was you," Hilda said. "I had to get you away from that man long enough to give you this so you could put it away properly before all hell breaks loose."

"All hell has already broken loose," Caroline pointed out. "Claudia de Vries is dead, and Douglas is having an affair. How much worse could it be?"

"That Detective Toscana is going to show up here any minute to arrest me."

"You?" Caroline gasped.

"Of course," Hilda said calmly. "Whom else would he come after? Even you should be able to see that I'm the most likely suspect. Once that happens, they'll get a search warrant, go through this room, and the contents of this envelope will be up for grabs. So while I go turn myself in, I suggest you do something with this. Put the envelope somewhere safe so that Toscana and his henchmen won't find it."

The fact that Caroline's mother was about to be arrested for murder was utterly unthinkable. "You're going to turn yourself in? For what?" she asked. "And what about having a lawyer there with you? Shouldn't you have one? Everyone else does."

"No need," Hilda replied. "It's nothing but a delaying tactic. I didn't kill Claudia de Vries, although, truth be known, I sure as hell wanted to. No, my turning myself in will give you time enough to get rid of the envelope. Then, when they find the real killer, they'll let me go and everything will be fine, and you'll have what you need to get yourself a great settlement. Judges don't just hand those out for no reason, you know," she added. "You have to have the goods on an erring husband in order to do that, especially when the erring husband is a member of Congress. But not to worry. You do have the goods, so take good care of them, while I freshen up and put on some makeup. If I'm going to be arrested,

I'm going to be photographed. It wouldn't do for the new owner of Phoenix Spa to be hauled off to jail looking like something the cat dragged in, now would it."

With that Hilda went straight to her closet and paused there, studying the contents. "Which do you think, the navy suit or the fawn?"

"Navy would be better," Caroline supplied.

"Good," Hilda agreed. "That's what I think, too. It does a better job of showing off my hair."

Taking the blue suit with her, Hilda disappeared into the bathroom. Caroline stooped over and picked up the envelope that still lay on the floor where she had dropped it. It was addressed to Mrs. Hamlin Finch, and the postmark was dated weeks ago. From the weight of the envelope, Caroline could tell that it contained many sheets of paper. If each of them meant a separate report, then the surveillance had been going on for some time. So had Douglas's betrayal and infidelity.

Caroline was still standing and staring at the envelope when the bathroom door opened once more. "Are you still here?" Hilda demanded. "You've got to do something with that, and you've got to do it now. Otherwise, it's going to be too late."

Nodding wordlessly, Caroline retreated upstairs to her loft. Not only had her mother bought back her cello, she had bought back the case as well. The case had a secret compartment concealed in the lid that had been known only to Caroline, her mother, and the person who had made the case. She pressed the pressure point just to the left of the topmost latch, and the satin lining sprang away from the leather to reveal a letter-sized, fold-out pouch. She slipped the envelope into the pouch and then closed up the lining.

Once the damning envelope was out of sight, the weight of all that had happened washed across Caroline and brought her to her knees. It was too much. The pain of her husband's betrayal, the shock of Claudia's death, the prospect of her mother being arrested — it was all more than Caroline could handle. She leaned against the bed with her head buried in the silky cover of her feather-soft duvet while a wild storm of weeping shook her very being. She stayed that way for a long time.

"Caroline?" her mother called up the stairs at last. "Are you still here?"

She stifled a ragged sob. "I'm here," she answered.

"I'm going, then," Hilda said. "I just wanted you to know."

"All right," Caroline managed. "Do you want me to come with you?"

"No. I'm sure you're in no condition to deal with any more stress. You stay here and try not to worry. Everything will be fine."

Everything won't be fine, Caroline wanted to shout at the top of her lungs. My marriage is over. My life is a wreck. My mother is being arrested for murder. But she didn't say any of those things aloud. Instead, she reached out her hand and touched the long, clean neck of the cello. She let her fingers trail along the smooth surface, allowing her fingers to find comfort there. When the door slammed shut behind Hilda Finch, her daughter reached over and removed her bow from its holder. Then she wrested the cello upright and carried it over to the dressing table chair.

Ignoring the ravaged countenance that stared back at her from the mirror, she planted the instrument between her sweats-clad legs and pulled the bow across the strings. The cello was so far out of tune that the shrill sound made her wince. It took her several minutes of tuning before she had it right, but when she did, she launched into the haunting strains of Camille Saint-Saëns's Cello Concerto no. 1. As the music washed over her it brought her the same relief it always had. It was through the cello that she had been able to endure all those years of arguments between her parents. It was music that had seen her through the loneliness of being an only child in an apparently loveless marriage. She had assumed, mistakenly, that once she fell in love — once she found the perfect mate — the peace granted her by music would no longer be necessary.

Wrong, she told herself grimly. Absolutely wrong.

And then, keeping her mind firmly turned away from Nero and his fiddle and the fire consuming Rome, she sat there and played her heart out, waiting for someone to come and tell her that her mother was under arrest.

Even without the benefit of practice and despite having been away from her music for months, Caroline Blessing played better than she ever had before. She played flawlessly because she meant to and because she was playing for her mother. Because somehow, Hilda Finch had known that her daughter would need that cello again. In spite of whatever difficulties had presented themselves, she had gone out and found it.

"Thanks, Mom," Caroline murmured as the last strains of the concerto died away. And then the tears came again.

Phyllis Talmadge entered the interview room, followed closely by her lawyer, Marsha Rollins. Wearing spike heels that clicked ominously on the marble floor, Rollins marched into the room with her laptop in hand and with a three-inch-deep chip on her shoulder.

"I want to object to the fact that you interviewed my client earlier under entirely false pretenses," Marsha Rollins announced. "I'm serving notice right now that anything my client said in the course of that interview will be considered inadmissible."

"Wait a minute, Ms. Rollins," Vince said calmly. "To begin with, your client came to me. I didn't send for her. She came in and spoke to me entirely of her own accord."

"She thought you were a producer," Rollins objected while Phyllis Talmadge nodded furiously. "She thought you were

156

there to interview her . . ."

Vince smiled. "I *was* interviewing her," he said.

". . . for an appearance on *The Today Show*," Rollins finished. "She thought this was something that had been set up by her publicist."

Vince looked past the attorney. "Why are you here, Ms. Talmadge?"

She blinked. "Because you said I had to be. Like everybody else."

"No, I don't mean why are you here in this room. Why are you at Phoenix Spa?"

Phyllis shrugged. "For the same reason everybody else is, I suppose. I have a cover shoot in a few weeks, and I want to look my best. So I thought I'd come here and shed a few pounds. Get in touch with my core being, you know. That kind of thing. In my line of work, centering is very important. Otherwise I can't tune in to the universe and learn what I need to know."

"What is the universe telling you about Claudia de Vries?"

"Really, Detective Toscana, you can't expect my client to answer . . ."

But Vince had hit Phyllis Talmadge where she lived, in her ability to see deep into other people's hidden lives. "Shut up, Marsha," Phyllis told her attorney. "I want

157

to answer this question. It's important. Claudia de Vries was an evil woman. She preyed on other people her whole life. It's hardly surprising that she finally got what she deserved. In fact, what I can't figure out is why it took someone so long to come after her."

"Did she ever prey on you?" Vince asked.

"Phyllis, please," the attorney objected. "You don't have to say anything."

"She tried to," Phyllis Talmadge said, as her eyes narrowed dangerously. "But I didn't let her get away with it. I told her to back off, and she did."

"When you say prey, what do you mean?"

"Blackmail," Phyllis said simply.

"She was blackmailing you? How and why?"

Phyllis shrugged. "She knew I had had a bit of a drinking problem, years ago. Then my first book came out and she went to my publisher and tried to convince them that I was a fraud, that I had become a psychic by taking a correspondence course when I was locked up at home with three little kids. That was a lie, of course. I only had two."

"And it worked?" Vince asked. "The

correspondence course, I mean."

"Sure it worked," Phyllis Talmadge replied. "It turned out I already knew how to do it, it's just that I didn't know I knew. It's like radio waves, you see. As long as the station is on the air, the waves are there. The only reason you don't hear them is you haven't turned on your receiver."

"I see," Vince said. "So do you ever help with criminal cases?"

"Detective Toscana, this is utterly uncalled for . . . ," Marsha Rollins began.

"Do you?" Vince asked.

"Sometimes," Phyllis Talmadge said. "Not very often, mind you. But sometimes."

"Would you be willing to help us on this case?"

"You mean professionally? Not as a suspect?"

"Absolutely," Vince said. "As one professional to another."

"I'd have to think about that for a little while," Phyllis Talmadge said. "I'd have to go outside by myself. Maybe down by the lake and think about it."

"Why don't you do that," Vince said, nodding sagely. "You go think about this case. Tune in to whatever radio waves you need to in order to be able to tell me what's going on here, then you come back and tell me what you learned."

"You mean in less than eight weeks," Phyllis said. "Eight weeks is usually my limit. Any longer than that, and the results may not be reliable."

"You take as long as you need, but I'd appreciate something sooner than eight weeks. That's a little longer than I had in mind."

Phyllis was nodding, and Vince knew he had her. He had appealed to her professional ego. If she knew something — incriminating or not — the woman would be stumbling all over herself and her bull-headed attorney to spill the beans.

Then, just when he should have been asking Phyllis for her verbal agreement to go along with his plan, there was a knock on the door. Damn.

"What is it, Mikey?" Vince demanded as the door opened a crack. "Don't you know I'm busy in here? I thought I told you I wasn't to be interrupted."

"Yes, sir. I know, sir, but I thought this was important."

Vince sighed. "All right. What is it?"

"There's someone out here demanding to see you."

"That's a switch," Vince Toscana said.

"Somebody actually wants to see me for a change? Sure it isn't another one of them damn lawyers?"

"It's that Finch woman. She says she's come to turn herself in."

Vince turned back to Phyllis Talmadge. "I'm sorry about the interruption," he said. "There's another door over here. If you wouldn't mind, you can go out the back way. And then, after you've spent some time down by the lake, you can come back and tell me what you've learned."

She shook her head. "No, that won't be necessary."

"What won't be necessary?"

"My going to the lake. I've already tuned in. Your assistant here is absolutely right. The Finch woman — I believe her name is Hilda — is the one you want."

"You're saying she killed Claudia de Vries?" Vince asked.

Phyllis frowned. "That's still a little fuzzy. The message isn't quite coming through, but the person you're looking for is Hilda Finch. I'm quite sure."

Mike was standing in the doorway with the door half open behind him. Now someone knocked on it hard enough that it bounced off his back and the doorknob whacked him in the hip.

"Well," Hilda Finch demanded loudly, "is he going to see me or not? If he can't be bothered, I suppose I could always go outside the gate to where all those television cameras are stationed and tell the reporters there that I tried to turn myself in but Detective Toscana was too busy doing other things to be bothered with arresting me."

Toscana turned back to Phyllis Talmadge and her fuming attorney. "If you ladies would please excuse me," he said, ushering them to the back door. "This sounds important. I'd better handle it."

The detective let them out, closed the door, and then turned back to the other door in time to see a limping Mike let Hilda Finch into the room. At the crime scene, Hilda hadn't looked her best, but now she did. With a daughter in her midtwenties, Hilda had to be somewhere in the mid-fifty range, but she didn't look it. In fact, the broad looked as though she was a high-powered CEO ready to make a speech in front of a corporate board of directors.

"What can I do for you, Mrs. Finch?" Vince asked politely.

"You can arrest me for the murder of Claudia de Vries. The woman was a black-

162

mailing bitch, and I'm glad she's dead."

"Being glad isn't the same as being guilty."

"Maybe not, but you need to arrest me anyway."

"Does that mean you're confessing?"

"Not exactly. But surely I'm under suspicion."

"Everybody here is under suspicion," Vince told her. "The problem is, at this time, I don't have enough evidence to arrest anyone, including you. Have you been advised of your rights?"

"I'm not some little wimp, Detective Toscana. I don't need my rights read to me, and I don't need an attorney present, either. I'm entirely capable of talking to you on my own."

"Why did you do it?" Vince asked.

"Do what?"

"Kill her?"

"Claudia was a very annoying woman," Hilda answered.

"You killed her because she was annoying?"

"And did you know she'd had a face-lift?" Hilda continued. "Here she is, spouting the age-reversing benefits of all these natural herbs and supplements, but she's gone out behind all her clients' backs and gone under some plastic surgeon's knife to smooth out the wrinkles. If that isn't flying under false pretenses, I don't know what is. In fact, I'd be surprised if someone didn't file suit against Phoenix Spa for false advertising practices."

"How long had you known Mrs. de Vries?" Vince asked.

"Long enough," Hilda Finch answered. "Since college."

"And how many years would that be?"

"I refuse to answer that question," Hilda answered. "It's rude to ask a woman her age like that. Didn't your mother ever teach you any manners? Anyway, it doesn't matter. I plead the fifth."

"So you'd been friends since college."

"I said we'd known one another since then. That doesn't mean we were friends."

"But you've been in business together."

"I've been in business with her," Hilda agreed. "But Claudia didn't know she was in business with me. She thought her silent partner was an attorney from Atlanta. I can give you his name and number if you like." She reached into her purse, pulled out a business card, and handed it over to Detective Toscana. He took it without looking at it.

"And now you own the business?" Vince asked.

"Something like that," Hilda replied.

"Don't you think Dr. de Vries would have something to say about it?"

"Raoul has nothing whatever to do with it," Hilda said. "Talk to my attorney. You'll see that there's an ironclad survivorship agreement. As spa physician, Raoul has been an employee here, nothing more. He's never had any ownership in the spa. I don't think Claudia thought him entirely trustworthy."

"You're aware that he's a convicted felon?"

Hilda raised an eyebrow. "No," she said. "But it's not too surprising. It also might make his continuing on here problematic. I wouldn't want Phoenix Spa's physician to have a blemished record. He might have kept it quiet up till now, but after this the world will know. That will make it difficult to attract and keep the kind of clientele we need to keep the bills paid. As you can well imagine, this isn't an inexpensive operation."

"Funny you should mention that," Vince said casually, tapping the stack of file folders he had laid out on the tabletop in front of him. "I've pulled everyone's folders, yours included. My plan is to take them back to the department to go over them one at a time. I would imagine they'll turn out to be some pretty interesting reading, wouldn't you?"

For the first time, Hilda Finch seemed to falter. Her eyes darted from Vince's face to the stack of folders and back again.

"Aren't you interested to see what is in your folder?" Vince asked.

"I have no interest whatsoever. I suppose it's all about what treatments are used and what kinds of results the client has over the course of a stay here."

"You might say that," Vince agreed. "So as a partner, even as a silent partner, you'd be aware of monies paid out over the course of time."

"I receive quarterly reports, if that's what you mean," Hilda replied. "At least, my attorney receives them, and he forwards them to me."

Vince thumbed through the folders and picked up Ondine's. "Would you happen to know why Claudia de Vries gave Ondine over a million bucks the last time she was here?"

"I beg your pardon?"

"Maybe it was just a trick-or-treat gimmick, since Ondine checked in on October thirty-first. She received a hundred and twenty-five thousand dollars that day and another hundred thousand every day for the remainder of her ten-day stay. You know anything about that, Madame Silent Partner?"

"Why that low-down bitch! You mean to tell me she was skimming that much off the top and giving it to somebody else? If I'd known that, I really would have killed her — with my own bare hands."

"But you didn't."

"No," Hilda admitted. "I suppose not."

"So what's all this charade, then? What's with this I want him to arrest me crap?"

"I did want you to," Hilda told him. "I still do. So I'd be safe."

"Safe from what? What do you mean?"

"I'm afraid that now, as the new owner, I may become a target, too. I thought the best way to be protected would be for you to put me in jail."

"Sorry," Vince told her. "No can do."

"Well, then," Hilda said with a sigh, "I suppose I could just as well go back to my cabin and change into my sweat suit since there won't be any photographers after all."

Just then, they heard a scream. Vince Toscana leaped from his chair and ran to the back door. He pulled it open just as Marsha Rollins came careening up onto the deck. "Come quick," she yelped. "I can't swim, and somebody's got to help her."

"What is it?" Vince demanded. "What's wrong?"

"It's Phyllis," Marsha answered, gasping for breath. "I came back from using the rest room and found her floating facedown in the lake. I think she's dead!"

7

The detective had turned the conference area into a makeshift squad room. Several maps of the spa had been tacked onto the back wall, along with a half dozen postmortem photographs of poor Claudia. Loose scraps of paper had been posted scattershot, certain items underlined in red, but Caroline couldn't read the words from where she was standing. Mounds of what looked to be notes and official documents hid the top of the circular black table he was working on. He smiled at her with watery eyes, pointed to an empty chair. But Caroline elected to stand.

"You actually revived her," Caroline stated. She was in awe. He had shown himself to be a man of action. Passivity, the mainstay of her personality, was probably not in his vocabulary.

Toscana shrugged. Revived her? Not exactly. But he did get the old lady breathing. The psychic was still unconscious.

Caroline said, "Do you think she'll make it?"

169

Again, Toscana was less than forth-coming. "I'm not a doctor, so I can't answer that. Is something on your mind, Mrs. Blessing?"

Caroline couldn't get the words out. Her eyes were fixed on the grisly photos of Claudia, face caked in mud, a sick parody of a vaudeville minstrel.

Toscana blew out air. "Your mother isn't here, if that's what you wanted to know."

"Did you arrest her?"

The detective tried to keep his face flat, but it didn't work. He must have thrown her a highly nasty look because the young woman recoiled, taking several steps backward and bumping into the wall. He said, "No, I did not *arrest* her. I *detained* her. I took her down to the precinct to have her questioned officially. Which is what I should have done with the lot of you when I was originally called down."

"Why didn't you?"

"The spa's a cash cow. Our city's revenue base is limited, if you haven't noticed. But I can't operate like this, tippy-toeing around a bunch of . . ." He caught himself, bit his lip to hold back venom. Not good to lose it in front of a suspect. "What can I do for you?"

"Does my mother have a lawyer? Caroline asked.

"Several of them."

"Your lawyers or *her* lawyers?"

"I think she has both."

Caroline tapped her toe. "Can I talk to you, Detective Toscana?"

Again, he pointed to the empty chair. She sat down on the opposite side of the table, taking him in. No-nonsense eyes peered out of a weathered face. Stubby fingers. She noticed them when he lit a cigarette. He saw her staring at him.

"What?"

"Smoking isn't allowed here," Caroline said weakly.

He took in a deep drag, then blew it out, away from her face. "If it bothers you, I'll put it out. But if you're afraid of my breaking some rule, don't worry about it."

"It doesn't bother me."

Vince was surprised. "No?"

"No." Caroline looked at her lap. "My father . . . he used to smoke cigars until my mother finally won *that* battle. Even so, every time she went away, he used to sneak a few. Before she came home, we'd spend hours trying to fan out the smell." She chuckled as her eyes swelled up with water. "It never worked. Mom always knew."

"I can believe that." He raised his brow.

"You talk about your dad like he's . . ."

"He is."

"I'm sorry."

"So am I."

A voice with a drawl interjected. "Where should I put this, sir?"

Caroline looked up. A handsome man in his thirties was carrying a coffee maker, a can of MJB coffee, a jar of coffee whitener, a box of sugar, and some thermal cups. He had dark hair and blue eyes. He was wearing a wedding ring. She twirled her own band around her finger, playing with the mockery.

Toscana said, "Anywhere you can plug it in, Mikey." He looked at Caroline, then at his man. "Officer LeMat, this is Caroline Blessing, wife of Douglas Blessing."

"The congressman?"

"The congressman," Toscana confirmed. "That means we gotta be nice to her."

Caroline said, "You're being condescending."

"Not possible," Toscana replied. "You folks own the monopoly on condescension. If it weren't for that woman over there" — he pointed to the photos of Claudia — "I'd say you all were funnin' with me. You know, let's have some yucks over the Southern crackers out here."

"You're not from the South."

"No, I'm not." He tossed her a bitter smile. "I'm from Philly, Mrs. Blessing. But I can assure you and your gang of high rollers that Virginia takes murder very seriously."

"No one thinks this is funny," Caroline said.

"Coulda fooled me," Vince said. "Mikey, you mind making up a pot of coffee?" He paused. "You want a cup, Mrs. Blessing? Or is caffeine against the rules, too?"

"Probably."

"Would you like a cup? Yes or no?"

"Yes."

"Make the entire pot, Mikey."

LeMat put on the pot and left. The room fell quiet, the only sounds coming from the gurgle of the coffee maker. Caroline licked her lips. "Any idea who pushed poor Ms. Talmadge into the pond?"

"Who said she was pushed?" Toscana answered.

"I just assumed . . ." Caroline stared at him. "Are you saying she tripped and *fell* in?"

"It's a possibility."

"But no one heard her scream."

"And if she was pushed in, you don't think she might have screamed?"

Caroline was silent.

Toscana said, "Do you know anything about the woman?"

"Not a clue."

"Nothing about her personal habits?"

"Meaning?"

"Did she drink?"

Caroline absorbed his words. "You think she was drunk?"

"Possibly. Wearing heavy shoes and being a bit tipsy, she could have lost her balance. If she was more than a little tipsy, her reaction time might have been off its prime, gone under before she realized she needed to do something. She might have tried to scream, but water's a pretty effective muffler."

"Did you smell alcohol on her breath when you revived her?"

"No."

"Then she couldn't have been that drunk."

Toscana sat back in his seat. "Not necessarily. What I smelled was lots of perfume and lots of mint in her mouth, like she was embalmed in wintergreen. You drink and you don't want anybody to know, what do you do?"

"You suck on a breath mint," Caroline answered.

Toscana nodded. "There you go."

"So her drowning was an accident?"

"I didn't say that. I'll know more once she's conscious — if she regains consciousness." The detective evaluated his subject. "Why are you here, Mrs. Blessing, and without a lawyer? Suddenly stricken with a bad case of conscience?"

"I thought that maybe . . ." Caroline looked at the ceiling. "You know, if we pull together some stuff . . . information . . . maybe we can solve this thing together."

Toscana smiled. "Now that's a *great idea!* Do you want a thirty-two or a Beretta semiautomatic, Annie Oakley?"

Caroline was silent.

Toscana sighed. "Look, Mrs. Blessing. You seem like a sweet kid. A real thin one, too. Why on earth are you here?"

"For my mother's sake. After Dad died, my husband . . ." She almost choked on the word. "We thought the trip might help get Mother through a difficult time."

"That's nice." He smiled. "That's really nice."

"The whole thing has been a disaster!" Caroline got up and began to pace. "Since my mother is the majority shareholder in this place, we both have a vested interest in solving this mess."

"Did she send you here?"

"No, she didn't. I actually came here on my own. I *am* capable of independent thought."

"I don't doubt it."

But he did doubt it. Caroline could see it in his eyes. "I want this to work for her. For her sake as well as my own. When she's happy, she leaves me alone."

"So what are you holding back?"

"If I tell you everything I know, will you tell me what you know?"

"Probably not. But give it your best shot . . . ah, the pizza." He shoved some papers off the table and onto the floor. "Put it right here, Mikey. Take a piece for yourself."

"Pizza!" Caroline cried out.

Toscana regarded her face. The woman needed a life. He slid the box over to her. "Knock yourself out."

Her eyes traveled to the postmortem snapshots. "I'm too sick to eat it now."

"Suit yourself." Toscana opened the box, took out two wedges and made himself a sandwich. "Great stuff! I can almost taste home in every bite. Go on. Give it a shot."

Dutifully, Caroline liberated a piece from the box and set it down on a napkin. She began to pick at the cheese.

"So . . ." Toscana swallowed and wiped his mouth. "What do you know?"

"If I talk freely, will it come back to haunt me?"

"Maybe. But if you don't talk, your conscience will most definitely haunt you."

Caroline dipped her finger into the melange of sauce, oil, and cheese and licked the tip with her tongue. "Claudia de Vries was arguing with someone the night before she was murdered."

Toscana picked up a pencil. "How do you know?"

"I overheard them fighting in the middle of the night." She perched on the edge of her chair and began the slow recount of what had happened when she had overheard Claudia talking to someone. How she had been hiding in the bushes, crouched like a cornered animal. Maybe she had been the lucky one.

Toscana regarded her with confusion. "Why were you hiding?"

Caroline felt her face go hot. "It's embarrassing."

"A tryst?"

"With a bread stick!" She looked up at him. "I had raided the kitchen for food! I was on my way back to my room when I heard someone behind me. So I hid and

. . ." She let the words die out.

Toscana cocked his head. "You got an eating disorder?"

"No, I just didn't have enough for dinner. The portions here are very *skimpy*."

"And *how much* did you pay to stay here?"

"Would you like me to continue?"

"Please." He finished off his pizza and started on another slice.

Caroline picked off a slice of pepperoni and nibbled on it. "Actually, I don't have much more to say. Claudia was having a vitriolic argument with somebody. It scared me, the anger and nastiness."

"But you don't know who it was?"

"No."

"Did the voice have an accent?"

"Not that I could hear . . . Oh, you're thinking of Thong Guy, the Adonis who pulled Claudia out of the mud. What's his name?"

"Emilio Constanza. He was there when you and your mother entered the bathhouse. Which means he was possibly the last person around to see Mrs. de Vries alive. He's also being questioned as we speak. You all are going to be grilled. Extensively. So if you have something to tell, it's better for you if you get it out early."

The man was making it difficult. His off-putting manner only strengthened her resolve to do the right thing, whatever that meant. Coolly, she said, "For your information, I also found an empty bottle of Jack Daniel's in the brush. I know that Mr. Fondulac confessed to you that he drank some Jack Daniel's last night."

"Who told you that?"

"Mother."

"Go on."

"I know that drinking is against Claudia's rules. I was under the impression that Mr. Fondulac came here to dry out. Mother told me that Claudia had personally searched Mr. Fondulac's baggage — just to make sure he wasn't sneaking in any contraband. If that were the case, where did he get the bottle?"

"Alcoholics are wonderfully adept at hiding things."

"You've implied that Ms. Talmadge might also imbibe. So *I'm* suggesting that maybe the bottle was hers." For reasons she didn't understand, she refrained from telling Toscana about Phyllis and Fondulac having been in rehab with King David.

"Jack Daniel's is a popular brand of whiskey."

"A more likely explanation is that they

had been drinking together."

Toscana wrote it down in his notes. "What else do you want to tell me?"

Caroline hesitated. "I know that my mother thinks Claudia was skimming off profits through Ondine."

"What do *you* think?"

"I don't know! I'm just a simple musician, an ex-musician at that."

"It's impossible to be an ex-musician. Just ask an old geezer like King David. Good Lord, his face looks like a truck ran over it. He is way past the prime meat rating. Some people just can't get past high school." Toscana drank his coffee. "What do you think of him?"

Caroline felt heat in her face. Toscana must have picked up on it and that's why he was questioning her about him. "He's a jerk."

"What specifically makes him a jerk in your opinion?"

"For starters, he's been bothering me, scaring me."

"Oh?" Toscana sat up. "Tell me about it."

"He told me he came here to look for something. He was certain that Claudia had it. Now, for some reason, he thinks I have it."

"But you don't know what he's talking about."

"No," Caroline lied.

"Very mysterious, Mrs. Blessing. And vague enough that I can't pin you down on anything. Why should I believe this ambiguous tale?"

"Why shouldn't I be believed?"

"Because, Mrs. Blessing, your mother has more than a little motivation for wanting Claudia de Vries dead, starting with the fact that Mom now owns the majority stake in the spa."

"Then why didn't you arrest her when she wanted to be arrested?"

"Because, silly old me, I still honor a thing called due process." As far as Toscana was concerned, Hilda's little drama was nothing but a ruse. "*If* there's something you want to tell me, please speak up. You want to help your mom, don't you?"

"Of course," Caroline insisted. "But I've told you everything I know." She hoped her words rang true to his ears.

"Then let me ask you this. Why are you so intent on setting up David King —"

"King David —"

"First, you tell me about a mysterious voice arguing with Ms. de Vries. Then you tell me about David King looking for some unknown thing —"

"King David —"

"Whatever."

There was something about her that reeked of honesty, or more specially, naïveté. For one thing, she was a congressional wife, talking without a lawyer. "Maybe King David was making a move on you?"

"Perhaps," Caroline admitted. "But when that didn't work, he became aggressive, insisting that I hand over something that I don't have and don't even know what it is." Again, her eyes watered. "Now I don't know what to think."

Toscana sighed inwardly as he watched her face. This wasn't just a simple "I'm scared" reaction. This was "I'm seeing my life pass before me and I don't like what I see."

No doubt she was weeping for her deceased father, for her overbearing mother. And judging from the way she was playing with her ring, pulling it on and off her finger, she was in the process of making some drastic decisions in the matrimonial department.

Toscana said, "You got a package today, Mrs. Blessing. Mind if I ask you what was in it?"

Caroline dabbed her eyes. "A cello. My

own old cello, actually. My mother traced down the person I sold it to and bought it back for me. It's in my room. Go take a look if you don't believe me."

"So you're a classical musician."

"Once upon a life, I was even symphony caliber."

"What happened?"

"I got married."

"And . . ."

"And it's a boring story." She smiled with wet eyes. "The main thing is that my mother actually did something selfless for me. Hunting down the instrument. That took effort. My mother made an effort to do something lovely for me."

"And that's unusual?"

"Extremely unusual."

"What's her usual style? Hiring a PI to take dirty pictures of your husband with other women?"

The shock registered instantly. Caroline snapped her head upward. "That was totally uncalled for."

Toscana regarded the look on the young woman's face. It made him shrink. It was one thing to be tough, another thing to be cruel. "That was terrible. I'm sorry."

She stood up. "I think we're done."

Toscana said, "If that's what you want. Again, I'm sorry."

"No, you're not. I'm sure this fits nicely into your stereotype of me — a stupid, innocent girl getting shafted by her husband."

"You're not stupid, Mrs. Blessing. Furthermore, you don't have to be stupid to be shafted. I nearly lost my entire IRA on a stock tip. It almost cost me my wife as well. That's why I'm here, to placate my spouse. Up to me, I would have never left Philadelphia. But you do things to keep the marriage going. You compromise."

"Up to a point!" Caroline said.

"Up to a point," Toscana repeated. "May I ask how long you have known about your husband's indiscretions?"

Tears pressed onto her cheeks. "Since this morning. When my mother gave me the envelope."

Toscana shook his head. "Why would she do that? Shove those pictures in your face. It seems to me that she wants you as miserable as she is —"

"Oh please! Haven't you said enough things for one day?"

"Probably."

Caroline glared at him. "How'd *you* find out about them?"

"I saw them when I visited your cabin."

Once again, Caroline was outraged. "You must have been snooping, then. I hid the packet quite well."

"Hid it?" Toscana was confused. "You left the pictures out in the open —"

"I did not! I should report you."

He offered her his cell phone. "You want the number of my superior?"

She pushed the phone away. "If you even *think* of using those pictures in your investigation —"

"Mrs. Blessing, even if I had found a smoking gun, I couldn't admit it into evidence. You've gotta know that I broke the law by entering your room without permission. I know it's not nice, but it's not murder."

"You don't seem bothered by prying into my personal effects!"

"The pictures were left in plain view, Mrs. Blessing."

"I didn't even open the envelope." She threw daggers at him with her eyes. "You opened the envelope, didn't you? You found the envelope, opened it, and left the pictures out for all to see!"

Toscana said, "Mrs. Blessing, I would never open sealed mail. That's a felony. You can sit here and protest your little heart out, but I didn't find your hiding place. Which means that someone else busted into your room. So why don't we cool down and try to figure out who would go through your things. Please. Let's start over. When did you hide the envelope?"

She thought about it. "I'd say about three hours ago."

"Okay. I went into your cabin right after I revived Ms. Talmadge. Since everyone was at the pond — out in the open — I took the opportunity to poke around. That was around two hours ago. So someone else was in your room between two and three hours ago. First person who comes to my mind is your mom. She certainly has easy access to your room."

"Except that she was the one who gave me the envelope and told me to hide it," Caroline said.

Toscana flipped a page on his notepad. "Maybe that's what she told you. But maybe she wanted to make it public so there would be no turning back."

"No, you have it wrong. She told me not to expose the bastard!"

"And if she had asked you to expose the bastard, would you have done it?"

Caroline was silent.

"So maybe she thought she was helping you."

186

"It wasn't Mother. She'd be mortified if Douglas's infidelities came out. It would sully her reputation."

"Why would it hurt her? Gossip would be great for the spa's business."

"It wasn't Mom!" Caroline insisted. "It had to have been King David. He did this to warn me that I should give him what he wants or else he'll have the photos published."

"If he was going to use the photos for nefarious purposes, I'd think he'd steal them, then go to your husband for blackmail."

"Well, someone opened my mail! Someone invaded my private life . . . such as it is." She looked at the remnants of the pizza. The cheese had leaked enough axle grease to oil down an auto lot. Just looking at it made her sick. She wanted to go home. Except where was home now? Certainly not with Douglas. And she wouldn't go back with Mother. "When can we leave this god-awful place?"

"I'm taking you all down to the station, one by one."

"How long will it take?"

"Not too long," Toscana lied. "Why don't you . . . I don't know. Take a nice long walk. But be careful, and don't go too far."

She glared at him.

"Okay," Toscana admitted. "A walk is a poor idea. Your mom went to all this trouble to get your cello back. Why don't you, you know, noodle around with the thing until it's your turn to be officially questioned?"

Toscana's cellular chimed. He opened the latch. "Detective Toscana."

Caroline saw his eyes grow wide.

"Okay, I'll be right down!" Toscana pressed the end button. "Psychic Beauty has awoken, thank God."

"I want to come, too!"

"This is official business, Mrs. Blessing."

"And I'm married to an official of the state of Tennessee . . . for the time being." Caroline stood up tall. "Don't make me pull rank!" But a moment later, she crumpled and pleaded to him with baleful eyes. "Please get me *out* of here, Detective!"

What could it hurt? Having a congressman's wife with you was good for the brass. He shrugged. "The only reason I'm agreeing to this is I don't want problems with the politicians."

"Fine. Neither do I!"

"Don't get in my way. Don't say anything, especially about what we were discussing!"

"I understand." Caroline let go with a genuine smile. "You actually trust me, don't you?"

"Yeah," Toscana sneered. "I trust you. I also trusted my brother when he gave me that stock tip —"

"Your *brother* almost lost you your entire IRA?"

"Ain't that always the case?" Toscana said, putting on his coat. "Family. You can't live without 'em, but you sure can dream."

8

Lauren didn't know if it was good for her face or not. She didn't care. She was chilled to the bone and she just wanted to be warm again.

Lauren Sullivan untied the sash of her pale green terry cloth Phoenix Spa robe and let the covering fall from her smooth, milky-white shoulders. Her carefully pedicured toes wriggled with appreciation as they padded across the almost hot cedar planks that covered the sauna floor. Nimbly, she climbed up to the top tier of the benches that lined the walls, spread out a towel, and lay down, stretching out her nude, lean body gratefully as the warmth of the toasted cedar began to seep through her back. She luxuriated in the hot, dry air that enveloped her exposed skin.

She was relieved to have the sauna to herself. Today she wasn't in the mood to take the normal scrutiny she went through as part of her daily life as a celebrity. The last thing Lauren wanted was some strange woman assessing her. Lauren knew full well that, later, the voyeur would brag to a friend that she had seen the famous Lauren Sullivan in the sauna and the movie star was thinner, fatter, shorter, taller, prettier, homelier, more relaxed, more haggard, younger looking, or older than she appeared on the movie screen.

She ran her tapering fingers through her tousled red hair and fanned it out across the warm cedar. She played with it lovingly, knowing that when she went back to Hollywood it was all coming off. Her next film role demanded a short, boyish haircut. It didn't really matter, Lauren reflected. It would all grow back. Or perhaps she would just keep it short. They said really long hair didn't become an "older woman."

Older woman! At thirty-seven, she wasn't really old by most people's standards. But by the Tinsel Town yardstick, it had been time to get some face work done, before everyone started saying she needed it.

The thin fingers patted ever so gently beneath her eyes, barely pressing on the recovering skin there. The dark circles under her eyes could be covered by a makeup artist's expertise. But during the filming of her last movie, it had reached the point where no amount of ice packing had succeeded in alleviating the puffy bags that developed under her expressive eyes.

Lauren continued pressing gingerly. The swelling had gone down now, and the last of the blue and greenish-yellow bruising was disappearing. The plastic surgeon, one of Hollywood's best, had known what he was doing. He had said the bags were hereditary and asked if her mother or father had them as well.

Good question.

It was one of the many questions that Lauren had been afraid to ask for most of her life. Who were her parents? What did they look like? Why had they given her up? Did she have any siblings?

Questions she hadn't dared ask the succession of foster parents over the years. She didn't want them to know and be angry that she often fantasized about her "real" parents and secretly wished that they would come and claim her and take her with them.

Some of her caretakers had been better than others. But none of them had been like her, either physically or temperamentally. Lauren couldn't help speculating about her gene pool.

Most of her life she had held back from pursuing the answers to her questions.

Finally, an emotional wreck, Lauren had gone into therapy. But therapy didn't work unless the truth was spoken. A year after she sat in the psychiatrist's office and tearfully described the tragic automobile accident that killed the most loving foster parents, Lauren knew she had to summon up the courage to come to Claudia. Claudia de Vries had the answers to her questions. Lauren was sure of it. If only Lauren had been able to get the information out of Claudia before she was killed.

Lauren cringed internally but kept the expression on her face calm as she heard the sauna door open. Footsteps caused the floorboards to groan. Lauren wanted to keep her eyes shut and not acknowledge the visitor or feel obligated to talk. But with Claudia's death, Lauren's radar was in a state of high alert. Anyone could be a danger. It was necessary to be on guard.

She turned her head and her gaze fell upon the towel-wrapped head of Caroline Blessing. Caroline climbed onto another sauna bench.

Lauren hated being stared at, and yet here she was staring herself. She turned her head back and looked up at the ceiling. The sauna was quiet save for the occasional creaking of wood expanding from the heat. It was Caroline who broke the silence.

"What do you think happened to Claudia?" Caroline asked.

"I really have no idea," answered Lauren in her famous throaty voice. "But I suppose the police will figure it out eventually." She hoped that her terse response would signal that she wanted to cut off the conversation.

But Caroline pressed on. "Did you hear that the psychic was just pulled from the lake? It looks like someone tried to kill her too."

Lauren shook her head back and forth against the cedar platform but did not answer.

Caroline ignored the snub. "I just came back from the infirmary. Looks like she's going to be all right, but I didn't stick around to hear all the gory details. The infirmary smelled like a hospital. It reminded me . . . well, I had to get out of there and clear my head." Caroline rolled over on her stomach and rested her chin in her hands. "This place is a nightmare. What about that Ondine? How could someone be that thin and live?" Caroline wondered out loud. "She looks like she could snap in two. Her breasts are almost nonexistent and her legs are knobby poles. If you ask me, Ondine looks more like a young boy than a woman. Can you believe that she is held up as an icon to millions of American females?"

Without responding, Lauren pulled herself up to a sitting position and climbed down to the sauna floor. Taking her robe from a peg on the wall, she wrapped it around her. As she pulled open the sauna door, she called over her shoulder, "If anyone wants rest, this is sure not the place to come. We should all demand our money back."

In the infirmary, Toscana sat next to Phyllis Talmadge's cot. "You're sure you didn't see anything?" he asked insistently.

Phyllis shook her head weakly against the white pillow. "As I said, Detective, I felt a sharp pain, and then everything went black. I don't remember falling in the water or being pulled out."

Toscana was not about to give up. "Go over it for me again, will you please, Ms. Talmadge? Tell me again what happened. I'm not sure I got it right the first time."

Phyllis looked at him skeptically. Toscana didn't miss a thing and they both knew it. Over the course of her psychic career, Phyllis had been called on to work with the police on some pretty tough cases. She knew the way the cops operated, asking a witness or victim to go over their accounts of what he or she recalled again and again until, sometimes, a new detail emerged.

"All right," she sighed resignedly. She closed her heavy eyelids as she tried to envision what she had been doing just before she was struck. "I was standing at the edge of the lake, trying to clear my mind of everything that was cluttering it. I wanted to get rid of all the negative energy and try to focus on Claudia and what had happened to her. I was hoping that something would come to me that would help in the investigation."

"And?" Toscana led.

"Nothing." Phyllis opened her eyes and stared defiantly at the detective. "I *told* you. I felt a blow and then blackness." The psychic's blue-veined hand raised around to the back of her head as she felt for the egg-shaped bump that throbbed there. Toscana almost felt sorry for her as he saw her wince. But his sympathy was replaced by contempt as he watched her turn toward Raoul de Vries, her voice dripping with sweetness.

"The first thing I remembered afterward was the concerned face of Dr. de Vries here." She smiled in a pathetic attempt at flirtation with the man who stood beside her bed. "What a dear man, taking such good care of me when he's just suffered his own deep and devastating loss!"

Toscana felt his gag reflex rising. Thank God, Phyllis Talmadge didn't remember being pulled from the lake. If she did, he, not de Vries, might be the uncomfortable recipient of the aging psychic's affections. Toscana glanced over at the gallant Raoul de Vries. The good doctor didn't look any too grief stricken to him. He noticed that Caroline Blessing, who had been standing just behind de Vries during the earlier questioning, had already slipped away — an important engagement, she had said. In the sauna. It was a tough life. Though he would be all too happy to leave Phyllis alone with her Sir Galahad, Toscana decided to give it one last try.

"Think, Ms. Talmadge. Think, please. Is there anything at all you can remember that could help us find the person who attacked you? Is there anything that you heard before you were hit? Anything you felt or sensed?"

Phyllis closed her eyes again, pausing

dramatically before she spoke again.

"Actually something *is* coming back to me now. I do remember something," she answered with surprise in her voice. She opened her bloodshot eyes and stared up at Detective Toscana. "Cigarettes!" she declared triumphantly. "I smelled cigarette smoke just before I got clobbered!"

In a private treatment room, safely away from Caroline Blessing, Lauren handed her robe carelessly to the attendant and climbed onto the sheet-draped massage table. As she lay prone on the padded slab, her mind was not on the mineral salt scrub she was about to receive at the strong hands of the hefty Marguerite. Instead she wondered how she was going to get away from Phoenix Spa.

If she had thought she would get rest, relaxation, and privacy here, she had been sadly mistaken. The atmosphere at Phoenix was not what the glossy brochures promised. Phoenix was far from serene, what with the police patrolling around the grounds and the media trawling outside the gates.

Lauren closed her eyes and sighed deeply as Marguerite's muscled hands swirled the warm lavender oil laced with coarse salt across her back. She tried to relax, but the abrasive rubbing felt like sandpaper being pulled across her skin. Lauren had to concentrate on keeping still.

Her mind raced. If she tried to leave now, the press would swarm down on her. Vultures. They would salivate to have a new angle for their "death at the spa" stories. She could see and hear the headlines now: *Lauren Sullivan, Top Box-Office Draw, Involved in Real-Life Murder Mystery!*

Just what she needed. More publicity.

Of course her agent and publicist would not be unhappy. As far as they were concerned, any mention of Lauren in the media was a plus, as long as they spelled her name right. They said so frequently and worked hard to ensure that Lauren's lovely face often stared hauntingly from the pages of *People* or smiled for the *Entertainment Tonight* cameras, dazzling the viewing audience. With yet another new Lauren Sullivan film set to be released next month, they and the movie studio would relish all the publicity she could draw.

Marguerite's sturdy fingers were kneading the backs of Lauren's slim calves when the door to the treatment room opened quietly. Lauren heard the soft squish of rubber-soled shoes as they crossed the terra-cotta floor. She opened her eyes.

"I'm sorry, Miss Sullivan," apologized the young woman Lauren recognized as the keeper of the appointment book at the reception area.

"What is it?" Lauren tried to keep the irritation out of her voice. Naked and covered with the gooey salt mixture, she was annoyed at having her precious privacy interrupted. Not to mention the constant awareness that how she looked would be reported to God knew how many other people by the person who saw her in her messy, vulnerable condition. That was just the way it was. People were fascinated with her, but Lauren never really got used to it. It left her feeling very exposed.

"Excuse me, Miss Sullivan," the receptionist said softly. "But Detective Toscana is on the phone. He's ready to speak with you now."

"Oh he is, is he? That's great." Lauren sighed deeply. "Well, all right. I've had enough here. Tell him I'll be ready to talk to him in fifteen minutes."

Moments later, she stood in the Swiss shower and felt her body cleansed by the warm water that sprayed from a dozen jet needle valves. As the oil and mineral salt slid from her exfoliated skin, Lauren planned what she would tell the detective.

Those Chinese healers had it right when they came up with this, thought Howard Fondulac as he lay on his back in the darkened room and enjoyed his reflexology treatment. The Chinese thought all the energy paths that ran throughout the body converged in the feet. That each organ of the body was represented by a corresponding reflex point in the foot.

The fifty-five-year-old movie producer lay on the table while the tiny blonde reflexologist slowly worked over muscles that he didn't even know were there. Howard liked the feeling of the young woman rubbing and kneading his feet. There was something decadent about it. He felt like a king being pampered by a maiden slave. It had been a long time since he'd felt like royalty.

Now the golden-haired servant was rubbing each toe.

"What part of the body does the toe correspond to?" he asked.

"The sinus. I push here to release blockages and help reestablish energy flow." The woman continued her gentle pressure on the pad of his middle toe.

"Ahhhh." Howard sighed deeply and tried to envision his sinuses clearing. This was just what he needed. He was always getting sinus headaches. His doctor said he should cut out the liquor and quit the cigarettes. But maybe if he had this reflexology bit done on a regular basis when he got back to LA, it would take care of the headaches. He didn't want to give up the booze and the butts, his two favorite vices. There was little enough he enjoyed these days, and a man was entitled to some fun.

He lay in the darkened room and listened to the taped sounds of flute music and ocean waves crashing on the seashore. He tried to relax and clear his mind. That was what he had come for. Partially.

He'd also come to Phoenix Spa because Claudia had told him that Lauren Sullivan would be here.

He needed something, and he prayed that Lauren Sullivan would be it. His career was on the skids. He had been unable to raise the money to produce a film in years and, though he hated to admit it even to himself, the Hollywood powers that be thought Howard Fondulac was a has-been. He couldn't get anyone to take his telephone calls, much less set up a face-to-face meeting with him. But if he could get

Lauren Sullivan interested in his project, those studio snobs would take his calls, all right. They'd be falling all over themselves as they lined up to kiss his massaged feet.

The blonde was firmly pushing her thumb up and down Howard's arch, and he smiled in pleasure as he imagined producing a Lauren Sullivan film. That would make him a player again. He had to get Lauren alone somehow. If he could just talk to her, he knew he'd be able to sell her on his project.

Even the jaded Detective Toscana was mesmerized as he watched Lauren Sullivan sweep into the room in her flowing purple robe. She was astonishingly beautiful. Toscana was careful to pay attention to the details of the movie star's appearance. He knew that when he got home Mary Elizabeth would be pumping him for information on her favorite screen star.

"Yeah, babe. She was gorgeous."

"No, honey. She didn't have any makeup on, but she still looked great."

"I couldn't be sure, sweetie, but I think that hair color is her own."

Mary Elizabeth never missed a Lauren Sullivan film. As often as she could, his wife dragged him with her to the movies.

Toscana would sigh and groan as if he was going along only to please his wife, but the truth of the matter was that he found Lauren Sullivan easy on the eye and enjoyed her acting. He and most of the men in America, he'd wager.

Now, in his makeshift squad room, the object of so many fantasies sat across the table from him. He watched Lauren as she glanced at the postmortem pictures of Claudia de Vries that were tacked onto the wall. She quickly averted her gaze, but not before Toscana saw her wince in repulsion.

"Do you mind if I smoke?" asked the detective routinely. Not waiting for her answer, he lit up.

Lauren sat quietly, waiting for the questioning to begin. Her graceful fingers played absentmindedly with a strand of hair that had fallen from the loose bun she had pinned to the top of her exquisite head.

"How is it that you came all the way to Virginia to Phoenix Spa, Miss Sullivan? I would think there are plenty of other spas you could have chosen that would have been more convenient for you."

Lauren shrugged. "I guess I could have gone to Canyon Ranch or Palm Springs. They are certainly closer to LA. But as you may have observed, Detective Toscana, I've just had some plastic surgery done, and I wanted to go someplace where I wouldn't be tripping over people I know from Hollywood. I wanted privacy and peace."

"Well, you certainly haven't gotten the latter here, have you?"

"No. Unfortunately, I haven't. And with those reporters prowling around outside, I'm afraid I might not get the former either."

Briefly, Toscana wondered what it must be like always to have people watching you. Not being able to take a walk in the park or run into the drugstore without someone gawking at you and telling friends that you bought a laxative. There was a price to fame. Suddenly, he was very grateful for his relative anonymity.

"Have you been to this spa before, Miss Sullivan?"

"Yes, sir. Several times."

"So you knew Mrs. de Vries?"

"Yes. I knew Claudia quite well." She had already decided that she might as well tell him. He would find out anyway. "Claudia is, ah, *was*, my aunt. She was my mother's sister."

The detective swiveled around to look at

the pictures of the dead woman. In the lifeless face it was hard to see any resemblance at all to the beauty who sat before him.

"If you are looking for a family likeness, Detective, I'm afraid you won't find it. You see, my birth parents gave me up."

"Well, I'm sorry for your loss," said Toscana solicitously. "Have you told your mother about her sister's death?"

"No. That isn't necessary. My mother and father were killed in an automobile accident last year."

Toscana was a bit flustered and struck by sympathy for her.

"Would you like a cigarette, Miss Sullivan?" he offered clumsily.

Lauren smiled weakly. "As a matter of fact, I would. I try not to smoke. It ages the skin, you know. But I think a cigarette would be nice right now."

Toscana pulled a cigarette halfway out, held the pack across the table toward the actress, and flicked his lighter for her.

She held the cigarette between her beautiful, tapering fingers and inhaled.

The fingers. Toscana stared at her fingers. They were long and delicate and somehow expressive. And familiar.

He had seen other hands that looked like

Lauren Sullivan's. He just couldn't quite remember whose.

But it would come to him.

Just feet from where Claudia de Vries's body had been found, Christopher Lund lay beside the crystal clear water in the pool house. He prayed that Claudia's death would be the end to his financial problems.

Christopher took his job as Ondine's manager very seriously. Ondine's income dictated his income. Booking the lucrative modeling assignments was only part of it. Christopher had to make sure Ondine was well rested, showed up on time, looked her best, and had the energy necessary to project whatever the client wanted her to project.

The magazine spreads and runway work at the fashion shows of the top designers paid very well indeed. So well that Christopher's fee, fifteen percent of Ondine's gross earnings, paid for his spacious loft in Soho, a beach place in Amagansett, a trip or three to St. Maarten each winter to get away from the gray coldness of Manhattan, and a Range Rover and the four hundred dollars a month it cost to garage it in New York City. His recreational cocaine use had grown to an everyday thing, and that ate up his money as well.

He thoroughly enjoyed his lifestyle and all the trappings of success. He was young and ambitious. He wasn't about to be giving up a thing — in fact, he wanted more. He wasn't getting any younger, and it was time to be thinking about acquiring wealth, like some well-chosen art and stocks, not just spending conspicuously.

All of this took money. And Ondine was his cash cow.

He didn't fear her overexposure. The more magazine covers Ondine appeared on, the more billboards she smiled from, the more restaurant openings, movie premieres, or parties she attended with the paparazzi snapping blindingly, the better he liked it. She was a star, and the more the public was aware of her the more powerful she became. Christopher drove her relentlessly.

At twenty-two, Ondine was still young, but the window of opportunity for the big bucks was relatively short. She was at the top of the profession now, but that could change anytime. There were always new, younger women coming along, eager to join the ranks of the supermodel. The public was fickle and, Christopher believed, had a short attention span. The new sensation was always just around the corner. There was no telling how long Ondine's time would last.

As Ondine's business manager, all the money flowed through Christopher. The companies that hired Ondine to tout their products made the checks out to The Lund Agency. Christopher, after taking out his fifteen percent, cut the checks to Ondine.

But Ondine paid little attention to book-keeping. She trusted her business manager and was not inclined to concern herself with the mundane details of banking. When Ondine had started making real money, Christopher had suggested that he make the deposits into her back account and keep track of her funds, neglecting to mention that he would have the power to withdraw money as well. He suggested that he take over having her tax returns prepared as well. Ondine had been only too happy to agree. Accounting bored her.

Almost imperceptibly, Christopher had increased his take on each modeling assignment. There were all sorts of ways to defraud her, and he rationalized his actions to himself with the knowledge that Ondine was still making an obscene amount of money for merely standing in front of a camera while he was busting his hump managing every aspect of her career.

The deal he had made with Claudia de Vries was especially lucrative. At least it had started out that way. Claudia had wanted to bring Phoenix Spa to another level. Not content with the spa's solid reputation, she wanted it to join the list of America's most exclusive spas. She thought Ondine could help her reach her goal, and Claudia had been willing to pay handsomely to realize her dream.

When she had first contacted Christopher about Ondine doing a spread for a glossy Phoenix Spa brochure, Christopher had convinced Claudia that her plan was too limited. Ondine was too huge a star to lend her famous name, face, and body to a mere brochure for a small spa in the Virginia hills. If Claudia wanted Ondine, she was going to have to think big and pay big.

The Lund Agency drew up a sophisticated advertising campaign and Christopher presented it to Claudia. She loved the ideas but not the price tag. So they scaled back the plan, finally agreeing that Ondine would come to Phoenix and be photographed amid the natural and man-made beauty. The photographs would be used exclusively in advertisements running in the fashion magazine that reached more readers around the world than any other and whose subscription base was the so-phisticated, discerning readers Claudia wanted to attract.

Christopher would be able to take care of it all, he promised Claudia. He would choose Ondine's wardrobe, book the best photographer, and deal with the businesspeople at *Elle*, making sure that the artistic ads were well placed. *Elle*'s base rate for a single full-page in black and white was sixty-five thousand dollars. Color cost seventy-five thousand. But Christopher impressed Claudia, saying he knew that if Phoenix Spa committed to running an ad in every issue for a year, *Elle* would negotiate a better price. Christopher tried to get Claudia to spring for the prized "second cover," which actually consisted of the back of the front cover and spread over to the next page. But at over eighty thou-sand dollars a pop, Claudia wouldn't swallow the idea. She said she had to draw the line somewhere, and budgeting almost a million dollars for the *Elle* ad placements was already keeping her up at night.

Christopher made two big demands. Ondine's modeling fee had to be paid up front and in cash if Claudia wanted to cut

Ondine's two-million-dollar price almost in half. And Claudia was not allowed to discuss anything with Ondine. Christopher claimed he didn't want his prize model to be bothered with any of the details of their business plan. He protected Ondine from the business aspects of her career, he explained.

Claudia, eager to get on with her journey to international success and save a million dollars, agreed. The spa owner invited Ondine and her manager down for a complimentary visit and, starting on Halloween Day of last year, began paying Ondine a total of $1,025,000. She paid the money directly to Christopher Lund and then marked the amount carefully beside Ondine's name in her spa records.

It had all been working well until Claudia had demanded to see some results. Christopher had been able to stall since last fall with a series of excuses. Ondine's schedule was packed. Ondine had some sort of flu, the result of a bug she had picked up during a photo shoot in Peru. Ondine needed to rest.

Christopher absentmindedly swept his fingers through the pool water as he anxiously remembered Claudia's anger at all the delays.

"Well, bring her down here to rest, for God's sake!" Claudia had finally cried in exasperation.

"I will, I will, Claudia. I'll get her down there as soon as her schedule permits," Christopher tried to assure the spa owner.

"Well, her damned schedule had better permit it soon, or I'm going to hire myself the best lawyer money can buy and sue your ass off, Christopher! Sue your ass off and make sure that everyone knows what a swindler you are!"

He had tried not to panic. With Ondine none the wiser that her earnings had gone in Christopher's bank account, he had already spent most of the money Claudia had paid. Now it was time to pay the piper.

He laid the groundwork, suggesting to the already painfully thin Ondine that it looked like she was putting on some weight. As Ondine cried and fretted, Christopher came to her rescue, soothing her and telling her that he would take her away to Phoenix Spa. There she could work on losing a few pounds without the eyes of the unforgiving New York fashion world watching. So they had come here, ostensibly to get the fat off Ondine, but, in reality, to buy some time with Claudia.

Claudia wasn't going to be bothering him anymore.

After breakfast the next morning, Caroline took her beloved cello from its case and seated herself in the straight-backed chair that stood in the corner of her bedroom. She listened to the tones as she tuned the instrument. Caroline positioned herself carefully, as she had so many times before, and slowly pulled the bow across the cello's strings.

The two began to make their mournful music together. Caroline's long, thin fingers held the bow gracefully and moved it expertly back and forth across the strings. The prized cello faithfully emitted the haunting sounds the musician requested of it.

Caroline tasted salty tears as they slid down her cheeks and reached her lips. It was a relief to cry again. It was comforting to have the sad music as her companion.

This was not what she had planned. She had so wanted things to be different. Caroline had gone into the marriage with such high hopes and such wonderful dreams. But if Douglas had betrayed her with another woman, those dreams were shattered. How could she share her life with a man she didn't trust?

Caroline dried her eyes with the back of her hand. Why should she worry about protecting Douglas anymore? Douglas Blessing, the freshman congressman from Tennessee, the handsome young man with the high political aspirations, was no longer her husband in the finest sense of the word. He hadn't cared about her feelings or about his sacred vows to her. Why should she fight to guard him now?

Caroline had a good mind to march down to the gates right now and tell the media camped outside all that was going on inside Phoenix Spa. In fact, the more she thought about it, the better the idea seemed.

Let the chips fall where they may.

9

Caroline had stormed out of the cottage at full throttle, but halfway down the tree-lined drive that led to the gates of Phoenix Spa, she eased her foot off the gas. Behind the pillars and the elaborate wrought-iron barrier, a writhing mass of reporters stood before a backdrop of cars and television vans, their satellite dishes pointed toward the sky on long, slender stalks. As she approached, Caroline thought she could make out some familiar faces — a bespectacled, frizzy-headed reporter from CNN and, Lord help us, that guy with the mustache, Geraldo Rivera. Next to Geraldo stood a well-coifed reporter who reminded her of an anchor back home on Channel 5.

Home. That word again. It stabbed at her heart with a pain so intense that she sobbed and paused in her purposeful march toward the world and the truth to catch her breath. Where was home? The house where she grew up had long ago fallen to the wrecking ball. Her bachelorette bungalow on Forest View in Nashville had been sold. And she couldn't imagine returning to the Georgian-style row house on Thirty-first Street in Georgetown where Congressman Blessing had brought his new bride less than a year ago. The furniture, carpets, wallpaper, and fabrics that she had chosen with such care and joy held no more warmth for her now than the cold fist of anger and fear that seemed to be squeezing the heart right out of her chest.

Panic seized her, she recognized the signs. First a tingling in her fingers and toes, then a wave of heat that rushed up her neck, suffusing her face and scalp and overwhelming her with dizziness. Fool! Whatever made her think she was even capable of meeting the press? Caroline glanced about for a quiet spot to withdraw, but a serpentine wall of solid brick lined the drive on both sides. She could continue toward the braying pack of media hounds or retreat up the drive to the cabin she shared with her mother, to her loft bedroom, now the only home she had.

Caroline scurried to the wall, seeking refuge in one of its sheltering curves. Panting with relief, she sat on her heels and leaned against the brick, which felt deliciously warm through the sheer cotton of her blouse. Insanely, she wished for Douglas. Douglas had experience with the press; he would tell her what to do. To her right, the manic shouting of the reporters assaulted her ears. To her left, there was nothing but tranquillity — a twittering bird, the drone of a honeybee — and a young man, striding purposefully in her direction.

"Mrs. Blessing?" he called.

Caroline swiped at the tears that streaked her cheeks and turned her face in his direction. She could tell he was a staff member by his green Phoenix Spa polo shirt, but he was neither tall enough nor lean enough to be Emilio Constanza. "Yes. Who are you?" she asked unnecessarily as the fellow got closer and she saw the name tag clipped to his uniform. It said "Dante."

"I'm a masseur," he offered.

"What do you want?"

"Dr. de Vries sent me to find you. You had an appointment with him at two-thirty yesterday."

Caroline wrinkled her brow. "What appointment?"

"Everyone has them. Part of the package. You discuss your needs, he evaluates your general condition, then he plans out the best therapeutic course for you during your stay."

In the blinding sunlight Caroline squinted up at Dante. She couldn't believe it would be business as usual for the freshly widowed Raoul. "Of course, I remember now." She stood, dusted off her slacks, and walked toward him. "But how did you find me?"

Dante pointed.

She followed the long line of his arm from rounded biceps to tapered index finger. "That birdhouse?"

He chuckled and shook his head, sending his ponytail flipping from one shoulder to another. "Surveillance cameras. They're all over the place."

Caroline gasped. "Raoul's been spying on me?"

"Not spying, exactly. The security officer sits in a basement room in the main lodge while this software just flips from one camera to another, capturing it all on videotape."

"I'm on tape?" Caroline was incredulous.

As if sensing her next question, Dante laid a hand on her arm. "They're only for the spa entrances and the grounds. We don't have any cameras indoors."

Caroline said, "Well, that's a relief." She wondered if Detective Toscana knew about the security system and, remembering her midnight raid on the spa kitchen, was glad she had come clean to him about it. "Do the police . . . ?"

"Oh, yeah. That Toscana fellow and his goons have been all over security this morning."

Grateful for the interruption and glad of the company, Caroline turned her back on the reporters and accompanied Dante up the drive toward the main lodge. Exhausted and drained, she walked in silence. As they passed the kitchen wing, the smell of food teased her nostrils.

"Mrs. Blessing, do you mind if I make a suggestion?"

Caroline had been thinking about her meager breakfast and how much she now regretted passing up the whole-grain Belgian waffles with fresh fruit in favor of some dry toast. Her stomach rumbled noisily. "What?"

"After you finish with Dr. de Vries, come see me." Walking slightly behind, he laid his hands on her shoulders. "You're tied in knots. Stiff. Your spine's coiled as tightly as a bedspring."

Caroline rotated her shoulders. "I know."

"I have an opening at three." He removed his hands. "Have you ever been Rolfed?"

Caroline laughed. "Rolfed? You're making that up, surely?" But when he didn't smile she said, "Is it anything like shiatzu?"

Dante shook his head. "Not at all. Rolfing's a deep-massage technique that works on the connective tissues. Quite frankly, it's not for everybody, but I've never seen anyone who needed Rolfing more than you."

Caroline smiled up at the masseur, thinking, What could it hurt? "I'll mention it to Raoul," she promised.

"Ordinarily, we suggest an eight- to ten-week course of treatment," the young man continued. "But let's do an introductory session and if it sccms to work for you, I'll recommend a practitioner for when you get home."

Wherever home might be, she thought ruefully. Forcing her lips into a smile, she looked up at Dante. "Okay, then," she said. "Pencil me in."

Through the half-open door, Caroline could see that Raoul's office was the June cover of *Architectural Digest*, from the brocade draperies to the foil-backed wall covering right down to the oversized art books carelessly but expensively arranged on the Louis XV coffee table. To the right, built-in bookshelves held matched sets of leather-bound classics. To the left, a globe the size of a basketball, each country delineated by encrustations of semiprecious stones, was centered on a narrow credenza.

If Raoul had a medical degree, Caroline could see no evidence of it. On the other hand, a boasting, black-framed diploma would hardly have been in keeping with the decor. As proud as Caroline was of the diploma from Juilliard that hung in her own study, it wouldn't have taken much arm-twisting to persuade her to replace it with one of the Mirós or Klees that hung in carved, gilded frames over Raoul's credenza.

Near the fireplace, a tabby cat, undoubtedly chosen by the decorator to coordinate with the rusty gold medallions in the Turkish carpet, had draped itself casually across the back of an overstuffed wing chair. When Caroline entered, the cat opened an eye, studied her, determined she was of no importance, and returned to its nap.

Raoul was hardly napping. Piles of papers and what Caroline took to be case files littered his desk. He was shuffling through them frantically, oblivious to her presence.

"Raoul? You wanted to see me?"

"What?" His eyes were enormous behind his glasses. "Oh, Caroline. So good of you to come." He shoved the folders aside until the space on the desk directly in front of him was clear, anchored the tallest pile with a substantial brass paperweight shaped like a propeller, whipped off his glasses, and stood. "Sit down. Sit down."

Raoul emerged from behind his desk and motioned Caroline into the armchair. The cat didn't budge. The handsome widower arranged himself opposite Caroline on a two-cushion sofa, beautifully upholstered in a reproduction of a medieval tapestry. Considering the money that had clearly been lavished on this place, it could have *been* a medieval tapestry.

"Frankly, Raoul, after what happened yesterday, I'm surprised you're keeping office hours," Caroline ventured after a moment of uncomfortable silence.

"What are my alternatives?" He spread his hands wide. "I've got a spa to run, as your mother keeps reminding me."

"That surprised me as much as it surprised you."

"Surprise is not the word I'd choose," he said. "Surprise is for Christmas presents or birthday parties. It's fair to say I was shocked, appalled, devastated." He massaged the bridge of his nose with a thumb and index finger. "Claudia must have known something about your mother's financial interest in Phoenix. You must have suspected."

Caroline had no answer for him, so she changed the subject. "Why did you send that fellow to find me, Raoul? It wasn't just to discuss my treatment program, was it?"

"No." He flushed to the lobes of his exquisite ears.

"Well, what then?"

"I wondered if you could tell me what your mother's plans are for Phoenix Spa."

"Mother and I were never all that close." She paused to swallow the lump that had taken up residence in her throat.

Raoul bowed his head. "I feel like a fish out of water. When Claudia was alive, I knew exactly what I'd be doing every day. But now . . ." He looked up. "Your mother can be difficult."

"What did Mother say to you?"

"She ordered me to stop mooning about and get on with it." He shook his head, and Caroline could see he was close to tears.

224

"Carry on with *what*, for Christ's sake. I have a wife to bury!"

Caroline reached across the coffee table and laid her hand on his. "I'm so sorry, Raoul. Sorry about Claudia. About Mother . . ." She took a deep breath. "About everything." She patted his hand, then settled back into the comfortable recesses of the chair. "Is there anything I can do?"

"Nobody can do anything until the police release Claudia's body, and who knows when that will be." He leaned forward, fingers laced together, his elbows resting on his knees. "They're not even sure how she died. Everyone assumes she was strangled." He shuddered. "But what if she was still alive when whoever shoved her face into the mud?"

"Don't even think about it, Raoul. It'll make you crazy."

"I can't eat. I can't sleep." He fixed his eyes, unseeing, on the wallpaper behind her head.

"Raoul . . ."

He shivered, seemed to snap out of it, then turned to look at Caroline as if seeing her for the first time. He reached across the table, covered her hand with his, and stood up, pulling her up along with him.

"Caroline, Caroline! Please forgive me. I've been babbling like a fool."

Caroline thought the man was hardly a fool. Quietly, she extracted her hand and began to stroke the cat.

Raoul seemed unperturbed. "We're supposed to be talking about you."

That's a subject best avoided, Caroline thought. Aloud she said, "Tell me about that young man you sent to find me. Dante. He's booked me in for a deep-tissue massage after lunch."

Raoul beamed. "Splendid! Should do you a world of good. He's quite the expert, Dante. We hired him away from the Broadmoor in Colorado Springs. Claudia considered it quite a coup!"

While Raoul pontificated on the solid-gold credentials of Dante, otherwise known as Daniel Shemanski, and oozed on about macrobiotics, homeopathy, and the miracle of colonic hydrotherapy, Caroline inched her way toward the door, hoping to escape. "Join me at my table for lunch?" Raoul inquired.

Caroline felt her stomach knocking against her ribs. If she didn't get something to eat soon, she'd end up looking like Ondine. "Of course," she replied. "Why not?"

Vince Toscana stared at the plate in front of him and considered where to begin. A scallion, its topknot fringed and curled, sprang like an astonished bird from the top of a pink, spongelike cube. A quartet of tiny shrimp flanked the scallion, each nestled in a rose-cut carrot curl set on a nearly transparent cucumber round, sliced thin as a lab specimen. The whole mess was arranged on a bed of limp yuppie lettuce that reminded him of dandelion greens.

Vince nudged his salad with his fork. Whatever happened to iceberg lettuce, he wondered. Saw off a hunk, pour on some Catalina dressing straight from the bottle. Now, *that* was a salad.

Across the table from him Stick Girl had moved one shrimp to the edge of her plate where she was using a knife to cut it into four pieces. One tiny quarter went into her mouth where she chewed it, he swore to God, one hundred times while gazing at nothing in particular, as if all her energy was going into the chewing of that infinitesimal lump of seafood.

Vince noticed her painfully thin arms and winced. Girls that skinny shouldn't wear sleeveless clothes. But sitting just to her right, Christopher Lund was staring at Ondine with more than the usual agent-to-client interest, so Vince thought, well, what the hell did he know? He was just a happily married old fart who was going to die of starvation himself if he didn't solve this case soon.

At a table for four near the kitchen, Raoul de Vries sat with the congressman's wife and that bitchy mother of hers. Vince would have given a Philly cheese steak with everything on it to overhear their conversation. Hilda was a no-go, but perhaps he'd be able to worm something out of Caroline later. As for Raoul, Vince had been avoiding the spa doctor ever since yesterday when the man had caught him practically red-handed in the file room. With only seconds to spare, Vince had stuffed Ondine's folder back into the proper box and managed to cover his presence in the room by swinging into his rambling, rumpled-raincoat, cigar-chomping TV cop routine.

Chewing thoughtfully on a carrot curl, Vince allowed his eyes to wander. In front of the swinging doors that led from the dining room into the kitchen, he noticed King David deep in conversation with Emilio Constanza. Emilio started to say something, but the rocker raised a hand

and cut him short. Emilio shrugged and watched King's back as he approached de Vries's table and rested his paw on the back of the empty chair. Almost without looking up, Raoul waved King David away. But it didn't take the rock star long to find another luncheon companion. Soon His Majesty and that actress were sitting at a table by the window with their heads together, jabbering away like long-lost friends. Their four luncheon companions, with painful self-consciousness, dutifully ate their salads and tried not to gawk at the famous pair. So much for Lauren Sullivan's claim that she didn't know any of the other guests.

Vince dragged the tines of his fork across the pink sponge on his plate and tipped the fork onto his tongue. Salmon mousse. The meal disappeared in three bites — shrimp, carrots, cukes and all. Vince chewed on some corrugated box tops that passed for bread in this godforsaken place, then snagged a bunch of grapes from the tray of a passing waiter.

He popped a grape into his mouth and turned, at last, to the girl. "So, Ondine is it?"

The girl looked up from her plate, a bit of cucumber balanced on the end of her fork. "Yes, sir."

"Got a real name, Ondine?"

"Ondine *is* my real name."

"What's the rest of it?"

She glanced at Lund as if seeking his approval to answer the detective, then turned her high cheekbones on Vince in a full-frontal assault. Suddenly, even without the makeup, Vince saw what hundreds of photographers and millions of magazine readers must have seen — the gamin beauty, the childlike vulnerability of the woman. Her smile was dazzling. "Just Ondine."

Christopher Lund waved a knife. "Like she said, Ondine. Had it changed legal."

Did these people think he was a complete idiot? Vince polished off the last of the grapes and sighed. He considered starting on the floral centerpiece. "Look, miss," he said. "You went to kindergarten, right?"

She nodded.

"So what name did they put on your report card in kindergarten?"

Ondine laid down her fork, propped the knobs she had for elbows on the white tablecloth, and considered his question with a slight smile. "Mary Louise Thorvald."

"Thorvald." He grunted. Probably had some fancy punctuation marks over the vowels. At least she wasn't another goddamn Italian. "What kind of name's Thorvald?"

"Norwegian."

"So, Ms. Thorvald," he began.

"I haven't been a Thorvald for years, Detective. I was a foster child. Changed my last name as often as my hair style." She dabbed at her lips — the only plump thing about her — with her napkin, then folded it carefully and laid it down next to her fork. "I was a bit of a problem, you see. Nobody wanted me for long."

Vince stared at her in silence. What did it matter what her name was, Vince thought. Ondine didn't have the strength to knock off Claudia de Vries. She could hardly lift a fork, for Christ's sake, let alone strangle a one-hundred-thirty-pound woman and drop her into a tub of mud. Claudia would have broken those fragile arms in twenty-seven places.

A waiter balancing a stack of dirty dishes on his left arm materialized at the model's elbow and, as Vince watched incredulously, Ondine waved away her barely finished meal. Vince gazed hungrily at the lump of salmon mousse remaining on the lapis lazuli plate. "Aren't you gonna finish your salad?"

Ondine shoved the plate in his direction

231

with two well-manicured talons. "Knock yourself out, Detective."

Caroline leaned over the marble counter in the plush reception area while Ginger, the receptionist and keeper of the master appointment book, helped her select a body lotion, some moisturizer suitable for extra-dry skin, and an assortment of hair care products. Perhaps twenty bottles of various colors, shapes, and sizes, each bearing the spa's distinctive silver label, were lined up along the counter. "I don't know," Caroline said as she studied the label on a bright lavender bottle of lotion. "This one's got coconut oil in it. I *hate* the smell of coconut oil."

With a well-trained, plastic smile, Ginger plucked the bottle from Caroline's fingers. "That's about it in the body lotion department, Mrs. Blessing. Unless . . ." Ginger turned, knelt, pulled open a drawer, and began to search through the neat rows of boxes it contained. While the receptionist's back was turned, Caroline reached over the counter and flipped the pages of the appointment book back a day. Reading upside down, she noticed that the facilities had been busy yesterday afternoon about the time Phyllis Talmadge took her nose-dive into the lake. Of the names she recognized, Lauren Sullivan and Ondine had been in at one-thirty and two o'clock, respectively, while Howard Fondulac had managed to drag himself over for a reflexology treatment at three. Her mother, to her surprise, had found time to spend the hour from three to four working out on the StairMaster while Christopher Lund was signed up for something, she couldn't decipher what, in the weight room at five.

"Here we are!" Ginger turned to Caroline in triumph, offering her a slender white bottle with some green leaves looking suspiciously like marijuana embossed on the label. "This stuff is wonderful, and not a speck of coconut oil!"

Caroline took the time to read the list of ingredients as carefully as if it were a logic problem on the SATs. Lanolin. Aloe. Hemp. She unscrewed the cap and sniffed, enjoying the unexpectedly light, clean scent. "Yes, this might do quite well."

A few minutes later as she lay on the massage table of softly padded leather, facedown, naked, a sheet lightly covering her legs and buttocks, she found herself thinking about King David. Maybe it was the hemp that reminded her. Caroline had told Detective Toscana about her conversation with the rock star, of course, but why had she failed to mention the key King suspected Claudia of having? In his gruff, big-city way, Toscana had been as kind to her as he knew how, even letting her tag along like Junior Miss Jessica Fletcher while he interviewed Phyllis Talmadge after her near-fatal plunge. She owed him. She should have told Toscana about the key.

Caroline had been massaged before, so she recognized the effleurage when it began: long, gliding strokes of Dante's hands, open against and never losing contact with her skin. He'd prepared her for the deep massage with warm essential oils — marjoram for grief and sandalwood for depression — and even tucked hot oiled stones between her toes. "I feel like such a hedonist," she drawled.

He bent down until he could look directly into her eyes. "And I forbid you to feel guilty about that. This is all about you, you, you."

Caroline prayed that this focus on me, me, me would make her feel important, worthy, loved.

But right then, all she felt was boneless.

As his hands and fingers, skilled as a surgeon's, worked over her traumatized body, she could feel the muscles loosen, the adhesions breaking and falling away. She moaned. Once, as he loosened the contracted muscles along her spine, she screamed. This was normal, he told her. To be expected. As he worked to release the tension in her thighs, Caroline bit her lower lip and tried not to cry out. Was this what childbirth felt like? she wondered. Exquisite agony?

Childbirth. She had hoped to have children. Douglas's children. Now that would never be, and her biological clock was ticking, ticking, ticking.

But she had a sister somewhere, or a brother! She counted backward to the year her mother was at Brown, 1962 or 1963. Her half-sibling would be thirty-something today. Had they ever met — on the metro, at the library, at a fund-raiser — without realizing the relationship?

She could be sister to the cashier at Bread and Circus, to the mechanic at VOB Volvo, to her stylist at the Toka Salon. Even to Ondine! No, Ondine was too young. But Lauren? Christopher Lund? And how about Dante? As his hands massaged her feet and ankles, she wondered about Dante. It was hard to tell with him; his amber eyes were wise, but his face was unlined and somehow ageless.

In her mellow state, Caroline wasn't sure whether she felt them first or heard them, but she gradually became aware of helicopters chop-chop-chopping overhead.

"Relax!" Dante warned. "Ignore them. It's nothing to us." His hands moved up to her shoulders.

Helicopters! Silly of Raoul to think he could keep the press out of the grounds of Phoenix Spa forever. It had to be the tabloids, she thought dreamily, training their telephoto lenses on the grounds below, hoping to catch Lauren Sullivan without her makeup or Ondine without her clothes. Vultures! She remembered fuzzy photos of a lover sucking on a topless Fergie's toes and knew that the tabloids would pay big bucks for a photograph of Congressman Blessing's wife with another man's hands grasping her upper thighs. Caroline was thankful that she lay indoors beyond the reach of their prying cameras.

As ordered, she ignored the helicopters, and for the next ten minutes she wallowed in forgetfulness. Cocooned, she felt limp, drained. Maybe she'd died.

"Caroline!" Douglas's voice spiraled down to her, as if from the end of a long tunnel. Dante's hands paused, resting lightly against the small of her back. With great effort, Caroline willed her head to rise and turned it toward the door. She stared at her husband with languid eyes.

He filled the doorway. She wondered, vaguely, why he was wearing jeans and a yellow cable-knit sweater instead of his usual three-piece suit. Brice, his pilot and sometime bodyguard, loomed large behind him, and Douglas must have brought other people along, too, because Caroline could hear the receptionist making fruitless stop-you-can't-go-in-there noises.

"Go away, Douglas." She rested her cheek against the soft, terry cloth covering on the table and waved a sluggish arm.

Douglas indicated to Brice that he should wait outside, then closed the door behind him. Caroline mused that Douglas would have liked to get rid of Dante, too, but the masseur's hands began their final assault on the tendons in her neck, and she once again became one with the table.

Douglas seemed to sense the wisdom of keeping his distance. He stood near the door, slim, tall, elegant as always even in his casual attire. Through half-closed eyes, Caroline was pleased to note that the suave self-assurance he showed in front of the television cameras and before his constituents had evaporated. His arms hung at his sides and he repeatedly opened and closed his hands, as if they were cold. "Caroline," he blurted at last, "I need to explain."

"Don't waste your breath, Douglas."

He took a step toward the table. "Honey, it's not what you think!"

Reluctantly, Caroline pulled herself up into a sitting position. She had never felt uncomfortable being naked in front of Douglas before, but now her nakedness embarrassed her. With elaborate care, she gathered the sheet around her, smoothing the fabric over her bare legs and twisting it into a knot at her breast. She skewered him with her eyes. "Congressman Blessing, you are full of crap!"

"Honey . . ."

"Don't you honey me!"

"But I can explain."

"Okay. So explain this. Eight-by-ten glossies. Dates, times, and places."

Douglas's jaw dropped. "You hired a private investigator?"

"I didn't, Mommie Dearest did." Dante's strong arm steadied her as she slid off the table and hopped to the floor.

"Where are the photos now?" Douglas asked.

"They were in my room . . ."

"Thank goodness! Then no one . . ."

"Depends on what you mean by no one." She gave him a tight-lipped smile. "I had them hidden, but somebody searched my room yesterday. *Somebody* found them." She watched her husband's face as the news sunk in. "Detective Toscana saw them when he searched our cabin, but when I got back to my room later, they were gone."

For an instant, Douglas wore that little-boy-lost look and Caroline felt her heart soften. But just as instantly, the look was gone, masked by what she had come to recognize as his press conference face.

"That's right. You'd better get on the phone to the damage control team." With one arm, she shoved her husband aside and disappeared through the door that led into the sanctuary of the women's sauna. "But tell those spin doctors not to waste any time working on *me!*"

From her post at reception, Ginger Finnegan was accustomed to hearing the occasional scream coming from behind the massage room doors. As she noted Mrs. Blessing's departure time in the proper column of the appointment book, she wondered, not for the first time, why anybody'd want to put herself through all that poking, prodding, and manipulating. With that new guy, Dante, there seemed to be more screaming than usual, but when the clients emerged, they seemed to be all smiles, so go figure. You know what they say. No pain, no gain.

With a few clicks of a mouse, she transferred information on the late afternoon schedule from the appointment book into the computer, thinking she had the most boring job in the world. Dr. de Vries had promised to give her a raise, but that had been before yesterday, before that wife of his had died and that other woman put herself in charge. Now all bets were off. Raoul had always been the voice of reason around the place. Didn't he put a stop to that foolishness when Claudia had wanted to call the spa attendants "guides" and the treatments they provided "journeys"?

Ginger nibbled at her thumbnail, scraping off the violet polish with her lower front teeth. She made up her mind to talk to de Vries about her future when he came through on his rounds at four-thirty. She looked around and, feeling guilty and a bit reckless, crossed to a console on the wall and turned a dial that silenced the singing whales. Enya, rain forests, and all that inner child crap. She just didn't get it.

She thought about the issue of *People* magazine that waited for her in the top drawer of her desk. Mel Gibson, now that was a subject she understood. But reading magazines on the job was a big no-no. Nevertheless, she had already slid the drawer half open when Howard Fondulac breezed into the room, a cell phone clamped to his ear.

"Can I . . . ?" she began, but he held up an index finger to silence her.

"We have a *deal*, buster, and don't you forget it!" His head bobbed vigorously. "Yeah, sure, sure. You do that." Fondulac punched the End button, then tucked the cell phone into the pocket of his exercise pants.

With a casualness born of long practice, Ginger slid the drawer shut over her *People* magazine. Honestly! First that congressman bursting in with his thugs, and now this jerk. "Cell phones aren't in the spirit of the spa," she reminded him sweetly.

Fondulac leaned over the counter and grinned at her. "I know that, sweetheart. But now that the old witch has cashed in her chips, who's gonna stop me?" He reached out and tapped the name tag pinned to the breast pocket of her uniform. "You?"

Ginger slapped his hand away and scowled. Fondulac was definitely not her type. "Don't mind me," she said. "I just work here." She stood, making herself as tall as possible in her sensible flat shoes, until her eyes were level with his. "How can I help you, *sir?*"

He pointed to his name in the appointment book. "It's Fondulac. I'm supposed to meet Gustav in the weight room."

With a slight nod, Ginger indicated the door on her right. "This is the bathhouse, sir. The exercise center is just through there, down the path a little ways and to the left. If you get to the lake, you've gone too far." Suddenly remembering that Fondulac had once worked with Mel — her Mel — she aimed a thousand-watt smile in his direction. "Gustav will be waiting for you."

Ginger watched thoughtfully until the swinging door had closed over Fondulac's narrow backside, hoping that Gustav would teach that arrogant SOB a thing or two. Gustav had come to Phoenix Spa after a twelve-year gig with the Russian weight-lifting team. She smiled. Gustav, now he was someone she could get cozy with. Or that hunky Detective Toscana who was out on the meadow just then dealing with that delicious congressman's helicopter. She liked her men older. Road tested.

When Ginger first came to Phoenix Spa, all the girls had been goo-goo-gah-gah over Emilio Constanza, but what a waste of time that had turned out to be. She'd actually engineered a date with Emilio, until Jean-Claude, the dietitian, had taken her aside, raised one artfully plucked, bleached-blond eyebrow, and drawled, "Honey, you may be standing on the platform, but that train is not coming in for *you*." Back then her competition had been Steve, the pool man, but lately Emilio had been hanging out with the assistant pastry chef, a short, hairy-chested creep named Geoff. Ginger pulled her magazine out of the drawer and balanced it carefully on her knees where it would be hidden by the desk. Mel, she read, had a wife and seven children. Tried-and-true. She rested her case.

It could have been minutes or hours later when somebody screamed. Ginger dismissed it, assuming that Dante must really be giving his four o'clock client the business. But then the screams came again and again, long and shrill, like somebody twisting a cat's tail, and Ginger realized they were emanating from the exercise center, not from Dante's cubicle.

She deserted her post — another no-no — and followed the sound, flying out the door and down the path, straight-arming her way through a set of swinging double doors and bursting into the weight room. It was that skinny model, Ondine, who was screaming, tugging with scrawny arms on the long, leather straps of the Pilates machine, her narrow face flushed and tearstained. "Oh, help! Help!"

Ginger puffed air out through her lips. Jeez! What with all that screeching you'd think she'd caught a boob in the contraption or something. Except the poor girl didn't have any boobs. Maybe she'd mashed a finger. Wondering where Gustav had gotten to, Ginger rushed forward to assist the model.

Ginger knew all about the Pilates machine. Claudia de Vries had demonstrated it to her when she first came to work at Phoenix Spa. Mrs. de Vries had read about Pilates — pronounced puh-LAH-tease, if you please — in the *Washington Post* and had decided, right away, that her spa should have one. This model was called "The Reformer," which Ginger thought perfectly appropriate for an exercise device that looked like a cross between a hospital cot and an autoerotic rowing machine. It came equipped with straps, stirrups, springs and bars, a brace for the neck and shoulders, and a sliding pad to support the torso.

Howard Fondulac's torso was being supported just fine and so was his head, but someone had fully extended the leather straps, wrapped them around the producer's neck like dog leashes, and tied them off in a macabre bow. When Ginger got close enough to see Fondulac's face, she took hold of Ondine's shoulders and pulled her gently away. "I think we need to call Detective Toscana," Ginger soothed. She folded the sobbing woman into her arms and began rubbing her back vigorously, right where Ondine's shoulder blades stuck out like marble wings.

But Ginger knew by the way the straps bit tightly into Fondulac's neck, by his contorted face, and by his eyes, wide and bulging as if astonished by something written on the ceiling, that there was not much Detective Toscana or anybody else could do. They might have been able to revive that psychic lady yesterday, Ginger thought, but Howard Fondulac, Hollywood producer, was tee-totally dead.

Detective Toscana felt as if he were in a nightmare. Here he was staring down at another corpse, and he had not the faintest idea who had killed him or why. Howard Fondulac was as dead as Claudia de Vries had been, if not quite as spectacularly, and it was unfortunately just as obviously murder.

How he wished it could have been suicide! That would have tied it all up nice and neat and he could have left this artificial place and these artificial people, and especially their itsy-bitsy food, and gone home to a sane woman who knew how to cook and was handsome and fun and wasn't obsessive about her appearance.

But before he could go anywhere, or have a square meal rather than a flat one, he had to find out who killed Claudia de Vries and Howard Fondulac, and please heaven before anyone else turned up strangled, drowned, or otherwise terminated with extreme prejudice.

The wraithlike Ondine had been shepherded away by Christopher Lund, an irritating cross between a nursemaid and a guard. His relationship with the girl was an interesting example of codependency. Toscana wondered just how much they needed each other as opposed to how much they thought they did. Ondine was unique, at least until someone else became the model du jour. But Lund could be replaced by any other ambitious young man with an eye for a golden chance when he saw it.

Who made the money, both of them, or only she?

And what was Ondine really doing at Phoenix Spa? Trying to put a few curves onto her bones, so she looked a bit more like a woman? Not on the scraps of rabbit food they fed people here! He didn't know how anyone kept body and soul together. If it had been starvation that killed the two victims, he would not have been surprised, but Howard Fondulac had most definitely had his throat crushed by the leather straps of this infernal machine. It even looked like a contraption designed to torture or kill, invented by the Spanish Inquisition. It was a pity he couldn't use it to get the truth out of someone.

The medical examiner and the crime

scene technicians were on their way, but unless there were fingerprints, there was nothing they could tell him that he couldn't see for himself. Since the machine was part of the spa equipment, all the guests could reasonably say they had used it and justify their prints being found on the handles and adjustable parts, so that avenue of evidence seemed closed.

Detective Toscana turned away with a sigh. It was back to interviewing everyone and asking all the same old questions, of comparing the answers to try and spot a lie or, better still, a meaning! A meaning would be good! Lies were a dime a dozen with this bunch.

Caroline Blessing was about the only one who seemed like a real person. She was quite decent, and she looked so wounded. Hardly surprising, considering the death of Claudia de Vries and the discovery of her body, not to mention the shock of learning the truth about her husband. She was a nice little thing who could use a bit of comfort about now. But he would wager a meatball and pepperoni pizza she'd get damn little warmth from her mother!

Ondine stared at Toscana with watery

eyes. The poor girl looked like something you put on charity posters to make people give donations. "This could happen to you, too!" sort of thing.

"Why did you go into the gym?" he asked her again. Her frailty made it highly unlikely that she meant to use one of the machines herself. "I'm waiting, Miss, uh, Ondine!"

She lowered her gaze, staring down at her hands on her lap, like a sulky child. "I was looking for Emilio Constanza," she replied.

"What made you think he'd be in the gym?"

"Nothing! It just seemed a good place to look."

"When did you see him last? Had you agreed to meet him someplace?"

"I can't remember when I saw him," she said crossly. "Yesterday or the day before. And no, I hadn't agreed to meet him anywhere."

"Why were you looking for him then?"

She looked up at him with disgust. "Do you really need me to spell it out for you, Detective?" She was waiting, one perfect eyebrow arched enquiringly.

"Humor me," he said. "I've forgotten what it's like to be twenty, and I never knew what it was to be a world-famous model."

She stared at him and gulped air.

He waited.

The expressions crossed her face one after the other: anger, humiliation, fear, confusion, anger again. She settled for self-pity. "No," she agreed soulfully, "and you probably don't have any idea what it's like to be lonely! People want you only because it boosts their egos to be seen with you, or because you can make even the most shapeless clothes look good, or because you can bust your butt selling their lousy rags that people wouldn't touch otherwise! I needed to speak to someone who wasn't looking for what he could get out of me!" She leaned toward him. "I knew Emilio. Well, let's just say he wouldn't want to date me — or any woman."

Toscana thought her words had a ring of truth. "Do you do that often, Miss Ondine, confide your loneliness to the hired help?"

She blushed scarlet, the color rising in a deep wave up her pallid face. She stood up sharply, tipping her chair and almost sending it over.

"Sit down!" he ordered.

She remained standing, but she did not leave.

"All right, suit yourself," he said, sliding back in his own seat. "When did you last see Mr. Fondulac alive?"

She thought about it for so long he was almost certain she was concocting a lie, judging what she could get away with.

"I can't remember," she said at last, looking him straight in the eye. "Maybe breakfast, or I might be confusing it with another day."

He leaned forward suddenly. "Tell me exactly what you saw as you went to the gym. Start from when you left your room. Who did you see, where, and when? Who were they with and what were they doing?"

She started slowly, obediently, like a child reciting a lesson. "Christopher and I had been talking . . . actually he had been talking, I just listened, or pretended to. He doesn't know the difference. I left him in my cottage and walked down to the edge of the lake. Then I saw that psychic, and I thought I'd quite like to talk to her." She shrugged. "You never know, she might be for real. But actually she was a terrible bore. All she talked about was herself, although how she could do that for fifteen minutes without actually saying a thing, I'll never know."

"You were with her for fifteen minutes?"

251

"About that. It seemed like longer." She pulled an expression of disgust. "I saw King David going up toward the gym." She was watching his face quite carefully. "Then he came out again within a minute or two . . ."

"Be more exact! How many minutes?" he demanded. "Two — five — ten?"

She smiled, that slow, dreamy smile with wide eyes that she used for the cameras when she was advertising an exorbitantly expensive perfume that was supposed to have men hurling themselves at your feet. "I'm not any good at time," she said sweetly.

"Try!" He meant to keep his voice level, and failed.

"I can't. It matters too much," she protested. "You're asking me to say something that might cost a man his liberty, even his life!"

An idea flashed across his mind with sudden illumination. "You went to see Howard Fondulac because you're fed up with being a clotheshorse, and you want to be an actress! Howard Fondulac's comeback, and Ondine's first movie!" He grunted. "You'd be good at it."

"Do you think so?" she was very obviously pleased.

"Sure!" he said. "You know how to play all the tunes, and you wouldn't know truth from fantasy if it rose up and bit you!"

She drew in her breath slowly, then let it out again without speaking.

Toscana did not speak either. Did he really think Ondine might have killed Fondulac? Why should she? He needed her far more than she needed him. Unless, of course . . . Another idea struck him. What if Fondulac had managed to persuade Lauren Sullivan to commit herself to working with him? Then he might have rebuffed Ondine.

"That's all," he dismissed her. "For now."

Lauren Sullivan greeted his question with laughter, full-throated, easy hilarity, as if it were the one truly funny thing she had heard in all this miserable affair.

"Good heavens, Detective," she said, controlling her mirth at last. "I'm sure you don't mean to be insulting, but I assure you, I have no need whatsoever of descending to work with a man like that. I'll pretend you didn't ask and tell you frankly that I was vaguely sorry for him, but even he had more sense than to imagine I would agree, and more dignity, even when he was drunk, than to ask me."

There was something about her luminous beauty that enthralled Toscana even though he kept telling himself she was a suspect. Sitting here talking to her, hearing that wonderful voice, he felt as if he were part of someone else's story, and they would all live happily ever after, however unlikely it now seemed. She may look guilty, circumstantial evidence might pile up against her, but in the end it would all unravel and it would be someone else who was the killer.

"When did you last see Mr. Fondulac?" he said aloud.

"About ten minutes before that awful scream," she replied. "I was in the shower just through the passage from the gym."

"Did anybody see you?" he asked.

Her eyebrows shot up and she gave a sudden, delicious laugh. "No! I'm an actress, Detective, and I accept that I court the public eye a good deal, but there are some things I do not perform for viewing, and taking a shower is one of them!"

He felt the heat rise in his face and could have kicked himself for his clumsiness. He started to explain, to apologize, then stopped abruptly. It was time he reexerted his authority.

"This is a double murder investigation, Miss Sullivan. I need to know the truth so I can arrest whoever is responsible before it becomes a triple murder, or worse."

She sobered up instantly, and the pallor of her face made him realize how fragile her control was. "I was probably the last person to see him," she admitted. "Apart from whoever killed him, and that certainly wasn't me. I walked through the gym because I was looking for Hilda Finch and I'd seen her going that way, but she wasn't there, so I gave up and had a shower. It wasn't all that important."

"Mrs. Finch was going that way? When?"

She bit her lip. "Almost five minutes before I did." She looked at him steadily, very well aware of what she had said.

"Why did you want to see her?" he pressed.

"She owns the spa," she said reasonably. "It was to do with treatments, and . . . personal."

He let it pass. He would never prove otherwise anyway. "Thank you, Miss Sullivan. That's all for now."

She rose and left, walking with her own individual grace. He could not help watching her, and the image stayed in his mind for several minutes afterward.

Naturally he sent for Hilda Finch next. She kept him waiting fifteen minutes, answered all his questions simply and briefly, and denied any responsibility for either Howard Fondulac's or Claudia de Vries's deaths.

"For heaven's sake, Detective!" she said tartly. "I own Phoenix Spa. Do you imagine I want any more deaths here? Claudia spent millions advertising this place. One death is difficult to overcome, but with hard work it might be accepted as misfortune. A string of them is a catastrophe!"

Looking at her sharp, elegant face with its penetrating eyes he could believe the reputation of the spa was her chief concern and the murders potentially a financial problem. He certainly learned nothing more from her, and she left him feeling more confused than ever, wondering whom to see next and what to ask.

Caroline had refused to see Douglas after their first sharp and very brief encounter, but she knew that a showdown was inevitable sooner or later. She couldn't remain locked in her room indefinitely. And she would not allow him to make her a prisoner, damn him!

It happened early the next day down near the lake with the sun glittering off the water and a very slight breeze carrying the scent of flowers from the bushes around the cottages. She saw his familiar figure striding toward her, and for an instant she felt the old pleasure, as if nothing had happened and everything was perfect, as it had been only a week ago.

Except that of course it hadn't. If she were not so naive she would have known that. She turned to face him, swallowing hard and straightening her shoulders.

He stopped in front of her.

She struggled to keep control and use her brain instead of the emotions boiling up inside her: grief for what she had lost and hope that perhaps it wasn't totally gone after all; shame for the fool she had been to be taken in by him; and rage at his duplicity, the way he had used her. "Yes, Douglas, what is it?" she said a little breathlessly.

"Have you had time to reconsider your decision regarding a divorce?" He was straight to the point. It startled her that he did not try any charm or prevarication at all. It was unlike him not to attempt the easier way first. He believed in his own power to win people, and to be honest he had had good cause to. Damn it, *she* had given him good cause! When had she ever failed to melt into his arms when he tried hard enough?

"And why should time make any difference?" she asked icily. "Would a day, or a year, change the facts?"

His smile was chilly. She used to think he was so handsome, almost beautiful because of the confidence and the charm and the kindness inside him. Now he was ugly. There was a slackness somewhere, a meanness of spirit.

"Time could change your perception of the facts," he answered. "You might develop a much clearer idea of what is important and what isn't."

"You mean I might acquire your idea of it!" she said witheringly. "Please, God, I hope not! The day I believe power and office mean everything, and honesty means nothing, I'd be better off dead!"

"Yes." He shoved his hands hard into his pockets and stared down, then up again quickly. "Well, death is a whole other subject. One I'd prefer to avoid, if possible."

She felt a chill ripple over her, and it was not from the breeze off the lake.

"I care about my career, Caroline," he went on. "And I intend to succeed. I don't think you have fully appreciated that."

A tingle of danger passed over her, but she ignored it. "Of course I appreciate it!" she said angrily. "And I wanted to help you with it. I imagined being by your side . . ." She was forced to stop by the emotion almost choking her. Why was it so desperately, agonizingly difficult to watch a dream die?

"I intend that you shall be," he said, and for an instant he seemed uncertain whether to try being charming or not. The smile was there, but then it faded and the hardness returned. Perhaps he realized it was too late.

"I won't!" she retorted, and now she sounded like a petulant child.

"Grow up, Caroline!" he said sharply, staring across the lake, his face hard. "It's time you started to think like an adult and faced a few realities of life. This is not kids playing games where you can throw your toys away and storm off in a sulk if it doesn't go your way." He turned back to her. "If you don't want to get very badly hurt, then you'd better start thinking of the consequences of your behavior."

She exploded with a bellow of laughter, rough edged with fury and indignation. "That's wonderful, coming from you! I'm not the one whose career is in jeopardy because I went whoring around the place with anything that wasn't nailed down or had four legs! And was careless enough to be photographed doing it!"

He blushed dark red, but she wondered if it was shame for having done such things, or embarrassment at his own stupidity in having been caught and recorded for posterity, in particular for the newspapers and the divorce court. She was afraid it was the latter. She might have forgiven him had it been the first.

His eyes were hard and bright, far colder than the sun glittering off the blue lake. "I intend to deal with that," he said between his teeth.

"Oh yes? How?" she jeered. Anger was easier than tears. Self-pity would destroy her. It opened up like a great hungry pit in front of her, filled with the death of her dreams, the most tender and vulnerable and precious dreams she had ever known. That was a kind of murder as well. She would have to learn to hate him for that! The deceit of it, the deliberate cruelty.

He was impatient. "Well, for a start, you are going to forget about the whole incident and behave like the loving, loyal, and admiring wife you were last week. You are going to —"

"I am not! I am going to divorce you," she shouted. "And if you think for half a second that you are ever going to touch me again, you're out of your mind!"

His eyes widened. "My dear girl, I don't give a damn whether I touch you again or not! As no doubt you are now aware, I can take my pick of any number of very beautiful and willing women."

"Don't be so squeamish, Douglas. There are names for women who are willing to be so obliging. And usually you have to pay them for it!"

He gave an abrupt little laugh. "I've got dozens of friends who'd understand me very well; they can't afford not to!" He shook his head, and his voice was brittle. "No, Caroline, you'll play the loyal and trusting wife in public, whatever we do in private, because I intend to get into the Senate one day, possibly even the White House. I have no intention whatever of allowing you to parade your small-town outraged virtue to stop me."

She was aware of a sense of danger, and yet she couldn't help herself from going on. "Small-town virtue, as you put it, has stopped more powerful men than you, men who were better at not getting caught!" she said witheringly. "Good heavens, Douglas, even if your 'friends' in power don't care about your appetites, surely they have enough sense to care about your crass clumsiness at getting caught! A villain is one thing, a fool is quite another!"

She felt the satisfaction run warm all through her at the fury in his face and the knowledge that out here where anyone might see them, including any wandering reporters, he dared not even let the rage show in his body language, much less actually hit her. She very nearly smiled.

"Talking about getting caught," he said deliberately, his lips thin. "A bit careless of your mother getting 'caught' when she was at college, wasn't it? Not like the Hilda Finch I know. But of course she wasn't Finch then, was she!"

Caroline felt the blood drain from her face. How could he know that? For a moment she was dizzy, the sunlight was glaring, blinding her.

"Don't tell me you didn't know?" Douglas's voice came from far away. "But of course you know, or what I'm saying wouldn't mean anything to you, would it? And you wouldn't look like you'd just seen ghosts walking."

"How could you?" she demanded. "She would never have told you! She doesn't trust you and never did!" She was challenging him as if the fact that he shouldn't know meant that he didn't. What did it matter how he knew? He did, that was the only ugly, horrible reality that counted.

"Claudia de Vries, darling! Who else?" Now he was mocking her. "Really, I'd have thought you could have worked that out for yourself. You're a disappointment, Caroline. Not only are you a prude and childishly unrealistic, but you're slow-witted as well. Don't make me spell all this out for you. Just acknowledge the facts and behave like a well-bred congressional wife."

"Or what?" She wanted to sound defiant, brave, and above all confident. She only sounded panicky and defensive.

"Oh, please!" he said wearily. "Do we have to play this all out to the bitter end?"

Caroline's mind raced, horrible possibilities crowding one after another. Would Douglas try to blackmail her mother as Claudia de Vries had? What would he do now? Did he merely know about the child because Claudia had told him, or could he prove it?

Anyway, these days who cared? Quite possibly it would simply add a little mystery and glamour to what had previously seemed a very staid and shallow, boring life. Her father was not around anymore to be hurt or embarrassed about it. Who was socially ruined because of a youthful tragedy these days?

And there was the other question she would like to have avoided ever asking. How much did she care, anyway? She and her mother had never been close, and the few rare confidences over the last two days did nothing to undo a lifetime's pattern. Would she live the rest of her own life tied to Douglas, living out a hideous charade of a marriage, to save her mother from possible embarrassment?

No, definitely not. Hilda could clean up her own mess.

She put her hands on her hips. "I suppose you also took Claudia's proof of this event?" she said with raised eyebrows.

"What do you think I'm going to do, blackmail your mother?" he said in surprise.

"Aren't you?" she countered. "Or, more exactly, blackmail me?"

"Hardly over that!" He dismissed it with a wave of his hand. "At least, not exactly," he amended. "Who cares if Hilda Finch had an illegitimate child thirty-something years ago? It would hardly be headline news."

Caroline was startled how deeply she resented his casual dismissal of her mother. It stung her pride, and she found herself instantly defensive, which was very odd. If ever there was anyone completely capable of looking after herself, it was her mother. But still she retaliated. "Not like a congressman caught on camera in what I imagine were some *fascinating* poses!" she said. "That would be news, illustrated news at that. A little difficult to deny . . . darling!"

His face was white, his eyes glittering. "I think there's really only one person interested in your mother's indiscretion, but he would be very interested indeed, especially when he knows that it was Claudia de Vries who told me."

"My . . . my half brother? I gather it is a brother, because you said 'he'?" she asked, finding herself breathless, her heart pounding.

"No, fool!" he said tartly. "Detective Toscana!"

It was all hideously clear now. She saw it in the triumph in his face, the leering knowledge that he had terrified her, and she could not conceal it.

"Rather a good motive for murder, don't you think?" he went on calmly. "All the

265

years of hate, blackmail, power. Not to mention the little matter of inheriting all this rather lucrative little business?" He gestured widely around him at the buildings, the lake, the trees and flowers, the cottages in the distance. "A lot of people have killed for a great deal less, never mind greedy women like your mother, who have endured years of humiliation and fear of exposure."

Caroline's mouth was dry, her heart pounding so violently she was sure she must be shaking with it.

"You . . . wouldn't . . ."

"No, of course not," he agreed, leaning a little toward her. "I'll help you conceal your mother's crime, *darling*." He emphasized the last word sarcastically. "Just as you'll help me conceal my little affairs . . . won't you!"

She stared at him. "I . . . I can't! I told you before, I haven't got the pictures anymore. Someone took them!"

"Oh, please! Can't you do better than that?" His tone was one of exquisite derision.

"It's the truth!" she said desperately. "I haven't got them! Douglas, I swear it!"

He looked as if she had hit him. He stood motionless for several seconds, fear and rage equal in his face. Then he mastered himself again and stared at her venomously. "Then you'd better find them, hadn't you? Or your mother is going to be arrested for murder, and this time it'll stick!"

"I . . . but . . . ," she started.

"Find them!" He turned on his heel and marched away, his back stiff, his shoulders rigid, feet almost silent on the grass.

She was amazed how intensely it mattered to her. She never even considered not trying to save her mother. The pain that had existed between them was irrelevant. All she could think of was the cello, as if that one act of kindness had obliterated all the quarrels, the criticisms, and the loneliness. She must find the photographs and give them to Douglas — whatever it cost. She'd deal with leaving him afterward, after Detective Toscana had found out who had killed Claudia and Howard Fondulac. Or if Toscana didn't, then she would find out herself . . . and prove it. Damn Douglas. Damn him, damn him, damn him!

11

Caroline's ears were red with anger, and the blood pulsed through her temples with such force that she thought her brain might explode, shooting shrapnel out through her eyes. As long as some of it went through Douglas's heart, she didn't much care.

Detective Toscana was standing on the patio by the swimming pool, a glass of something brown in his hand. He waved through the pool fence at her, but she ignored him, stalking past with her head down, eyes firmly on the ground. The image of him, peering through the bars of the fence like a big brown bear in the zoo, stuck in her mind. That's how he'd like to see her mother, no doubt — behind bars, waiting for her daily mammal biscuit!

Out of sight of the detective, she hesitated. Her mother would be in their cabin, and she wasn't in any mood for company, no matter how sympathetic. She didn't think she could stand even the soothingly professional attentions of the spa staff.

What she did want was her cello — a stormy workout with Zeller to exorcise the worst of her fury, then half an hour of Bach. JSB could calm the most aggravated spirit with the beauty of his singing logic.

The fingers of her left hand twitched, aching for the throb of the metal strings, the solid mellow wood of the cello's neck. But the cello was in the cabin with her mother, and she wasn't fit to be near another human being right now. She glanced around, desperate for a refuge, someplace out of sight of everyone.

Wind stirred in the branches of the trees behind the main building, bringing her the sharp, clean scent of pine resin, a faint olfactory echo of her cello. Mind made up, she turned toward one of the paths that led beyond the compound and marched off, into the beckoning green depths of the wood.

"I'd say that lady isn't very happy with her husband, eh, Detective?" Emilio Constanza rocked back and forth on the soles of his spotless white sneakers, tray balanced negligently on one hand. "What do you figure all that was about?" He nodded toward the scene of the recent argument, to which he and the detective —

to say nothing of the maintenance man cleaning the pool filter — had been unwitting — but certainly not uninterested — observers.

"You got me." The sun was hot, and the metal bars of the pool fence were warm on Toscana's face; he pulled back and took a deep, meditative sip of the iced tea Emilio had brought him. "Ooh, that's good."

The waiter smiled. "Special recipe. Phoenix sun tea, brewed with orange pekoe, green tea, ginseng, and ginkgo. A dash of papaya enzyme, a drop of kiwi nectar, and Bob's your uncle!"

"You don't say?" Toscana squinted into the depths of his glass, sniffed suspiciously, then shook his head. He nodded toward the lawn where Douglas Blessing still stood, spine stiff with anger. His aide had popped up out of nowhere — that lady reminded him of some kind of mosquito, the way she was always appearing out of nowhere, whining in somebody's ear — but Blessing was ignoring her, fists clenched by his sides as she murmured urgently to him, one hand on his rigid arm. Toscana drained his glass and set it back on Emilio's tray.

"Tell you what, pal. Why don't you go tell the congressman I'd like to see him for a minute? Bring some more of that up to the office, huh, maybe bring the pitcher and two clean glasses?"

"*Clean* glasses," Constanza said gravely, inclining his dark shock of hair. "I'll make a special note of that, sir."

Karen McElroy was searching through the leaves of the planter full of English ivy that lined the wall of her tiny manicurist's studio, when she saw a pale face rise up behind the glass-brick wall above the ivy. Big eyes bulged in a ghostly face surrounded by something that looked like water weed, and the mouth opened in a soundless fishy gape.

"Ahh!" She jumped back, sending the trolley with the hot-wax burner rocketing across the room, spraying a metallic rain of cuticle nippers, sanding blocks, and callus graters in its wake. The door opened.

"Ohmygodohmygodohmygod." Karen pressed a hand to her ample bosom, as though to keep her heart from leaping out of her chest and going *splat* in the aloe-citrus lotion bath. "I thought you were a ghost!"

"I'm sorry." Ondine hesitated in the doorway, looking almost as scared as Karen. "I didn't mean to startle you. Are you . . . could you . . . well, never mind, I mean, it's not important . . ."

"No, no! Come in, come in!" Karen clasped Ondine by the wrist, relieved to find her warm. The poor thing looked just like a living skeleton, but the important word was "living," after all. "I was just lookin' for my gargoyle, when I come to catch sight of you through that glass. I just come from the lounge, where they was talkin' 'bout that lady what fell in the lake. I was thinkin' of that, and then I saw you right there, all white-faced and your hair all —" Karen made a vague gesture at her own neat blonde ponytail, indicating Ondine's floating cloud of hair. "Thought you was drowned, I surely did."

Ondine's look of alarm hadn't noticeably faded as a result of this explanation. "Gargoyle?" she asked.

"Yeah, you know, one a them little stone guys? Sits on top of churches?" She waved upward, indicating some imaginary Gothic edifice, ringed with stone guardians. "One of my clients brought him to me from France. He's from Notre-Dame, like in that hunchback movie," she said proudly. "I keep him up there" — she waved at the edge of the planter — "cuz he looks so cute, hidin' in the leaves. He keeps fallin' in, though. The guy who does the plants don't see him and knocks him off when he does the watering. But that don't matter none, I'll find him later. Can I do somethin' for you?" She smiled, dying to be helpful.

Ondine smiled back, charmed, as guests always were, by Karen's eager kindness and West Virginia drawl. "Well, I don't want to bother you, it's just . . ." She extended one long, pale hand, showing one of the rosy nails snapped off short. "Do you think you could fix that for me?"

"Bother me? Lawdy, what you think they pay me to do 'round here?" Karen laughed heartily and waved Ondine toward the padded cream-leather chair behind her mirror-topped worktable. "Sit down, honey. I'll take care of that in no time."

She set to work at once, removing the rose-colored polish with businesslike dispatch. Besides the broken nail, two more were split; one of those had a chunk taken out of the side. Karen clicked her tongue over the damage as she took out the brushes, powder, and acrylic liquid.

"Mercy, girl, what you been doing there?"

A faint pink rose under Ondine's skin. She wasn't what you'd call pretty, Karen thought, but she sure Lord did have fine skin. Except for that little bit of discoloration near her eye, not a freckle, not a mole, not a single pore in sight. The blush — if you could call it that — looked just like a white rose blooming, thought Karen, pleased at the poetic thought.

"I caught my hand on a piece of gym equipment," Ondine said. "It got away from me and snapped that nail right off." She waggled the injured finger in illustration.

"Oh, yeah, I see that kinda thing *all* the time." A quick dip into the liquid, a tiny ball of powder, and a beautiful smooth surface spread over the split nail, sealing the tear and hiding it immediately. " 'Specially on the Pilates thing, but . . . oh! But you wouldn't have been usin' *that.*"

Karen shook her head, appalled at the memory of what the other staff had told her about that poor, poor man who got strangled in that contraption, the one with the name that reminded her of melted cheese — fondue, that's what Momma called it, but it was just warm Cheez Whiz to Karen. No big shock there; Karen was only surprised accidents like that didn't happen more often.

"Oh, no," Ondine said. "No, of course not."

Eyes focused on her work, Karen couldn't see Ondine's face, but she sounded shook up, Karen thought, and no wonder. She frowned slightly, the tip of her tongue caught between her teeth in concentration as she wrapped and shaped an artificial tip to repair the torn-off nail.

Momma had been on the phone every half hour since the news of Mrs. de Vries's death came out, wanting Karen to quit and come home. When Mr. Cheez Whiz got choked, Granny McElroy started in to calling, too. She'd finally unplugged the phone, so as she could get a little work done, but Karen would admit that she'd had her doubts about staying. She jumped whenever she heard a sound behind her, and she had a feeling all the time like mice were crawlin' up her spine.

But whatever in heck was going on at the spa, Karen couldn't see how it might have anything to do with *her*. And this was the best job she'd ever had; it paid like three times as much as doing nail-tech work in the city, and it wasn't but half the work, either. And besides, she'd told Momma and Granny both, the police were right *there*. That nice detective walked through her building now and then, and waved and smiled. He wouldn't be letting any killers bother her, she was sure.

"There." She admired her repair work; all the nails were once more long, smooth ovals, gently shaped and glossy. "You got *such* nice hands, honey. Those long fingers, and nice long nail beds, too — see, that's the part of the nail's attached to your hand, that's what you gotta have for elegant nails. Mine are so short." She waggled her free hand briefly in illustration. "Even if I put long tips on, they're never gonna look great, but yours . . . you know, I could swear I seen hands just like yours someplace lately. Not *quite* the same, but real close. Now, you want to pick you out a nice color? How 'bout I do you a pedicure, and we can put it on your toes, too?"

Leaving Ondine mesmerized in front of a wall rack filled with dozens of bottles of custom-blended Phoenix nail polish, Karen went into the small alcove where the thronelike pedi-spa, her pride and joy, sat in splendor under a cool blue light, designed to make the client feel as though she were a mermaid sitting at the bottom of the sea, with reef fish nibbling at her toes and the soothing scents of kelp and sea salt all around.

Caroline's long, thin, neatly manicured

fingers twitched unconsciously against the leg of her jeans, her left hand fingering the reaches as she played the allegretto of Saint-Saëns's *Danse Macabre* in her mind. She was some way beyond the spa buildings now; the sea of leafy green had closed over the slate-tiled roofs like a cleansing flood, as though the place had sunk like Atlantis. Good riddance.

Her pace slowed, and she wandered aimlessly, summoning up bits of her long-neglected repertoire, pleased to find that the music came back effortlessly. She knew it wouldn't be that easy to reach performance level with the actual instrument, but it was both a thrill and a relief to find how much she remembered, how instinctively her fingers flexed and reached for the notes that thrummed in her inner ear.

She left the path, and her feet shuffled through layers of crumbling dead leaves, damp with the residue of summer rain. The light filtering through spruce and beech wood was a soft blue-green, and the susurrus of branches in the wind could have been the sound of distant surf. But these were quiet woods sounds and made no interference with the music in her head.

Dum, da-da-da-da dum, da-da-da-da dum, dum, dum, dum . . . The music conjured images, as it always did: imps, dancing with unholy glee, tossing things into a magic cauldron, leaping back as the contents erupted in a shower of firework sparks.

Dee, deedle-deedle dee-dee-dee, dee, deedle-deedle dee-dee-dee — She stopped abruptly, as she realized that the high-pitched violin part was not coming from her inner ear but from someone singing it, near at hand.

She swung around, hands half raised in instinctive defense.

"Deedle-deedle, dee-dee-dum!" Phyllis Talmadge finished and bowed, with a smile of fulfilled performance. "I knew you wouldn't forget," she said, straightening up. She was still smiling, though with a look of remoteness in the back of her eyes, as though she was looking at something beyond Caroline.

Caroline was at once startled and flustered by the intrusion. Finding no words to protest, she said rather weakly, "Forget what?"

"What?" Phyllis's wispy gray brow lifted. "Your music, of course. I used to watch you, you know, when you played with the symphony. Even as part of the orchestra, you played with such . . . such life! And in the solos, you were simply magnificent, my dear." She shook her head, sighing.

"You heard — oh." Caroline was still flustered but undeniably pleased at this echo from her past. "I didn't know you were a music aficionado. Do you play, yourself, or did you just know the violin part from performances?"

The older woman had started to walk, and Caroline fell into step naturally beside her.

"Oh, I play a bit, but I'm not up to your level, by any means." She flipped a dismissive hand.

"Neither am I, anymore," Caroline said, a little wistfully. "Maybe again, but not yet. Not until all this" — she waved a hand in the direction of the spa buildings — "is settled." She cleared her throat, suddenly aware that Phyllis had herself been attacked, or evidently attacked.

It occurred to her that they were quite alone here. Caroline brushed a hand casually across her thigh, reassured by the weight of her cottage key with its heavy ornamental fob. It wasn't much of a weapon, but she was younger, taller, and stronger than the elderly psychic.

"Uh, are you sure you're feeling all right, Ms. Talmadge? Should you be out walking?"

Now that Caroline took time to notice, she saw that the older lady was in fact looking very pale and insubstantial, her skin nearly the same gray as her hair. Phyllis paid no attention to the question, though, instead focusing her eyes intently on Caroline. "It's very important that you play," she said. "That's what I came to tell you. Don't let anything that happens here stop you."

"What do you mean?" Caroline's initial startlement at the psychic's sudden appearance was rapidly giving way to distinct uneasiness. "What's going to happen?"

The psychic tilted her head to one side, almost as though she were listening to someone — or something.

"You don't need to know that," she said.

"*What?* What do you mean, I don't need to know that?"

"Things will happen," Phyllis said mysteriously, "but you'll be all right. Some people close to you" — she turned her head, wearing the listening expression again — "people *very* close to you," she amended, "may suffer harm. But you'll be all right."

"Who? Who do you mean? My mother? Is something going to happen to my mother?"

This is ridiculous! Caroline thought. *Absurd!* If asked half an hour previously, Caroline would have expressed complete skepticism of the concept of psychic ability and profound disinterest in anything said by anyone professing to have any. Now, the first inkling of some personal relevance, and she was agog as any caller to the Psychic Hot Line.

On the other hand — a ripple of unease snaked down her spine — she *knew* she hadn't been humming aloud, and yet Phyllis Talmadge had come in with the violin part, precisely in the right spot. *Danse Macabre,* indeed!

"That," said Phyllis enigmatically, "is up to you. But you must play your cello. It's very important."

Caroline closed her eyes in momentary frustration and drew in a deep breath through her nose. "Now, look," she began, in a determined tone of voice, opening her eyes, "you can't —"

But she stood alone in the middle of a small grove of oaks. The glossy leaves rattled faintly in the breeze, and an acorn tumbled down through the branches, rolling to a stop at her feet. Nothing else stirred.

"Ms. Talmadge?" she said, and her voice

sounded weak to her ears. She cleared her throat and called again, louder. "Ms. Talmadge!"

No one answered. The wood stirred gently around her, but the solitude was no longer soothing. It was only as she turned to make her way back toward the spa that she recalled. Hadn't they said that Phyllis Talmadge had been taken to the hospital following her attack? Had she been released, or had Caroline just met a . . .

"Nonsense!" she said aloud and, turning on her heel, strode determinedly back toward the spa.

Karen turned on the taps of the pedi-spa and dumped a handful of sea lavender–scented bath salts into the swirling water. Leaving the basin of the footbath to fill, she went back toward the door to the studio, pausing on her way to pick up a cuticle nipper that had fallen to the floor when she'd been startled earlier.

"Forget it!"

She was startled again, this time by Ondine's voice, pitched low but furious. A male voice answered, also low, and grimly commanding.

"Oh, no, baby. I'm not about to forget it. And neither are you. Where is it?"

"I don't know what you're talking about!" There was a scuffling sound, then a sharp intake of breath from the girl. "Let go! Howard had it. Now he's dead, and it's gone. Somebody took it."

"Yeah? Well, if 'it' is what I think you mean, then you're the most likely person to have taken it! Ow!"

Holy shit, Karen mouthed silently to herself. What was "it"? Drugs, maybe. Mr. Cheez Whiz sure looked like he was taking *something.* And if he had enough for somebody to kill him for, he was maybe a pusher, not just a user. If it was Ondine, a coke habit would sure explain how she kept so skinny!

She craned her neck to one side, trying to see the man who was talking to Ondine, but couldn't see anything save a few wisps of the model's hair against the curtain of ivy, as she tossed her head, hissing at her companion.

"Let go! I'll call for help!"

"No, I don't think so. You can't afford to do that." The man's voice was low and self-assured but not loud enough for Karen to say for sure who it was.

Call for help. Karen licked her lips and glanced into the shadowy blue alcove. There was a phone there, back around the corner where she kept the canisters of sea salt scrub and peppermint lotion. Wiping her sweaty hands on her pale-blue uniform, she took one stealthy step toward the phone. One more, careful not to let her gum-soled shoes squeak on the white marble floor.

She could call the main office. If the man heard her talking, he'd be scared off, but that was okay. Ondine could tell the detective who he was, and then . . .

Her hand closed over the receiver. She held it to her ear for a long, heart-stopping moment of silence before she remembered that she'd unplugged the phone earlier. Fingers trembling, she fumbled for the phone jack, her hands sweaty with fear. The voices had gone silent for a moment. Was the man gone?

Someone else spoke, a different voice, one she knew, but — The dial tone sounded loud in her ear. It was a cordless phone; she huddled as far as she could get into the cupboard alcove, close to the wall, back turned to the studio. She punched the three-digit number for the office and pressed the receiver tightly against her head to muffle the sound of ringing. *Ring . . . Ring . . . Ri—*

A white light bloomed inside her eyes,

and the receiver fell from her hand, bouncing and clattering off the slick white marble. There was a sound of dragging, a splash, and Karen McElroy's blonde pony-tail fanned out, waving gently in the blue-green water of the footbath like some exotic seaweed.

"Hello?" said a tinny voice from the fallen receiver. "Phoenix Spa. Hello?"

A finger poked the Off button on the phone, and it fell silent. Then the switch for the pedi-spa. The whirling water spun slowly to a stop, a few final bubbles of lavender scent bursting to the surface. Tiny tendrils of crimson unfurled in the silent water, but the surface lay still and blue over the manicurist's submerged face.

On the white tile by her hand, a small gray stone gargoyle grinned through jagged teeth.

The congressman's aide *was* a mosquito, Toscana decided, and just as hard to swat. She kept insisting that she had to be with the congressman, she must sit in on the interview, after all, this wasn't really official, was it? And the congressman would need advice, she'd call his attorney . . .

Toscana thought he maybe should have asked Constanza to bring a can of Raid, instead of the pitcher of Phoenix sun tea, but he succeeded at last in keeping the pesky aide out and the congressman in.

"Sit, sit," he said, waving Blessing to a seat. He picked up his glass and gestured invitingly at the sweating pitcher. "A little tea?"

Blessing waved away the tea impatiently. From his earlier behavior, Toscana expected him to start cutting up rough again, but no, not a bit of it. To his surprise, the congressman sat down, leaned across the table, and said, "Detective, you have to help me! Please!"

Sheer astonishment prevented Toscana from saying that no, the congressman hadn't quite grasped the situation here — *he* was the one supposed to be helping. Instead, he set down his glass of tea, carefully, to avoid splashing any on the polished granite, and sat down at the table across from Blessing.

"Help you, huh? What with?"

"With my . . . with my wife." Blessing was looking pretty strange. Red one minute, white the next. His hands were clenched into fists on the desk, and the knuckles stood out like the joint on a drumstick.

"Your wife," Toscana repeated carefully.

"Well, see, Congressman, it's like I told you. Nobody can leave here until —"

"That's not what I mean!" Blessing's features contorted, his teeth gritted, his eyes squeezed into slits. He looked like a politician who'd taken the lid off his garbage can and found a *National Enquirer* reporter nestling inside.

Toscana stole a look at the pitcher; it looked like a big chunk of glass, heavy enough to conk somebody. Was it, though, or was it some of that plastic stuff that just looked like glass?

Before he could put a casual hand on the pitcher to check, Blessing got control of himself. He breathed like a marathon runner coming down the stretch, and his face went from red back to white, but at least he'd quit shaking.

"I'm sorry," he said, and his voice was so quiet Toscana had to strain to hear it. "I didn't think it would be this hard."

"Don't you worry," Toscana assured him, with one eye on the pitcher, just in case. "Police officers hear all sortsa stuff."

A ghost of a smile crossed Blessing's face. "You aren't going to tell me it goes in one ear and out the other, are you, Detective?"

Toscana contented himself with a shrug

and a noncommittal murmur, but it seemed to help. Blessing sat slumped in his chair, exhausted. Toscana — who really had heard almost everything imaginable in his career — knew when to talk and when to listen. This was a time to keep still and wait. At last, Blessing nodded, like a man making up his mind.

"I'm being blackmailed," he said.

At this point, the news came as no big hairy surprise to Toscana, but he felt his heart jolt in his chest anyway. A break! Goddamn, was he finally going to get a solid break in this case? "Yes, sir?" he said politely. "What about?"

Blessing's long, muscular throat moved as he swallowed. "I was adopted as an infant," he said. "I had no idea who my birth parents were and no reason to think it mattered. But then . . ." His jaw clenched involuntarily, and he had to force it open to get the words out. "I met Claudia de Vries at a fund-raiser last year. She seemed interested in the issues. . . ."

Toscana snorted, by reflex, and Blessing's head shot up. "Yeah," the detective said, waving a hand in dismissal. "Issues. Yeah, that too, I'm sure. So?"

Blessing's jaw was bulging again. "So," Blessing got out, "I met with her . . . now and then. She made contributions to my campaign fund, large contributions." Toscana made a casual note on his pad: check the congressman's other contributors, just in case.

"Illegally large?"

"Certainly not!" Red, white, red again. The man could get a job as the flashing light on a caboose, Toscana thought. He went back to the noncommittal grunt.

"I wouldn't countenance anything of the kind," Blessing said. "And that's what . . . well, eventually, she started conveying . . . messages. From other contributors. About things they'd like to have happen, votes they'd like to go a certain way."

"So Claudia was fronting, huh? Who for?" Toscana was more than interested and didn't bother trying to hide it. Blessing had made up his mind to talk, and he was going to do it, if he had to fight himself every inch of the way.

"I don't know. I have guesses, but I don't know." Blessing gave a grimace that might have started life as an ironic smile. "The Mob? Is there still such a thing?"

"Oh, you better believe it," Toscana assured him. "Though a few of 'em have gone uptown." Hoo-boy. Well, *that* would explain a few things, wouldn't it? He drummed his fingers on the table, thinking. If you had a lot of dirty money — a chronic problem for anybody connected — a spa had certain advantages as a laundry. A little more class than a garbage company, a great front for funneling funds to political targets, and maybe, just maybe, cover for a few other illegal activities. You could hide a heck of a lot of things under a layer of mud and an herbal wrap.

Blessing cleared his throat, and Toscana came out of a rose-tinted dream of men in tailored suits and wing tips being herded en masse into the paddy wagon.

"So," Blessing said, with renewed determination, "when I made it clear that I couldn't be bought, Claudia smiled and went away — and then she came back, with the record of my birth mother's name. Hilda Finch."

"Hil—" The pitcher clattered to the floor, in a flood of ice cubes and sun tea. So it *was* plastic, Toscana thought dimly. "But Hilda Finch is . . ."

"My wife's mother. Yes, exactly." The deep lines still furrowed Blessing's brow, but he seemed relieved to have got it out.

"Oh, Jeez."

Blessing's mouth actually twitched slightly at that.

"Very eloquent, Detective. So you do see, I hope, why I need your help. I have to divorce my wife — or rather, make my wife divorce me."

Toscana was recovering from the shock. He flicked an ice cube off the table with one finger, eyeing the congressman. "Yeah? I didn't hear everything you guys said outside, but I heard enough. Sounded like you were doing everything you could to make sure she stayed married to you."

"If it sounded like that," Blessing said shortly, "then I did a good job."

"What do you mean?"

The congressman exhaled, shoulders slumping a little. "Claudia may be dead, but whoever she was fronting for isn't." He straightened up, with a sharp glance at Toscana. "Bear that in mind, Detective. I *knew* there was someone behind her, and that someone certainly knew the secret of my birth — and my marriage. Killing her wouldn't have helped me. It's put me in a much more difficult position," he added, with a nod toward the door.

The position was simple. When he had discovered the truth about his marriage, he had been overcome with horror. Unwilling to believe it at first, he had finally accepted Claudia's claim. Records could be forged,

291

but there was something else.

"Look." He stretched his hands out on the desk. They were neatly manicured, the nails buffed and glossy, long-fingered and graceful. "When you get a chance, look at Caroline's hands. They aren't identical, but the shape of the fingers is damn close. And then there's this." He held up his hands, palms toward the detective. The fingers of the right hand lay together; on the left hand, the little finger stuck out at an angle, with a space between it and the ring finger. "Caroline has it, too. It isn't obvious enough that anyone would notice unless he or she was looking." He folded his hands abruptly. "There are half a dozen other tiny things; that's just the most obvious."

All doubt erased, he had been confronted with a wracking dilemma. "I love her," he said softly, looking down into his lap, where his fists lay on his thighs. "I couldn't bear to tell her, to have her look at me with disgust, to recoil from me. But likewise, I *couldn't* . . ." He shrugged, helpless. "I *couldn't* . . ."

"Well, I can kinda see how that would be," Toscana said slowly. "But what you said? About being a good actor?"

Blessing nodded and took a deep breath.

"Whoever was behind Claudia, he — they — wants me to stay married. It helps the image" — he made a slight, instinctive grimace — "and more important, it keeps me under control. So I couldn't divorce her, they wouldn't have it. The only thing I could do was to try my best to make Caroline divorce *me*." He swallowed. "She might hate me, but at least she could remember having loved me. If I . . . if she knew the truth, she couldn't ever think of me without wanting to throw up."

He sighed. "So I did my best. I went off to the cabin with Miranda to make it look like we were having an affair" — he nodded toward the door, where his aide presumably still buzzed — "and gave that masterful performance outside." He looked up with a faint smile. "It might have sounded to you — and to Miranda — like I wouldn't let her divorce me. But Caroline's a proud woman. Being told, and told in brutal, shaming terms like that, nothing would drive her away faster."

Toscana pursed his lips, nodding. "What about those photos? Method acting, huh?" He quirked a brow at Blessing.

"Faked," the congressman said shortly. "You know there's nothing easier than to doctor photos."

"Yeah," Toscana agreed amiably. "Look at the *National Enquirer*. Elvis don't even look dead half the time. So, Ms. Mosquito — I mean, your aide, there — you think she's in with the people who were controlling Claudia?"

Blessing grimaced. "I don't know for sure. It might be just devotion to duty, but I *think* she's spying on me for them. She never leaves my side. It was a heaven-sent chance when you called me in and wouldn't let her come with me."

He leaned forward, dark eyes intense. "So now you know. And now you see, Detective? I have to have your help, to make my wife, to make my *sister*" — he paled slightly at the word — "divorce me."

12

Vince Toscana had never had any reason to give nail polish a second thought. But after today, he'd never again be able to watch his wife paint her nails without a shudder. No amount of life on a Philly corner could have prepared him for the scene that met his gaze in the manicure studio.

He stared speechless as the carved mahogany shelf unit that had contained the dozens of nail preparations was gently raised by his crime scene technicians, leaving behind it an incarnadine sea. Just as the ocean contained myriad shades of blue and green, there was now a glutinous pool of multitudinous tones of scarlet spreading across the floor. Carmine bled into ruby, magenta swirled through vermilion, cherry melted into plum. And through it all, glass shards stuck up at random angles, polish sliding viscously down them to join the rest of the drying mess that Vince feared would soon be rigid as vinyl siding.

And at the heart of the horror, curved

like a gathering wave, lay the crushed heap of bones and skin that had once been Ondine. Only her toes were untouched, sticking out from the red sea and looking incongruously pale. "Jesus," Vince sighed. "The only way we're going to be able to tell blood from nail polish is when it sets."

As he waited for the technicians to complete their work on the crime scene, he walked through to the consulting room where Karen McElroy's hair still swirled gently in the foot spa, the coppery smell of blood mixing with kelp and mineral salts hitting his nostrils as he bent over her, careful not to disturb anything. The trouble with working for a small department where there wasn't a lot of serious crime was that there was only one team of technicians. Just like always, Vince thought. The poor folk have to wait in line for the rich folk to get seen to first. He wished he could at least restore some small grace to Karen by draining the pink-tinged water, but he knew better than to touch anything before it had been processed by the experts. There was nothing dignified about these deaths, he thought bitterly. Anger began to burn like indigestion in his stomach. Somebody in this place didn't give a damn about human life. And even though he considered most of the people he'd encountered at Phoenix to be pretty damn worthless, they still had a right to their selfish little lives. It was his job to protect them, and so far he wasn't doing a very good job of it.

Fresh determination burned inside Vince as he gazed down at the murdered beautician. He was going to put a stop to this killing spree. And if that meant slamming every last one of these spoiled people in the county jail, then he'd damn well do it. Vince turned on his heel and marched through to the nail studio with a new sense of purpose.

Hilda yanked open another drawer. She didn't think Claudia had ever thrown anything away in her life. The banks of filing cabinets filled the entire walk-in storeroom that opened off the spa director's luxurious personal office. It was like an archaeological dig, ploughing through it. But although she'd found business correspondence dating back more than twenty years, brochures from every establishment Claudia had ever worked in, and folders stuffed with letters from grateful clients, Hilda still hadn't found what she was looking for. Somewhere, she knew, there must be

Claudia's secret stash. She'd made it her lifetime's work to get something on everyone she thought she might possibly make use of, and Hilda knew her well enough to realize it would be somewhere accessible. No bank vaults for Claudia; she'd have wanted her leverage where she could gloat over it at her leisure.

Hilda sighed. Another file of correspondence. She probed farther back in the drawer and came across a thick manila folder marked "College." Curious, she pulled it free and opened it. To her amazement, it was stuffed with mementos of Claudia's years at Brown. There were handbills for plays and concerts, notes from fellow students, ticket stubs for movies and football games, even a faded corsage, pressed and preserved to recall some distant evening. Hilda was amazed. She'd never have credited Claudia with so sentimental an attachment to the past.

Fascinated, she flicked through the folder's contents, misty-eyed at the memories it evoked. She was sure they'd been to that performance of *Love's Labour's Lost* together. Yes, she remembered now. They'd gone on a double date with those two seniors that they'd met at the Harvard–Yale football game. Claudia had spent the whole evening sulking because the more handsome of the two boys had clearly preferred Hilda. Hilda's present smile was pure malice at the recollection.

Right at the back of the folder was a thick wallet of photographs. Suddenly, Hilda's memory provided its own snapshot. Claudia, filled with delight over her parents' Christmas gift, one of the new Kodak Instamatic cameras, gathering her friends into groups and making them pose for pictures. "Smile, everybody!" had become the words most often on Claudia's lips that semester.

Intrigued to see what had survived of her own past, Hilda opened the flap and pulled out the faded color photos. The first half dozen were an assortment of girls from the dorm. Hilda herself appeared in three of them, her hair perfectly lacquered in a beehive, showing off her small, neat features to their maximum advantage. Her face relaxed as she drifted back in her mind to those cozy dorm chats, drinking hot chocolate and eating cookies late at night, girls perched on narrow beds and pillows on the floor, gossiping about their lives and loves. They'd still believed the world was theirs for the taking, convinced the golden days would run forever. God, she wished she'd known then what she knew now.

The next picture hit Hilda's nostalgic mood like a cold pool after a sauna. Claudia had framed her subjects perfectly. They were leaning against a car. Hilda was in profile, head thrown back, mouth open in laughter, her arms thrown around the slim hips of the boy who was pulling her close to him, his own narrow, triangular face grinning sheepishly at the camera. "Tad Blake," Hilda hissed, her lips pulled back tightly over her teeth.

She had forced Tad Blake from her memory with the systematic efficiency she'd brought to every area of her adult life. The foolish conviction that she'd been in love, the fumbling passion that had left her life in ruins, Tad's refusal to accept that her nightmare was anything to do with him, his protestations that she couldn't expect him to believe he was the only one she'd given herself to — it had all been consigned to a section of her memory marked "Do Not Enter." The temptation to rip the photograph to shreds was almost overwhelming. But she controlled herself. She didn't want torn photographs in the office trash to tell their tale to any passing police officer. She grabbed the photograph and stuffed it in her pocket. She'd dispose of it later, somewhere its remains wouldn't be found.

Her action revealed the next photograph in the bundle. It was Tad again, but this time he was the one seen from the side. An involuntary gasp escaped Hilda's mouth. Her mind rebelled. It couldn't be. Could it?

Intently, she studied the picture. Tad's flaming red hair had faded to a dull auburn as the film chemicals had degraded, but her memory supplied the missing tones. Okay, the hair was the same. But that was no proof of anything, not in these days of flawless hair tinting. But that profile was undeniable. The pointed chin, the high forehead. They were identical. Hilda pulled the other picture from her pocket. Substitute her neat little nose for Tad's, and you'd be looking at the unmistakable profile of Lauren Sullivan.

Hilda stared at the photograph, a confusion of thoughts and images tumbling through her head. It looked as if Claudia had left her a legacy that could yet prove even more advantageous than the spa. Lauren Sullivan. What a coup.

The encounter with the psychic had unsettled Caroline. Phyllis Talmadge was right. Playing air cello in the woods was no substitute for the real thing. She decided to head back to the cottage. She was going to have to face Hilda sometime; if her mother was there, at least she'd get it over and done with. Then she could open the windows and sit looking out over the lake playing one of the Bach cello suites. Number three, she thought. That would lift her out of this despair and rage and remind her that there was a place inside her where beauty could still live.

Caroline hurried through the woods, paying scant attention to her surroundings, already hearing those first haunting notes in her mind's ear. By the time she emerged on the path, she was almost trotting. She pushed open the door of the cottage, humming the theme of the first movement under her breath, and stopped short. To her astonishment, she found Raoul, not Hilda, sitting in the morris chair, looking as relaxed as if he were in his own sitting room.

"What are you doing here?" Caroline demanded.

He raised his perfectly shaped eyebrows. "Hoping for a word with you, my dear Caroline." She opened her mouth to speak, but he held up a hand to silence her. "I wanted to discuss the return of something that belongs to you."

She glared at him, suddenly putting two and two together. "It was you who left those photographs lying on the table for Detective Toscana to find, wasn't it? And then you came back for them later, didn't you?"

Raoul smiled. "Clever Caroline."

"But why?"

"I thought it might muddy the waters with the cops. You see, Claudia had a very profitable little sideline going. Some friends of hers needed a little political clout on their side, and your charming husband was in a position to meet their needs. Of course, he took a little persuading."

"Claudia was blackmailing Doug?" Caroline crossed to the sofa and sank into it. She knew her husband was a double-dealing, two-timing bastard when it came to love, but she didn't think his politics were as corrupt as his sex drive.

"Such a coarse word, blackmail. I prefer to think of it as oiling the wheels of commerce. And with your mother taking over my living, I figure I'm going to need all the commercial support I can find. I didn't want the cops stumbling over the real dirt that Claudia had on Doug, so I decided to serve them up a delicious little red herring."

Caroline frowned. "I don't understand. You mean she wasn't blackmailing him over his infidelities?"

Raoul laughed. "You're so naive. You really think in this day and age that your husband's constituents would vote him out of office because he can't keep his fly zipped? Oh, it might lose him a few votes here and there with the fundamentalists, but it would pull in a lot more from all the guys who would love to be doing exactly what he's doing. But thankfully, our local detectives are just as credulous as you are. They won't doubt for a moment that keeping those photographs away from you would be enough of a reason for darling Doug to do what Claudia asked."

"You're saying there's more?"

Raoul crossed his legs. He looked as pleased as a cat that had just incapacitated a mouse. "Here's the way I see it. While it won't harm Doug's career in the long run if the world finds out what a sleaze he really is, it would be better all around if things just continued as they are. I don't think there's any need for you to get a divorce, Caroline. Don't rock the boat. Keep things on an even keel. Make it easy for

Doug to earn the money he's going to need to keep me satisfied."

Caroline shook her head in disbelief. "You're crazy. I wouldn't stay married to Doug to save my life."

"Oh, I think you would. And that's just what you're going to have to do. Because what I know about Doug won't just destroy him. It'll destroy you, too. You'll be a social outcast. There's not an orchestra in the land that would give you a job. No, let me rephrase that. There's not an orchestra in the whole world that would have you. You'll be a leper for the rest of your life."

He was enjoying himself, she could see that. And she hated him for it. But there was something concrete underpinning his flesh-crawling confidence. "I don't believe you," she said defiantly. "Whatever Doug has done, it's his responsibility. It can't reflect on me."

"Oh, but it does, Caroline. Because you were a willing partner in this . . . enterprise."

"You're not making any sense at all."

Raoul uncrossed his legs and leaned forward, elbows on knees. "I assume you know about your mother's little indiscretion?"

Caroline's head came up, her eyes widening in astonishment. Claudia must have confided in her husband, she thought wildly. But what did this have to do with her and Doug? "You're still not making sense," she said, less certain of herself now.

"The child your mother gave up for adoption all those years ago went to a Mr. and Mrs. Blessing," Raoul said, grinning like a Halloween pumpkin.

Panic started to clench in Caroline's chest. She could feel her heart thudding, the cold sweat of fear breaking out on her neck. "No," she gasped, her pupils dilating as the adrenaline pumped into her system and her breath began to quicken.

"Oh, yes," Raoul said. "In keeping with that fine Southern tradition, you've been sleeping with your brother."

"You're lying. Where's your proof?"

Raoul got to his feet and crossed to her. Caroline shrank back against the soft cushions. He reached out and grabbed her left hand. "There's your proof. That angled little finger. You and Doug share the same genetic defect."

Caroline gazed at him in a long moment of stunned silence. Then her face crumpled and her shoulders started shaking. But she wasn't crying. It was laughter that shook her slender frame. "That . . . that's your proof?" she managed to squeeze out.

Raoul frowned. This wasn't how it was supposed to play. "You think incest is some kind of joke?"

Caroline struggled to take command of herself. With a final gulping hiccup, she managed to control her hysterical laughter. "My finger . . . It's not a genetic defect. I broke it badly when I was six years old. It happened at our cabin up in the mountains. By the time we got to a hospital, it was too late for them to straighten it out without surgery. So they just let it heal crooked." The stunned look on Raoul's face almost made her lose control again. "That's one of the reasons I took up the cello. My physical therapist said it would help to strengthen my hand."

Raoul took a step back, his scowling face a mask of suspicion. "You're making this up. Claudia had paperwork."

Caroline shook her head. She'd sobered up now and anger was beginning to assert itself. "Paperwork can be forged. Doug isn't my brother. Believe me, I'd know. And I'm warning you now. If a single word of your lies ever leaks out, I'll hit you with my hospital records and as many X rays of my hand as you care to see. Not to mention the DNA tests that would prove absolutely that you're a liar. It won't be me facing ruin, Raoul. It'll be you."

He was pale now, all his self-assurance gone. He was pathetic, Caroline thought. No wonder Claudia had made sure he'd had no financial stake in her business. She stood up, contempt in her eyes. "Now get out of here before I call Detective Toscana."

Raoul turned on his heel and fled, leaving Caroline with the first unmixed moment of triumph she'd felt since she'd raided the fridge what seemed like a lifetime ago. What a piece of work Raoul was. But at least she knew one thing for certain. He'd never have the guts for murder.

The technicians had finally completed their work on the crime scene that had been a state-of-the-art nail studio and had moved on to Karen McElroy's last resting place in the foot spa. They'd lifted the heavy shelving away from Ondine, and now Vince was left alone with the medical examiner. Dr. Richmond pulled a face as the tacky nail polish attached itself to her overalls everywhere she touched it. "God, Vince, this is terrible," she complained as her latex-gloved hands began their initial probing of Ondine's body.

"Isn't it always, Sarah?"

"Bodies, I don't mind. But I've always thought cosmetics were more trouble than they were worth." There was a horrible slurping sound as Dr. Richmond turned the body over. Vince tried not to think about it.

Sarah Richmond's expert fingers moved over Ondine's shattered body. "The skull's pretty well crushed. Blunt-force trauma everywhere." She glanced up. "Those shelves must be damn heavy." She ran her hands expertly down the supermodel's torso. "Broken ribs, sternum feels like it might have gone, too." She was talking to herself, requiring no response from Vince.

"Sounds like she'd have taken less damage if she'd been hit by a truck." Vince knew what he was talking about. He'd seen the crushed results of vehicular homicide more times than he cared to remember. "Has she taken a beating, or was it the shelves falling that killed her?"

"Hard to tell at this stage," Sarah said absently. "I'll be able to say for sure once I've done the autopsy and matched up her injuries with the shelf unit." Then she frowned. "Hang on a minute. This isn't right." She leaned forward, delicately peeling back the waistband of Ondine's jogging pants. "There's something here, Vince. Can you get a photographer back here?"

He called for the cameraman and stooped over the body to try to make out what Sarah had seen.

"Look," she said. "There's something taped to her body, just alongside the hip-bone." She leaned back to allow room for the photographer. Then she picked at one corner of the adhesive tape, pulling it free to reveal a small key. Vince reached into his pocket for a plastic evidence envelope and held it open for Sarah to drop the key in.

He held the envelope close to his face. "It may be small, but it's a serious-looking key," he said. "I'd guess a safety-deposit box or a safe. But I haven't seen anything around here that this would fit."

Sarah shrugged. "There's no reason why it belongs here. Maybe it's the key for a safe back home?"

"So why carry it taped to her skin? Why not keep it in her purse?"

Before they could speculate further, Mike rushed in, looking as pleased as a puppy dog who has finally mastered continence. In his hand, he clutched a videotape. "Vince, I think I've got something for you."

Vince brightened visibly. Anything that might move this bogged-down case forward had to be worth listening to. "Shoot, Mikey," he said.

"You know we've got a team going through all the security videos?"

Vince nodded.

"Well, one of the guys brought me this tape from the camera on the corner of the main building near the path to the lake. It's timed just before the attack on Phyllis Talmadge. You can see Ms. Talmadge walking into range and almost bumping into King David and Raoul de Vries. They've got their backs to the camera, but they're obviously deep in conversation. Then Howard Fondulac comes up behind Ms. Talmadge and listens in while she's talking to them." He paused expectantly, but his boss seemed more frustrated than excited by the news.

"Damn," Vince said. "Why the hell don't they have audio on these tapes?"

"Sir, we don't need audio," Mike replied, obviously bursting to reveal something extraordinary.

"We don't?"

"No, sir. See, my sister, she was born deaf. When she was little, I used to take her to lip-reading classes. I've always kept it up. And I could read Ms. Talmadge's lips."

Vince felt his mouth fall open. "You're kidding me."

"No, sir." He pulled his notebook out of his pocket and flipped it open. "This is what she said. I'm pretty much certain of it. 'I had to get out of that room. It's full of secrets. I could sense secrets and lies that touch all of us.' "

"You're sure about this?"

Mike nodded. "I watched it through a dozen times to make sure I wasn't mistaken. That's what she said."

"She never said a thing about running into those guys on her way to the lake," Vince said. "Why the hell would she keep quiet about something like that?"

Sarah Richmond stood up. "She's the one who got hit on the head and dumped in the lake, right? She might well have no recollection of it. Serious trauma to the head can often lead to patchy memory loss of the time immediately before the incident. There's probably nothing more sinister to it than that."

"Whatever. But we need to talk to the Talmadge woman. Now," Vince barked, delighted to have a purpose at last. "Let's head out to the hospital, Mikey."

"I checked with the hospital. She discharged herself this morning. She's back here, having a consultation with the nutritionist," he said. "She'll be done in about ten minutes."

"So what are we waiting for?" Vince demanded, heading for the door. "You did good, Mikey."

When Phyllis Talmadge emerged with her depressingly limited diet sheet, the two police officers were waiting for her. She seemed unsurprised to see them. "I had a feeling you'd want to talk to me some more," she said. "That crack on the head seems to have sharpened up my powers. I've already spoken to my agent about it, and she's arranging some press interviews so I can tell my public that far from being impaired by my injuries, my psychic abilities are stronger than they've ever been."

"Great," Vince said without enthusiasm. Just what the world needed. A reason for crackpots to smack their psychics upside the head when they didn't like their reading. He could hear the excuses now. *But, officer, I was only trying to help her get a clearer picture . . .*

"Here's an example," the psychic continued, undaunted. She pointed to the small plastic bag containing the key that was still clutched in Vince's fingers. "That bag you're holding, it contains something belonging to the dead woman."

"Which one?" Vince said cynically. It wasn't too much of a stretch to guess that an evidence bag in the hand of a detective engaged in a murder investigation would contain an item that had been in the possession of the victim.

Phyllis frowned. "Why, Claudia, of course. You mean there have been more victims?"

Vince nodded. "We've just found Ondine dead. And Karen McElroy, the manicurist."

Phyllis nodded sagely. "I'm not surprised. I sensed there would be more deaths before the day was over. But whatever you've got in that bag didn't belong to either of them. It was Claudia's. The vibrations are unmistakable."

Intrigued now, Vince opened his hand and revealed the key. "You're telling me this key was Claudia's?"

"May I?" Phyllis said, reaching for the bag.

"Be my guest. But don't take it out."

Phyllis took the bag and placed it between her hands, which she folded into the shape of prayer. She raised them to her face, the tips of her index fingers against her lips. She inhaled deeply, closing her eyes. Vince glanced at Mike, who was staring at the squat little woman with something approaching awe. He was surrounded by nutcases, Vince thought wearily.

Phyllis's eyes snapped open and her hands fell away from her face. "There's no mistake," she said. "This key was definitely Claudia's."

"I don't suppose your guiding spirits told you where I'll find the lock belonging to the key?" Vince said, struggling to keep the sarcasm from his voice.

"Not exactly," she admitted, handing it back to him.

"I didn't think so. Now, we have a couple of questions for you —"

"But it's somewhere in that room you're using to interview us," Phyllis interrupted.

"What?" Vince exclaimed.

"That key. Whatever it opens is in that room."

"But there's nothing in there with a lock," he protested.

Phyllis shrugged. "Suit yourself. But I trust my powers. There must be a hidden safe or something like that. When I was in there before, I was oppressed by the feeling that the room was filled with secrets," she added triumphantly.

Mike gasped. "That's what you said to King David and Raoul de Vries."

Phyllis looked puzzled. "I did?"

"On your way to the lake. You told them you had to get out of the interview room because it was full of secrets and lies."

"I don't remember that," she said, confusion furrowing her brow. "But you're right, I did experience the aura of hiddenness and fear there."

Vince rolled his eyes. "I guess there's only one way to check this out. We need to search that room."

If Christopher Lund had known what had befallen Ondine, he would have been in no mood for relaxation. But so far, he was ignorant of her fate, and all he was conscious of was the need to unwind. He had nothing to fear. Only Claudia had known about the terms of their deal. Now, if the payments came to light, he could explain that Claudia was paying up front for Ondine's endorsement of the spa, which would be completed with an illustrated brochure. So what if Ondine denied all knowledge of the arrangement? She seldom knew very far in advance what he had planned for her. That she didn't know about it meant nothing. He could explain it all away, if only he could keep calm.

The steam cabinet would help, Dante had assured him. It would sweat away impurities, leaving him cleansed and languid, ready for the gentle aromatherapy massage that would follow.

It was just as well he wasn't claustrophobic, Christopher thought. For someone who didn't like confined spaces, the steam cabinet would be a decent facsimile of hell. Only his head was in the open air. The rest of his body was enclosed in the cabinet, sealed with a padded collar. The temperature was thermostatically controlled by a feedback system that reacted to the sensors Dante had carefully placed in a dozen locations around his body. And as a fail-safe there was a reassuring call button in the armrest of the cabinet, which could be used to summon help if he felt he was overheating.

He closed his eyes and felt the sweat trickling down his face as he let the saxophone of Kenny G wash over him. He was glad he'd brought his own CDs along to the spa. Five minutes in the place, and he knew all they ever played here was the whale music and Peruvian rain forest sounds that he despised. New Age garbage, all of it. This was more like it. Cool music, hot steam, and the prospect of a couple of lines of coke waiting in his cottage when the treatment was over.

His blissed-out state was abruptly halted by the clatter of something falling to the floor. Suddenly alert, Christopher looked around him in confusion. The person standing in front of the control panel obviously wasn't a member of staff. And the screwdriver that was still rolling toward him wasn't part of any health regimen that Christopher had ever heard of. The person turned to face him, eyebrows drawn down in a ferocious glare. With a surge of fear that turned his insides liquid, Christopher realized he was looking into the eyes of a killer. A killer who had just removed the cover of the panel containing the thermostatic controls for the steam cabinet.

His first thought was the panic button. He fumbled for it, his fingers slick with sweat and steam. He pressed as hard as he could, feeling relief creep through him.

As if possessed of X-ray vision, the killer produced a predator's smile. "No point in hitting the panic button, Chris. I already fused the controls. It'll look just like a short circuit. It's just you and me now. You and me and the big heat."

318

"What's going on?" the agent stammered. "Why are you doing this to me?"

"It's called vengeance. You killed Ondine, now I'm going to kill you."

"What? Are you crazy? Ondine's not dead!"

The killer crossed the room in a few short strides and slapped Christopher's face. "You bastard. There's no point in pretending. I know what you did."

"Okay, okay. You say she's dead. But why would I kill Ondine? She's my meal ticket." Christopher's voice was a squeal of anguish.

"I don't know why you killed her. Maybe she finally got wise to your chiseling little schemes. All I know is that I saw you leave the building. You were running, like you were running away from something. And by the time I got inside the manicure studio, she was dead. You killed her." The low voice was hoarse with passionate anger. "And now you're going to pay with your pathetic little life." The killer stepped back and picked up the screwdriver, then returned to the control panel and began to tinker with it again.

"I don't know what you're talking about." Christopher could feel the temperature rising now. His fingers were starting to swell, his throat to dry up. "I swear," he said desperately. "I didn't even know Ondine was in the manicure studio. Let me out of here. You're making a big mistake. Kill me, and Ondine's killer walks free."

The killer ignored the desperate pleas and replaced the cover on the control panel, screwing it firmly down.

"You've got it all wrong," Christopher sobbed. "Let me out of here, I promise I won't tell a soul. We'll track down the real killer together."

The killer glared at him. "You expect me to believe you? I don't think so."

Terror gripped Christopher. He opened his mouth to scream, but it was already too late. As his jaws widened, the killer moved fast, a hand snaking out to grab one of the small towels on a nearby table. Powerful fingers stuffed it into Christopher's mouth, making anything more than a muffled mumble impossible, then pinched his nostrils tight between thumb and forefinger.

Watching Christopher's face turn from scarlet to purple, the killer didn't flinch. There was a cold relish in the eyes that stared down into Christopher's panicked gaze. At last, Christopher broke their locked stare, his eyes rolling back in their sockets and suddenly dulling. The killer waited a few moments to make sure that the cheating murderer in the steam cabinet would never breathe again, then pulled the towel out of his mouth and carefully wiped both sides of Christopher's nose. There was no point in risking the possibility that the police would be able to lift fingerprints from the skin. As promised, the death would look like nothing more sinister than an unlucky accident. Nothing could bring the beautiful, fragile Ondine back. But at least she had been avenged.

13

Vince Toscana came out of the steam house for a breath of air that didn't taste of parboiled human being and saw in an instant that if he didn't move right now, his rapidly decreasing pool of suspects was going to scatter to the four winds before sunset. And considering the financial resources of even the poorest among them, those winds might well carry the guilty ones beyond his reach.

Vince raised his voice to bellow, "Hey, Mikey!" The young cop was standing barely ten feet away, but it wasn't for his benefit that Vince had shouted. Every tense face, guest and spa employee alike, was now turned in his direction. Vince could feel the taut vibrations humming off them from twenty yards away. If you touched any of 'em, they'd twang.

"Right here, Vince."

Vince lowered his voice to a more normal level but kept his eyes on the skittish individuals on the other side of yet another line of yellow police tape.

"Mikey, we gotta get some calories into these people. Let's get a dinner together that's got some substance to it. You take charge of that. Talk to the cook — he'll call himself a chef, so mind your manners — and see if he's capable of cooking real food. If he is, have him put together an order and get your brother's market to deliver it. If not, put in a call to your cousin with the Italian restaurant and get him to send over anything on the menu that's got cheese or olive oil. Preferably both."

A wayward draft from the room in back of them prompted both men to take a step farther into the air, and caused Vince to add, "Maybe nothing too meaty. And ask your ma's bakery to bring us half a dozen cakes for dessert. Tall, goocy cakes." The kind Vince's wife would let him eat only about once a year.

"Tea and biscuits," said Mike unexpectedly.

"Biscuits?" Jeez, Vince thought: Southern cooking. "Nah, that chocolate cake with the icing that's six inches tall, or a coupla key lime pies, that kinda thing."

"No, no, I mean like in Agatha Christie, they're always giving people what my sister calls comfort food. Empty calories, you know? Sweet tea and cookies, they make people feel better. 'Biscuits' is British for 'cookies,' " he added helpfully.

"Whatever you say, Mikey. I dunno about comfort; I just don't want them keeling over on me. Get on it, would you? Have 'em bill the department."

As the young man trotted off, filled with the righteous anticipation of shoving a lot of unhealthful food down people who'd paid a small fortune for gussied-up celery sticks, Vince found himself wondering if the kid's police training consisted of anything but murder mysteries.

Agatha Christie. Bah.

Caroline stood alone in the crowd of people watching the young policeman jog away in the direction of the dining room and wondered mildly who would be the first to break. She herself felt like a cello string wound beyond tight: Would a slight weakness in the string be where it snapped, or would the bridge itself give way?

It was lucky for Douglas that he did not touch her. As it was, even his tentative pronunciation of her name made her jump as if she'd come in contact with a live wire. Had he laid a hand on her arm, she probably would have belted him one.

"What!" she bit off.

"Caroline, I —" he began, then stopped.

He looked wretched, so miserable that she nearly leaned forward into him and wrapped her arms around his chest. Why, oh why did her body persist in this nearly pathological gullibility, this insane trust in a man who had done everything short of striking her? And why, if he was such a feeble excuse for a husband, did he persist in looking so forlorn, so lost, so . . . lovesick?

"Douglas, what is it?" she cried before she could stop herself.

For a moment it looked as if he might crumble; he started to reach for her, and then with a clash of mental and emotional gears that was almost audible, he stepped back, the impulse to affection violently squelched.

"What on earth . . . Oh. Oh, my God," she said softly as remembrance cascaded down on her. She'd set out to find Douglas the moment Raoul left her room, but had been interrupted by the discovery of Christopher Lund's death, distracted by yet another round of redundant paramedics, another influx of urgent police, the further jarring festoons of yellow tape across the manicured Phoenix landscape. With her husband's involuntary step away from her, it all came back: that absurd yet primally shattering scenario Raoul had confronted her with, a scenario that was even now inhabiting her husband's mind in its full, raw horror, leaving no room for anything but the overpowering need to protect his wife from knowing that she'd been sleeping with her brother. Setting Douglas free from the all-pervading taint of incest would lift the misery from his face, she knew that. But before she could free him, she had to know one thing.

"Doug, did you sleep with that woman?"

She saw the denial in his face before he could stop it. She also became aware of a number of interested listeners. She took Douglas's knit sleeve and led him away to a bench situated to look over the glittering lake. Neither of them noticed the scenery.

Caroline went straight to the heart of it. "Douglas, you are not my brother."

The impact of these words was too great even to register on his face. He simply sat there, gaping at her as if she'd said something in Swahili or Cantonese.

"Doug, I don't know who told you that you were, but Raoul de Vries gave it to me, and I had to laugh in his face. It's true I have a sibling somewhere, but it isn't you."

"Claudia told me. It was Claudia."

"She said it was because of the hand, right?" Caroline reached for her husband's left hand and held it up, lifting her own beside it against the afternoon sky. The length of the fingers was similar, and the separation of the little finger, but nothing else: Her nails, straight thumb, and narrow wrist were from a different genetic heritage than his short nail beds, slim knuckles, and slightly retrograde thumb. "My finger was smashed when I was a kid," she told him, then shivered involuntarily, brushed by the vivid twenty-year-old memory. A furious slam of the cabin door, a soar of pain that didn't stop throbbing until the doctor numbed it days later, and the indelible link it created in her mind between parental anger and great pain. An accident, but Caroline had never whined at her mother again, and she'd often thought the injury laid the foundation for a lifetime of repressed emotion. She shook herself and returned to the present. "We'll have DNA testing if you want, but tell me: Do you really think we could have been brother and sister without knowing it?"

Now his face took on an expression of dawning wonder. "I thought . . . Oh God, Caroline, I knew I'd never hold you again. That's why I sent you the cello — went looking for it and bought it back to take my place — because I could then feel that if your arms were around it, they were around me, too; that when the body of it rested between your knees . . ." Douglas seized her hand, put it to his mouth, and began to sob.

Caroline patted his hair absently with her free hand, then said, "Doug? Douglas, sweetheart, I'm sorry, but — *you* bought back my cello?"

He raised his head but laced his left fingers tightly through hers; their wedding bands came together with a faint tap.

"Yes. For you. It cost me a fortune because the woman loved it so much, so I had to pay even more than I thought I would, but it had to be the real one, to set you back on the road you'd been on before I —"

"How much, Doug? I have a reason for asking."

"Thirty-four thousand. Plus shipping."

"Thirty-four? My mother told me she'd paid twelve!"

"God, no. I did ask her to pretend it came from her. I thought you wouldn't accept it otherwise."

"Thirty-four thousand dollars. And she knew I'd have some idea of what a stay at

Phoenix cost, so she just called it that and pocketed the difference."

"Your mother —" Douglas caught himself, and changed it to, "Your mother is a very strange woman."

My mother, Caroline thought sadly, is a damned monster. Hilda Finch's entire universe is Hilda Finch. Her husband had not mattered; her own daughter was more often than not just one more inconvenience to be manipulated away. The woman was hopeless.

Still, her mother's iniquities did not affect those of Douglas Blessing. Caroline pushed down the urge for adolescent romance, straightened her back, and retrieved her captive hand.

"Douglas, you still have an awful lot of explaining to do. You can begin with those photographs."

As Vince ducked under the tape to approach his group of captive (for the moment) witnesses and suspects, the congressman and his wife began to move away. Vince kept an eye on them, but they didn't go far, and he turned with satisfaction to the pale and ever-thinner group, the idea that officer Mike LeMat had planted shining away in his mind. If these

329

people wanted Agatha Christie, then old Agatha he'd give them. At least for long enough to keep the lot of 'em from bolting for the exit.

"It's three o'clock now, and I want us all to have a meeting after dinner," he announced. The statement caught their attention, he was pleased to see, although these seriously underfed men and women were probably more interested in the possibility of food than the potential revelations of the meeting. In either case, they wouldn't know what hit them. He could almost taste the pepperoni now. The thought made him smile, as did the next part of his suggestion: "How 'bout we get together in the library."

Only one or two of them looked at him suspiciously, but he pretended not to notice. Instead, he told them he wanted each and every person there to write down every little thing he or she'd done since the afternoon before Claudia de Vries had died. Pens and paper were in the dining room (as one, they twitched in reaction to the word "dining," as predictable as old Professor Pavlov's dogs). He added that anyone who wanted to go to his or her room should take a uniformed along, that dinner'd be early, at six-thirty (another

330

twitch), and thank you, ladies and gentlemen.

Most of them trailed away like a troop of
very young school kids, his authority a
comforting rock in the pounding surge of
fear and confusion. And like school kids,
they wouldn't think to object to the completely pointless writing assignment he'd
given them. It would keep them busy, all
this navel gazing, and who knows — it
might actually give him something useful.

Not that Vince would need it. He looked
down at the note from the crime scene
techs that Mike had brought him on his
way to town for junk food and full-sugar
soft drinks, and smiled. It was all over but
the shouting. And he'd be damned, after
the last two days, if he'd let anyone get
much shouting in now.

He looked up, startled by the sudden
materialization of a great deal of smooth,
exquisitely tanned male skin in front of his
face. Vince had seen this particular epi-
dermis a number of times now, but he
found it no less disconcerting than the first
time. The man was just too beautiful to be
real.

"Detective, we need to talk," the
bodybuilder in the tiny shorts began, but
Vince was already looking past him at the

two backs he didn't want to disappear on him.

"It'll have to be a little later, Mr. Constanza. I'm kinda busy just now." Vince glanced back to be sure that his uniformed officers were ready, then raised his voice to call, "Er, Mrs. Finch, Dr. de Vries? Could you two come with me for a minute?"

Caroline was just thinking that the bench, though scenic, was hardly the ideal place for a lengthy session of revelations and self-recriminations when she happened to glance over her husband's shoulder at a scene straight out of the evening news. In fact, seeing it enacted on the stage of Phoenix's bucolic landscape made it seem even less real than the televised version: the stereotyped shot of the handcuffed suspect, shoulders hunched against distant camera lenses, a cop's hand steering him by the elbow toward a police cruiser. The bizarre unreality of the scene only grew as she recognized the suspect as Raoul de Vries. And then she saw his companion, also handcuffed, also bent over, also urged forward by uniformed figures. Caroline shot to her feet, cutting dead the abject apologies of the man at her side.

Her mother was being arrested.

★ ★ ★

The minutes that followed later became somewhat confused in Caroline's mind. Douglas had held her back, and Caroline had raged at him, but even as she struggled against his arms and pounded ineffectually at his chest, a part of her had been quite aware that if she truly wanted to go to her mother's rescue, she had only to knee her husband hard and she would be free.

That she had not done so, Caroline reflected later that evening as she pushed around the remaining cake crumbs on her lapis-and-gold dessert plate, indicated both that she had not actually wanted to go to Hilda, and that some part of her had begun to anticipate a future need for Doug's more delicate plumbing. Torn between her mother's version of the truth and her husband's, Caroline's body had known which way her mind, and her heart, had chosen. She had not forced her way to freedom.

Still, there was a heavy load of apprehension and guilt and fury and despair packed into those confusing minutes on the lakeside. Which made it all the odder that, looking back, Caroline's most vivid memory of the entire afternoon was not of the shiny handcuffs riding above her mother's expensively manicured hands; nor of the prisoner's defiant protest at the door to the police car, Hilda irritably shaking off the protective constabulary hand that threatened to mess her coiffure; it was not even the memory of Douglas's strong, satisfying, and — yes — dependable arms encircling her, keeping her from harm.

The image that had stayed with her the rest of the day and through the substantial Italian dinner that followed, an image as crisp and clear as the late afternoon sunlight, was the brief communion of the two people left behind when the arresting officers moved away. The two most unmistakable figures in the whole gathering of strong personalities had stood shoulder to shoulder, waiting until the cars holding Hilda Finch and Raoul de Vries left the compound. And then Caroline, with a blink of astonishment, had watched King David turn and seen Emilio Constanza's arms go around the green-haired rock star, comforting him just as Douglas had been comforting her.

However, not even astonishment could last long, not in the wake of the past few days. Caroline had nestled the side of her face into her husband's shoulder, gazing across the corner of lake at the other pair, feeling nothing but a kind of mindless pleasure at the simple sanity of two humans holding one another.

With that, a third figure had come out of one of the cottages, moving with a quiet, self-controlled dignity that seemed to radiate pain. Lauren Sullivan, her coppery hair blazing as if to deny the soul's aches, had approached the two men. Their arms parted as they gathered her in, and the three of them had stood locked together, oblivious to the world.

Caroline had not seen what broke up the circle, because Douglas had decided the time had come to move on, and when she'd glanced across the water, King David and Lauren had been going slowly toward the cabins, his big hand resting across the nape of the actress's neck. Emilio had remained behind, deep in conversation with Vince Toscana, who had suddenly reared back, seized by some strong emotion resembling outrage. The detective had snatched something that resembled a small book out of Emilio's hand, thrown it to the ground, and stalked away. Constanza had picked the object up, pushed it into a pocket, then followed on Toscana's heels.

"I hate to be prosaic, sweetheart,"

Douglas had said at that point, "and I know we have to find out what's going on with your mother, but if I don't get something to eat pretty soon I'll starve to — I mean, I'm really hungry."

Pushing away the spotless dessert plate, Caroline now found that she was smiling at the memory: by all means, let us avoid using the word "death" with its air of dark reality. Douglas was a born politician.

"We may have to send your aide to town for a McDonald's," she had told him lightly, adding in saccharine tones, "right before you fire her."

"It's never a good idea to fire somebody who knows too much, darling," Douglas had protested. "Wouldn't it be better if I just found her a job somewhere else?"

"At a higher salary," the politician's wife had suggested.

And in amity at last, looking the very picture of the successful political couple, the Blessings had gone in search of food and information. Food they had found, and information they were about to receive, both of those commodities in greater abundance than they had dared imagine.

The dinner that Mike LeMat's various family members had provided was a smashing hit, a meal that went far to counteract the depredations of the last days — both on the waistlines and in the minds. After Mike's restaurateur cousin, grocer brother, and baker mother had done their parts (the spa's chef having taken to his bed in horror), everyone in the dining room was replete, stunned with the unaccustomed bounty, drunk on carbohydrates and fats (both saturated and un-), tipsy with refined sugars and the first caffeine most of them had had since setting foot on the premises.

And Vince Toscana saw that it was good.

However, Vince reminded himself sourly, Detective Vince Toscana was no longer the chief investigator here. He couldn't think about it without a jolt, the sight of that authoritative ID wallet in the hands of the near-naked man. If he hadn't made the calls to Washington and confirmed it, he'd have slapped the guy in cuffs, too, for impersonating an officer.

Well, he'd have tried to.

Vince had to hand it to the state of Virginia: Even Philly'd never thrown anything like this at him.

Okay, he decided, these jokers had stuffed in about as much food as any Italian mother could hope for. If he waited any longer, they'd fall asleep into their tiramisu. He caught Mike's eye, and they began to encourage the players to move next door. Into the library.

Caroline wondered for an instant who the gorgeous guy in the pricey suit was and then blushed furiously when she realized that the first time she'd come in — no, not in contact exactly, the first time they'd had relations — no! The first time she'd seen the guy, he'd been wearing rather less fabric than the scrap of paisley silk that was currently sticking out of his breast pocket. Adonis, Thong Man, the hunk-of-all-trades with the Italian name and the Oxbridge accent who'd hauled Claudia out of the mud bath, a man (a whole lot of man) she'd never seen wearing more than brief shorts and a briefer tank top, was dressed in a suit that made the custom three-piece that Douglas had changed into look like it came from Penney's. Constanza straightened from applying a match to the kindling in the stone fireplace, and the room could see that, along with several yards of wool and linen, he had donned an unmistakable air of authority. They all forgot instantly that Detective Toscana was there.

"Emilio," Phyllis Talmadge said sharply, "what is going on here?"

"Why don't you take a seat, Ms. Talmadge? We'll explain when you're settled." His voice was reassuringly that of his previous incarnation, and gradually, with curiosity now overlying their exhausted apprehension, the sadly depleted band subsided into the chairs circling the fire. Caroline and Douglas sat near the fireplace; Phyllis Talmadge, a bandage still on the back of her head, sat next to Caroline; Lauren Sullivan, the only one who had picked without interest at her rich food, was joined by King David, his multicolored Medusa locks tamed into a ponytail, the lines on his face carved into gouges by the strain of the last days. Dante the masseur was there, and his colleague Marguerite, with Gustav the weight trainer, Ginger the receptionist, Jean-Claude the dietitian, and a handful of others, including Geoff the assistant pastry chef, surely the most underemployed talent on the premises. Near the door, Vince and Mike stood watch. Emilio waited for their attention to return to him, and then he began.

"Normally, in such a case as this, the police would take your statements and let you go, and you would hear nothing more until you were called upon to testify.

"Because of the glare of publicity already generated by recent events, and because some of the people involved wish to keep what has gone on here as quiet as possible, it has been decided that you should be told everything, in the hopes that you will keep your statements to the press to a minimum. And since Detective Toscana had already set up this rather literary device of the meeting in the library" — here Constanza shot a glance at the back of the room; Vince Toscana's eyebrows went up in what might have been wry apology — "I decided that we may as well make use of it. I had to draw the line at the traditional denouement of the Golden Age mystery story, namely, the unmasking of the villains and their arrest in front of the other suspects. Modern police techniques render that irresponsible, as I'm sure you understand. As for the other, I trust you will forgive the melodramatic overtones."

Here he reached into the inner breast pocket of his suit to draw out the small leather booklike object that Caroline had seen Toscana throw to the ground. He flipped it open and handed it to Douglas on his left.

"You know me as Emilio Constanza. I

340

was hired under that name eight months ago by Claudia de Vries, who thought she was getting an herbalist from Bombay. My name is Jonathan Sassoon." ("I knew he was no paesan," Vince muttered.) "I actually was born in India, into the ancient Jewish community in Goa, although what I know about herbs I got from a book I memorized on the plane coming to take Claudia's job. My expertise," he said, "is drugs."

The leather wallet indeed identified the impressive figure before them as an agent of the United States Drug Enforcement Agency.

"The feds," murmured Douglas as he passed the article of show-and-tell on to Phyllis Talmadge, on Caroline's left. "No wonder Toscana looks pissed."

"You're also going to have to forgive a certain amount of apparently disconnected narrative as I go along," said Adonis the Fed in his plummy accent. "This case has roots that go back quite a way."

("I knew this case stank of ancient history," Vince said sotto voce to Mike. Mike did not respond; he was too awestruck by the man at the front of the room.)

"You have been the unfortunate witnesses to a series of deaths, all of them related in the sense that the deaths during an earthquake are related: They share the same underlying cause, if by different actual instruments. We have here five deaths and one assault, committed by three different individuals. I do not believe any of the other murders would have occurred had it not been for the first.

"The first to die, of course, was Claudia de Vries, and the means of death may be taken as highly symbolic — a patchwork shawl drawn tight, knotted around her neck, representing the tightening knot of her various crimes and deceptions that were pulled in around her."

He caught himself and looked mildly embarrassed. "Pardon the romance," he said. "It must be the surroundings. At any rate, Claudia de Vries was killed because she was a thief, a blackmailer, and a source of illegal drugs, and because there was a struggle for power among her fellow criminals. We will return to that aspect of the case in a minute.

"As I said, that and the other deaths have roots that go back a long time. My own involvement began approximately twelve years ago, when I arrested a very famous rock star for possession of heroin. That's right: King David himself."

The wide smile he gave the wrinkly rocker was eclipsed only by the electric return grin. The singer had, Caroline noted, surprisingly good teeth for a heroin addict.

"Fortunately for David, he had a clever lawyer, a clean record, and a malleable judge. Which would have been just another instance of justice for the rich, except for one thing: David actually wanted to rehabilitate. He'd been very close to someone, another member of the band, who'd recently died of an overdose. I see some of you remember this."

They did, even Caroline, who had been barely in her teens at the time and hadn't much cared for King David's kind of music anyway, but who had read the articles about the band's troubles with avid attention, wondering at the mix of the famous and the kinky.

"I went to see him in rehab and made him an offer: He'd pass on any information that came his way about dealers and suppliers, we'd work it into our cases, keep his name out of it, all that. It's the sort of thing we do sometimes, though generally we'll offer to reduce time. In this case, I was pushing the revenge side. Not that I had much hope — his sentence was so light we had no leverage, but a person can only ask, and besides, I thought that during our interview we had connected. Turns out I was right, though not in quite the way I'd thought." Again an exchange of knowing smiles, until the agent pulled himself together.

"Anyway, to my amazement, no sooner had I mentioned the possibility of his turning informant than he started to roar with laughter, as if I'd made an enormous joke. Turns out the director of the rehab center he was staying in had offered him a line of coke while they were filling in the admit papers. I couldn't believe it — we hadn't even suspected the place.

"The center was run by Claudia and Raoul de Vries, and although they got a lot more subtle over the years, their operation grew. And we grew with them. We knew something was coming together these last few months, and that's when I came in undercover."

(The skimpy turquoise thong he'd been wearing when she first saw him flashed through Caroline's mind. That was some disguise — nobody'd think to look for a cop underneath . . . She blushed again and told herself to behave.)

"Chris Lund and Howard Fondulac were two of her major distributors, Fondulac in Southern California, Lund all over, wherever Ondine had regular jobs. She, I hasten to say, had nothing to do with it." He shot another glance across the room, but this time, Caroline thought, it was aimed not at King David but at Lauren Sullivan beside him. "Howard was getting erratic and had been diagnosed with the early stages of liver cancer. He was pressing Claudia to give him more of the stuff to distribute, at the same time that he was holding back a heavy percentage of the profits — he badly wanted to underwrite one last blockbuster film and was desperate for the cash. In the end, according to her notes, he said he'd given her all he could and threatened to tell all: If he was going to die, he might as well bring the whole operation down with him. So he had to be removed, whether by Raoul de Vries or by Christopher Lund or by another remains to be seen. I imagine that one of them will take our offer of a deal and give evidence on the other. This investigation, I hardly need say, is going to keep a number of agencies busy for a long time.

"I believe we'll find it was Raoul de Vries, rather than Lund, who killed Fondulac. He'd already attacked Phyllis Talmadge, though not very efficiently. He knew that his wife had a safe filled with blackmailing material, but he couldn't get at it because of the continuous presence of the police. When he heard Ms. Talmadge's declaration that the room contained secrets, he thought her statement was based on clear knowledge rather than some vague psychic intuition, and he panicked. Howard Fondulac's death was similarly opportunistic, making use of the exercise machine, but you can be sure that this time his killer was watching, waiting for just such a chance.

"Christopher Lund's problem was that he'd started using more cocaine than he was selling. His death, although the timing is suspicious, may finally prove to be the accident it appears. The crime scene technicians haven't finished in there, so it's far too soon to say anything about it.

"But now we come to Ondine's death, which is the real reason we've brought you here. The precise details of her death are proving hard to pin down." (An unfortunate turn of phrase, Caroline thought, considering the way the poor girl had died. The inappropriateness seemed to occur to Emilio/Jonathan at the same moment. He went on hastily.) "From the position of the body, it is just possible that she came back in the salon, looked into the next room and saw Karen McElroy lying dead in the pedi-bath, and fainted. She was, after all, so severely malnourished that it wouldn't have taken much of a shock." Caroline thought he seemed determined not to look over at the rock star and the actress when he said this, and she wondered why.

"So Ondine could, possibly, have fallen against the shelf unit and had it come down on top of her. It was massive, but most of the weight was in the top, and as a result the piece as a whole was far from stable. The only problem with that theory is that we found two very clear sets of prints on the side of that freshly polished wood. One set up along the back." Here he gripped his right hand over an invisible object at shoulder height. "And another lower down." In illustration, he pulled with his right arm against the imaginary weight, pushing out with his left. The room winced at the silent crash of a shelving unit, laden with nail polish, onto the fragile bones of a prostrate but still breathing model-waif.

"Now, before I tell you about those prints, we need to look at the other skein in this tangle. For that we need to go back even farther than twelve years.

"I believe most of you were aware some

time ago that Claudia de Vries was a blackmailer. It should be obvious by now that she was a lot of things; anything that brought in money, she was willing to try. Some criminals stick to a specific area; others are generalists. Claudia was one of the latter.

"The first criminal act we know of was when she was in college and agreed to help a friend arrange an illegal adoption. For payment, naturally, to ensure that the friend's illegitimate baby went to a good, caring, if none too wealthy family. In fact, she dumped the child with a relative and kept the money."

Caroline realized that she was squeezing Douglas's hand until all their fingers were turning white. She eased off, made herself take a deep breath, and then jumped when another voice spoke up.

"That was me." The speaker, Caroline saw with incredulity, was Lauren Sullivan, beautiful and bruised. "My adult looks have taken me a long way, I know, but as a child I was difficult and funny-looking and incredibly shy. My acting career began young, when I constructed a storybook family, loving and stable and infinitely detailed, and imagined myself into their midst." She wasn't about to go into detail here, serving up her life history for these eager strangers to drink in every nuance. It was none of their business that a year ago, when her therapy reached the point that the imaginary parents really had to be dealt with, she simply killed them off in an equally imaginary car wreck, fiery and tragic. Adoring but dead parents were infinitely more comforting than the parents she'd had, and any crutch, even a twisted one, was better than no support at all. She continued with the abbreviated version. "It is a role I play still — to the extent that when he asked me, I gave Detective Toscana that fantasy version of my history automatically, without thinking about it. In actual fact, although I was taken in as an infant by Claudia's older sister, it didn't last long. I was passed from one family member to the next, then into a series of foster homes. Not until I was thirteen did I arrive in a family that actually wanted to adopt me. The week before the papers were finalized, the father came to my room. I had a baby at fifteen."

The library was so still the air reverberated, even the whispers of the fireplace seemed to pause. Into this hush dropped a name.

"Ondine."

Caroline must have made some sound, some protest, because Lauren looked up and smiled, tears quivering unshed. King David was holding her hand.

"It's a cycle, isn't it? My baby, too, was put up for adoption. Claudia's sister agreed to take me back, more or less permanently, but she couldn't handle a baby as well. Ondine was removed from me when she was two days old, and I never knew what happened to her. All I knew was that my baby was a girl and that she had a birthmark on her face, although the doctor said it would fade when she grew. On her eighteenth birthday we both registered to have our records released, but even then it took us years to find each other, the records were so confused. She was so beautiful." And then she wept.

The DEA agent cleared his throat, to take the room's attention off the weeping woman. Caroline's eyes, however, remained on the actress. Her sister.

"About three years ago, we became aware of another figure on the scene, directing Claudia and Raoul. A silent partner, with authority but working through a lawyer in Atlanta. Christopher Lund came into it around then, too, a clever young man with a growing appetite for money. There were several questionable deaths connected with the spa: two accidental deaths of the possessors of large estates; one due to a heart condition exacerbated by the extreme diet and exercise program assigned here; and the hit-and-run killing of a wealthy man about to divorce his wife (nothing was proved against her because she had an alibi). There were even a couple of late-term miscarriages that might or might not have been induced. Nothing we could pin down, except that the deaths all involved hefty inheritances or life insurance policies for their grateful families." (Such as Leticia Finnerman, Vince thought, of Newton, Massachusetts, killed by a brake failure on her way home. The macabre humor of that collection of falsified records in the conference room closet under the label "Dead Files." Typical of the criminal mind, so sure that no one would catch on.)

"So you get the idea. A lot of greedy and hard-to-prove illegalities, most of which were arranged by a known blackmailer. We're talking major income and influence. So when Ondine threatened to interfere with Chris Lund, that threatened the business's smooth running. The cold, mathematical logic of the psychopath: Lund was necessary, Ondine was a danger to Lund, therefore Ondine had to be removed.

"In truth, the deaths connected to the spa all seem to have been directed by a party other than Claudia and Raoul de Vries, a party concealed behind an Atlanta law firm, whose financial records are being subpoenaed and will, I have no doubt, reveal payments from a number of names close to the dead. And I'm very sorry to have to say this publicly, Mrs. Blessing, but we believe that person to be Hilda Finch. She was the one out to take over the operation as a whole. She was the one on hand to wrest power from the other surviving member of the triumvirate, Raoul de Vries. She seems to have had contact with family members of several of the spa clients who died under dubious circumstances. And certainly the only prints on the shelf unit that killed Ondine were hers, along with those of Karen McElroy, which belonged there."

Douglas tightened the grip on his wife's hand, but Caroline was beyond sorrow. The daughter of a smiling psychopath, she said to herself. That is what I am. Maybe she would feel sorrow later, when the numbness had passed, sorrow and guilt and revulsion against the blood that moved through her veins.

Emilio — hard to think of him as that other name — was going on, but Caroline heard only a part of it. Peddling influence, setting up a distribution network for their cocaine operation, and blackmail, that pool ever widening: business as usual for Claudia, only more so. Then he was saying something about a key.

"— on Ondine's body. Hilda obviously didn't know that Ondine had the thing, or she'd have retrieved it, but the key seems to have passed through several hands before the girl got it. Howard Fondulac's fingerprints were on it, so Ondine may have been given it by him, or maybe she found it when she was trying to get him untangled from the Pilates machine.

"I doubt we'll ever be certain. I do know that Ondine told David she would see him in his cabin tonight. I assume she would have given him the key then, to give to Lauren, whom Ondine did not wish to be seen with too often. Ondine knew that Lauren was looking for the key to a safe and thought this might be it; she had no way of knowing that David had an interest in the contents of that safe as well."

"But did she *know?*" Caroline interrupted. "Did Ondine know that her mother was . . . ?"

"Lauren told her the first night. They pretended to be strangers whenever there was a chance someone might overhear, but, yes, she knew where she came from."

That was who she'd seen with the model, Caroline realized, on the other side of the moonlit lake. Laughing or sobbing — or, more likely, both. Which also meant that if Lauren Sullivan was Hilda Finch's other, illegitimate daughter, Caroline had spent the first evening here in friendly conversation with her own niece. Those unexpected sparks of sympathy she'd felt for the achingly pretty younger woman were facilitated by blood ties. A spasm of grief took her, and she missed Emilio's next words, until:

"— Finch looks to me a fairly pure example of a sociopathic personality. Without a conscience, her concern for others a learned facade, her only interests self-serving. I haven't had a chance to interview her fully, of course, but I did ask her if she knew she'd killed her granddaughter in Ondine. She did not. There seems to have been a lot that Claudia kept from her silent partner — it was, as I said, more a triumvirate than a partnership. Claudia and Raoul, with the newcomer Hilda Finch anonymous behind the lawyer; all

354

three jostling for power, attempting black-mail to keep the others under control, making temporary alliances against the third, aiming for domination. It is the reason a number of you were brought here, so that Claudia could assemble her victims in a bid for power against the others. Once Hilda Finch revealed herself, warfare was open — with knowledge as the weapon. One of them would feed another information to undermine the third. Hilda, for example, told Raoul about a secret compartment in Mrs. Blessing's cello case; Claudia told Hilda about Raoul's felony record. Raoul may have told Hilda that Claudia had a safe, or Hilda may have figured it out on her own. In either case, Hilda did not know where it was at first, nor did she have the key. In the case of Ondine, it is possible that Claudia herself didn't know the identity of Ondine's mother, since she had not been involved in that adoption procedure. At any rate, Hilda's reaction, when I told her, was chiefly exasperation: She'd been overjoyed to discover that Lauren was hers, not from any maternal urge but because it would be a coup for the spa."

(Vince elbowed his assistant. "I toldja, didn't I? Anyone that didn't care about her own daughter had to be dangerous?" Mike LeMat nodded.)

"Her chief regret for Ondine's death was, I quote, 'Just imagine what I could have done with this place if I'd had both of them.' "

Caroline couldn't even wince. She'd known it was coming, had known since hearing of Hilda's hidden partnership with Claudia that her mother was not just impossible, she was downright evil. Looking back, Hilda must have known that Douglas was being blackmailed, and by what means, yet she had made no move to tell him the truth, to free him from the appalling images in his mind, to free Caroline to be happy in her marriage once again. Caroline studied her hands, feeling every eye in the room on her, the daughter, born to and raised by a creature like that. Only from Douglas did she feel empathy — Douglas and, oddly enough, King David. She straightened her spine and lifted her eyes to meet the tattooed gaze squarely: She did not want this disturbing man's pity.

"The key Ondine found opened one of Claudia's two safes. The one it fit was cleverly hidden inside a storage cupboard in the corner of the conference room Detective Toscana has been using. The other, the reason Claudia de Vries was in the bathhouse at that hour of the night, was in a very clever compartment beneath one of the mud baths. That safe had a combination lock. When we emptied the mud bath, we found the keys to the bathhouse door — you may have seen how heavily locked she kept that building — but not the safe key. That is because Claudia's killer knew there was a safe and recognized the key for what it was. However, either the killer knew as well that the safe was in the conference room and therefore inaccessible until the police cleared out, or else made the mistake of murdering Claudia before finding out where the safe was. Hanging onto the key would have been dangerous — if the police did a complete search of the grounds and found it, they'd know it had something to do with Claudia's death — so the killer gave it to Howard Fondulac. He was a drunk, but he wasn't stupid; he knew that he was being set up to take the fall and in fact told Detective Toscana as much, but he couldn't very well reveal the details without giving away his own illegal activities.

"The only person who fits into this com‐bination of inside knowledge and incomplete details is Hilda Finch. She gave Howard the key, knowing that eventually she could get the location of the safe out of Raoul, but in the end, Raoul did not know his wife had a second safe. The one in the conference room did contain a great deal of moderately secret material, but it was primarily a decoy. The bathhouse safe was where Claudia kept her real treasures — blackmail evidence and correspondence going back more than twenty years: letters, bank statements, blood tests, records of drunk-driving and prostitution arrests for dozens of people. And by the way, the material in both has been seized, but it will remain confidential. You have my word on that, any of you who might be concerned."

Phyllis Talmadge made a small noise and slumped into her chair, causing those around her to speculate what sort of document bearing her name might be inside one of those safes.

"Anybody got a cigarette?" Phyllis asked the room at large. When no one reached for a pack, she sighed gustily. "You know, until three days ago, I hadn't smoked in nearly twenty years. How's that for a health spa?"

(So much for the psychic's testimony that she'd smelled cigarettes before she was conked and thrown in the lake, Vince thought grumpily, leaving his packet firmly in his pocket. She'd been sucking mints to hide not booze but smokes.)

"So," Emilio was finishing up, "you understand why I have told you rather more than I would normally have done, by means of asking you to keep the gossip to a minimum. The press outside does not know of the familial links between several of the famous individuals here, and although the right to privacy is generally regarded in this country as a mild jest, I appeal to you to grant it to those who have already suffered enough. I leave it to your sense of honor. Of course," he added, his voice and eyes going hard as diamonds, "I need hardly add that if I am aware of a leak originating in this room, the DEA will be most attentive to the individual involved, for a long, long time. Thank you for your time, and now I think Detective Toscana will need to take yet another set of statements from a number of you."

Close on to midnight, there was no one else in the swimming pool. When Caroline had first stood with that once again pristine stretch of blue water at her feet she had nearly drawn back: It would be a long time before she was entirely comfortable with solitude, and the locked door to the ominous mud room still bore the police seal. But Douglas offered to stay with her, to float around quietly at the other side of the pool. That compromise reassured her, and the strong, steady laps she had swum in the silky water soothed her further. Soon, very soon, she would have to approach Doug with the offer to free him from marriage to a psychopath's daughter — ironic, really, considering his own efforts in practically the same cause. But not now, not here; it was more than time for a small fraction of the relaxation and ease she had come here to find.

When the three figures at the far end of the echoing, chlorine-scented room caught her eye, she was startled, but not badly so, and although she glanced to the side to make certain that Douglas was there (and he was, standing protectively upright in the hip-deep water), she put her head down and continued her measured strokes to the end, where she surfaced to prop her arms on the rim of the pool.

"We need to talk with you, Caroline." It was, strangely, King David who spoke, not the beautiful DEA agent whom she had decided had to be the rock star's lover. She looked from Emilio to Lauren Sullivan, then dropped back underwater to swim to the side and pull herself out. Retrieving her terry cloth robe from the bench, she belted it on and swept her wet hair back from her face.

"About what?" About how devastating it was to have a mother who murdered and blackmailed and God knew what else without a qualm? About the link she had to this stunning red-haired woman before her, a link neither of them could mention without drawing forth the deep shame of being birthed by Hilda Finch? About how miserable and lost she felt, with only Douglas left to her? And how being faced with the larger-than-life trio of a seven-figure actress, a drop-dead-gorgeous body-builder, and a six-foot-four rock singer with black and green hair, tattooed eyes, and more sheer animal magnetism than Mick Jagger (all three of them, moreover, fully dressed, and in clothing so expensive it showed no sign of the long day behind them) made her feel like a low-rent cock-roach? The three of them presented a united front, linked together in a bond that Caroline did not fully understand and felt that she personally would never again know. She faced them with her chin up

"You want to talk to me about what?"

The tattooed eyes gave a quick sideways glance to where Douglas stood. Doug Blessing, whose own looks and charisma faded in their presence as a star in daylight. She held out one hand to her husband, her eyes defiantly on those of the rocker, who nodded and waited until Douglas had sloshed from the pool and joined them.

"Let's sit down," the singer suggested. They sat, on two facing benches. His words, though spoken in a low voice, reverberated back from the mosaic tile scenes that lined the room, and as the blue water grew still again, the universe seemed to contract to where the five of them sat.

Caroline could not bear it. She seized the initiative and spoke first. "If you're here to tell me that Lauren Sullivan is my half sister, I already know it. And Lauren," she went on, forcing herself to meet that world-famous gaze, "I promise never to tell a soul that my mother had anything to do with you. I'd probably deny her myself, if I could. Is that all you wanted?"

"No," said the actress, her sultry voice ripe with some intense but unidentifiable emotion. "Dad, do you want to . . . ?"

She was, Caroline saw in disbelief,

speaking to King David, who stirred and reached into a pocket.

" 'Dad!' Did you call him — but . . . you told me you're, what? Forty-four?" Caroline objected, staring incredulously at the rock star. Even for someone as wild as King David, fathering a child at the age of, what? seven or eight? was a bit hard to believe.

He laughed, checked the two photographs he had taken from his pocket, and handed one of them to Caroline. "Detective Toscana found these on Hilda Finch when he arrested her."

Caroline dried her fingers on her robe and took the faded snapshot by its white-bordered corner. It showed a red-haired young man, in profile. She turned it over and read, in a girl's handwriting, "Tad Blake." "Okay," she said, waiting for the explanation.

"Hold it up," the singer ordered, and when she had done so he got to his feet and turned his head to give her the side of his face.

"Christ!" exclaimed Douglas, who saw it at the same instant: The picture showed the baddest boy of heavy metal music as a clean-cut, all-American college kid, before tattoos, heroin, and decades of late nights in smoke-filled rooms.

The singer looked down at Caroline, the lightning bolts crinkling in amusement. "Yeah, that's me all right. I dropped out a couple months after that was taken, went to San Francisco to become, if you can dig it, a folk singer. Instead of that, I discovered drugs. I woke up five years later, cleaned up my act a little bit, and discovered hard rock. But can you imagine somebody called Tad Blake eating live bats on stage? The name would be fine for a folk singer, I guess, but it just didn't have the right ring for where I wanted to go. So I changed it, got the tattoos to change my looks and my image, traded my gold-rimmed glasses for contact lenses, lied about my age — remember, these were still the days when we didn't really trust anyone over thirty. I wrote 'King's Revenge' in 1972, it went platinum, and I haven't been off the charts since. And now everyone just assumes that I'm in such lousy shape for my age because of all the years of drugs and parties. I don't have to let on about the vegetarianism and health spas."

"Tad Blake?" Caroline said, looking at the red-haired youth in wonder. Douglas nudged her elbow; she looked up to see a second photo being held out to her. She took it and nearly fell backward off the bench: Tad again, this time looking straight at the camera, his arms around a small, trim girl: Hilda Finch.

Caroline gaped at the man across from her, then at Lauren. "Dad," indeed; Lauren's resemblance to the boy in the picture was unmistakable. She covered her mouth to stifle a laugh, a slightly hysterical sound that caused the other four to eye her with concern. "Sorry," she gasped. "I was just thinking what Douglas's constituency would do if they found out that their congressman's wife was related, even second-hand, to King David."

"They wouldn't know whether to impeach me or ask for your autograph," Douglas replied, sounding rather uneasy at the prospect.

"You'd sure as hell dominate the heavy metal vote," the rock star reassured him, the sheepish grin on his middle-aged features eerily like that on the snapshot. "But hang on, it gets even weirder. You're right saying you're Lauren's half sister, but it's not through Hilda Finch that you're related."

"What? What are you talking about?" Caroline's mind seemed to slip gears fraction, then spin wildly. Her voice climbed higher. "Of course we're related through Mother, who else is —"

She broke off as King David and Lauren Sullivan, after a quick exchange of glances, rose as one and came to sit on the bench next to her. Without a word, Lauren lifted her right hand into the air and held it out, the palm toward Emilio. On the other side of her, the singer did the same, his thumb brushing her little finger.

"Now you," Lauren told Caroline. "No, the right hand."

Three hands held up to the air, the precise way she'd done that afternoon with Douglas. Only, where that comparison had denied the similarity, these three hands clearly differed only in size and muscular development: long nail bed, strong nails, thumbs without a hint of backward curve, prominent knuckles, an oddly long index finger, and a slightly outward turn to the smallest finger. King David's hand was the biggest, of course, and Caroline's fingers reflected long hours working the bow of her cello, but . . .

"Ondine's were just the same," Lauren said sadly.

"Would you look at that." It was Douglas, speaking Caroline's wonder.

Now Emilio spoke up, for the first time. "When Hilda got to her thirtieth birthday and had never been pregnant again, she decided she needed a child. I gather by the notes in Claudia's safe that your father was tested and judged not to be the problem. Eventually it was determined to be the result of some long-ago infection, perhaps just after Lauren was born, blocking her tubes. Surgery might have helped, but instead she went looking for Claudia de Vries, thinking that if her old college roommate had been able to get rid of one child, surely she could lay hands on another.

"As it turned out, she was right. Claudia never forgot an old friend, never lost track of someone she'd once used. She was one of the few who knew what had become of Tad Blake. By this time she had a whole staff of snoopers, one of whom found out that King David, in those good old pre-AIDS days of drugs, sex, and rock and roll, wasn't always punctilious in his use of birth control. Your mother was a sound technician on his road gang. You were three months old when she agreed to give you up, and Claudia handed you over to Hilda. Who, so far as I have been able to determine, had no idea where you came from. Claudia may have been saving that bit of information for the future."

King David now reached across Lauren to claim Caroline's hand and to take possession of her attention with that magnetic gaze that she had mistaken for a man's desire, when all along it had been a father's yearning that gazed out at her, just as the mesmerizing touch of his hand had been blood calling to blood. The key that he told her he was searching for, she suddenly knew, was not just a slip of metal, but something more. The beloved lost possession that Claudia had dangled in front of his nose to get him to come here was in fact herself, Caroline. His daughter. "I knew as soon as I laid eyes on you," he was saying. "That's why I couldn't take my eyes off you, couldn't help touching you. You look just like your mother. She was a beautiful, talented, big-hearted woman. Catherine was her name, although she called herself Cat. She died nine years ago, I'm sorry to say, but I have pictures of her for you. She didn't want to give you up, but it would have meant losing what she had worked long and hard for — a rock band on the road isn't exactly the place for a baby. She made the decision that it would be best for you to go to a loving, two-parent, relatively wealthy, and stable home. She couldn't have known. . . . And I should have taken responsibility, but it was the seventies, and we were touring nearly three hundred days a year, and frankly in those days I was just a hyped-up bastard. I'm sorry, I was barely aware of you. I have to admit, you and Lauren aren't the only ones."

Of course, he would say that Caroline's mother had been a paragon, even if he scarcely remembered her. But it was his last statement that snagged her attention: *more* siblings? A father — *this* father? And maybe, once she'd gotten used to the idea, a member of the band's road gang wouldn't be such a terrible mother figure. Lord, even an irresponsible, drugged-out groupie of a mother would be better than . . .

With that thought, Caroline shook off her father's grip and turned to lay a tentative finger on the slim wrist of the woman between them. "Lauren? I am so sorry about Ondine."

Emilio answered. "Giving those people in the library the fact that Ondine was the daughter of Lauren Sullivan was Lauren's own idea. Obviously, someone in the group will sell the story to the papers before th ashes in that fireplace are cold. We'd thought of it before, but after Ondine died, we wanted Lauren to keep it quiet. She said no, and she's right. Doing it this way will distract the media, giving them a bone to chew so they don't keep digging and get the rest of the story. If they found out that the four of you are tied together, by blood and marriage, the feeding frenzy would never let up."

Douglas looked ill.

"At least Ondine's death was quick," the actress said, although none of them believed she found much consolation in the fact. "That manager of hers would have killed her before much longer."

"Chris Lund?" Caroline was startled. "They seemed to get along so well."

Again Emilio's English tones gave the explanation. "Ondine had a huge life insurance policy, with Lund the benefactor. She was starving herself to death. Lund pretended he was against her dieting, pretended that he was on the brink of force-feeding her, but at the same time he was the one who had told her she needed to lose weight, and that was what she believed. Just before she died, they'd had word of a major contract cancellation, the second this year lost to younger models;

they could both see the writing on the wall. He decided to, as they say, cash in his chips."

"But I thought you said that Mother — that . . ." If Hilda wasn't Mother, what was she?

Lauren answered her protest, in a bitter voice. "Hilda pushed over the shelf unit, but Chris Lund put my daughter there, vulnerable."

Emilio clarified. "We think Lund killed Karen McElroy either because she'd noticed the similarity between Ondine's hands and Lauren's when she did their manicures, or because she'd overheard him and Ondine arguing and was calling the police. We found a blood spatter on one of his shoes that I'm pretty sure will turn out to be Karen's. Ondine either saw him, or found the girl shortly afterward. And as I said earlier, fainted."

Again, Douglas said what was foremost on Caroline's mind. "And you don't think Lund's death was a little . . . convenient?"

"An accident," Emilio said blandly, although a bit too quickly.

Caroline glanced at King David — at her father! — and saw him studying his hands, those oddly elegant, larger versions of her own, as if reading their history in the skin and bone. Then Lauren reached her right hand over and wrapped her fingers through his, before doing the same with her left hand and Caroline's.

A family, joined together, with one daughter's husband and the father's lover looking on. A family, rising phoenixlike from the ashes.

Yes, thought Caroline. Lund's death was an accident.

Much better that way.

But — "Wait a minute," she objected. Everyone tensed, willing her not to say aloud that it could not have been, but Caroline had something else in mind. "There was a polka-dot bikini in Claudia's hand when we dragged her out of the mud bath. If . . . Hilda . . . killed Claudia, where did that come from? And you can't tell me that my mother was wearing that thing." She fixed the agent of law and order with a look of accusation and was astonished to see those finely chiseled features turn a furious shade of red, flushing down to the neck of his expensive wool suit, and beyond (just how far beyond was a speculation that crossed the minds of all four witnesses).

Emilio gave a short bark of uncomfortable laughter and with great dignity told them, "It was mine. I'm afraid that, among Claudia de Vries's other sins and wickednesses, she was also guilty of the most blatant form of what I would have to call, er, sexual harassment."

He looked up at their snorts of laughter, none of them stifled with much success, and protested. "Honestly, she wasn't a very nice woman!"

The employees of Thorndike Press hope you have enjoyed this Large Print book. All our Large Print titles are designed for easy reading, and all our books are made to last. Other Thorndike Press Large Print books are available at your library, through selected bookstores, or directly from us.

For information about titles, please call:

(800) 223-1244
(800) 223-6121

To share your comments, please write:

Publisher
Thorndike Press
295 Kennedy Memorial Drive
Waterville, ME   04901

DUE